Annette,
Hope you enjoy.
All my best!
John Boland
6/18/08

S0-BLH-187

THE COLOR OF FRAUD

JOHN BOLAND

PublishAmerica
Baltimore

First printing

This is a work of fiction. Names, characters, places and incidents either are the product of the author's imagination or are used fictitiously. Any resemblance to actual events or locales or persons, living or dead, is entirely coincidental.

ISBN: 1-59286-402-3
PUBLISHED BY PUBLISHAMERICA, LLLP
www.publishamerica.com
Baltimore

Printed in the United States of America

*This book is dedicated to my children
Tim, Christine, and Sean*

Acknowledgements

To my wife, Pat, for encouraging me throughout the process of writing and publishing.

To Mary Divilly for reading the manuscript with a critical eye and making it a better story.

To John Davidson, my friend, who always shared his wisdom and offered me opportunities in my banking career.

To JD Richards who is a master of instilling confidence and a great writing teacher.

To Michael Castro who has taught and inspired me in my writing journey.

Photo credit: Linda Perry

1

David quietly finished his last day as an employee of Norbank in Des Moines and walked out into the parking lot where his pickup truck faced west. He thought it appropriate that his truck was already pointed toward his new job in California. His final day at Norbank brought no fanfare, no party to celebrate his departure. Like the frigid, windy winters that sweep across the Iowa plains, executive management treated him coldly for taking another job. His boss bought him lunch as a polite token of appreciation. Norbank disliked losing good managers. And David was a good loan servicing manager. He enjoyed a national reputation and could have any number of jobs servicing mortgage loans at national banks and mortgage lenders. He was leaving a good job hopefully for a more fulfilling one.

He had accepted an opportunity to build a loan servicing unit in Sacramento for a company much smaller than the mega-servicers his resume boasted. He had worked for Citybank and a large subsidiary bank owned by an automobile manufacturer. Norbank had tried to convince him to stay, but he wanted something different, smaller and more challenging. As one of the country's largest servicers of mortgage loans, Norbank management spent an inordinate amount of time at HUD in Washington and at Fannie Mae, the Federal National Mortgage Association, the largest investor in single-family residential loans. The travel and pressure had taken its toll on David. So had living in Des Moines for the last two years.

Des Moines was a quiet, proper and conservative city. It also had harsh, cold winters. Most people were friendly, but there wasn't much to do. David looked forward to a warmer climate and the endless attractions of California. He knew that his wife, Ann, was also tired of the long, windy winters. Dave pictured their hiking and camping in the Sierras. He could sail in San Francisco

7

Bay. He could lose himself in the glitter and the gambling in Tahoe. He smiled at the myriad possibilities as he climbed into his truck.

Dave sighed in relief. The constant pressure was off for a while. As he pulled out of the parking lot he recalled his first day at Norbank. He had felt nervous. Maybe he was in over his head with two million customers to service. He spent his first day meeting all of the employees individually. He walked from cubicle to cubicle introducing himself.

He remembered instances where he never met new managers in his career. They just materialized in a private office one day and quietly summoned people when the need arose. And when they left the company, they simply vanished from the organization chart. He had resolved to learn from those bad examples etched in his memory. To him employees were important. They made or broke a manager as well as an organization. And he needed their support if he was to be successful. He was successful because he truly cared about the people who worked for him. At times his staff loyalty was so high that other managers resented him. Employees looked for opportunities to transfer to Dave's departments because they knew that he was accessible and concerned about his employees.

He turned left at a downtown overpass onto the entrance ramp to I-80, the highway that would take him from Des Moines to Sacramento. No turns, just a straight road across the plains, two mountain ranges and desert into Sacramento, his new home. His wife, Ann, would stay in Des Moines until the moving van was loaded and ready to go. Ann was thankful to leave the gray and windy winters behind. She saw the move to California as an adventure, a warm place to live, and the promise of a good life.

After loading the truck and telling Ann goodbye, Dave once again pulled on to the interstate. He looked out at the cornfields for the last time. The corn stood mile after mile as far toward the horizon as he could see. No wonder we have the capability to feed the world, he thought. He crossed from Council Bluffs to Omaha over the Missouri River. After the two hours of interstate surrounded by corn, Dave welcomed the sights and the traffic of Omaha as a break to the routine of driving. Like any progressive city, Omaha was full of road construction, adding lanes to the highways while the suburbs sprawled into what once was prime cropland.

He found an inexpensive hotel in Grand Island, Nebraska. Tired from a day of work and driving the interstate, Dave fell into bed and slept soundly. By eight o'clock the following morning he was on the road again. On the console of his truck were a cup of hot coffee and a breakfast sandwich. Dave found comfort and assurance in the fact that he could stop and get fast cheap meals that wouldn't keep him off of the road for very long. Then, when he needed some time to get out, stretch and have a leisurely meal, he felt he could afford the time.

As mind numbing as the drive across Nebraska and Wyoming was, Dave found it a good time to reflect on his career to date. He thought of the various cities he had lived because of job transfers, and all the people he had met. He thought about what he wanted to do in his new assignment in California. They are the lucky ones, he thought. I get to put all of my years of training and experience to work in building something from the ground up. *How many times does a manager get to do that within the confines of big corporations?* he asked himself.

Three days later David pulled his truck into the Harbortown apartments in Sacramento. The relocation package gave him thirty days of temporary housing, which he hoped he wouldn't need. He disliked apartments. They were noisy and crowded, a storage facility for humanity until they bought a house or moved on, he thought. Apartments present a strange world to an unsettled homeowner. Too many years of living in houses made a short stay in a well-furnished apartment almost unbearable for David.

He carried in his belongings he had stuffed into his truck. He noticed that phone service had been installed. He stood at the counter bordering the closet-size kitchen and read the rules of apartment living, the welcome information from his company and the complimentary city map. He emptied his pockets of receipts collected in the last three days and headed back out the door. Groceries and housekeeping supplies couldn't wait. *Sacramento at last,* he thought to himself and smiled. Before he stepped back into the truck, he stretched luxuriantly. His mind was fresh, his butt numb and his stomach growling with hunger. The wave of new adventure surged through his body. He had no idea how much of an adventure it would turn out to be.

National Assets had humble origins in the Midwest. It started as a small loan company in a used mobile home near Chicago. For twenty years a small group of entrepreneurs, led by its founder Leo Pecunia, built the company into the major market shareholder of consumer loans and sub-prime mortgage loans. When the aged, founding father passed operational control of the company over to his son, the Sanford educated son relocated the headquarters to Sacramento. By 1994 National Assets was well entrenched in the Sacramento business community and quickly becoming a major employer in the area.

Soon the company expanded into small business financing, college tuition loans and home improvement lending. National Asset's foray into these new markets was an impressive success. The key to their marketing success was their toll free number and twenty-four hour access to loan representatives. They advertised heavily on television with commercials that appealed to the normal person who struggled to make ends meet and probably had a few bad credit ratings. The psychological appeal to the underdog consumer was a hit. The loan applications poured into the phone center where the loan representatives often gave instant approval to the applications. Until the last two years only one incident dampened their success.

Some of the tenured and politically powerful employees in Chicago refused to migrate to the new California headquarters. In an effort to appease both his son and his long time co-workers, Leo returned as chairman and established a policy that kept the accounting and investment functions in Chicago. His son was permitted to relocate the rest of the company to Sacramento to market, process and service the loans. Outsiders questioned the wisdom of this move. But the insiders wouldn't have to justify the move. National Assets was family owned and had not gone public at the time of this decision.

David met the president of the company, Will Eagleton, a month ago during his job interview. Will was a charismatic leader. They nicknamed him "Iron Will." His passions were building the business, wearing the finest business clothes money could buy, and physical fitness.

In his early fifties, his dyed and curled blond hair gave him an almost clownish look. But the hand tailored suits, shirts and exotic ties gave the impression that the business style magazine photographers were waiting for him in the next room. He spent his lunch hours at a gym where he rigorously exercised all body fat from his small frame. He wore shoes with elevated heels to push his height to almost six feet.

During his meeting with him, David recalled that Will did most of the talking. In near fanatic theatrics he talked about National Assets and regurgitated every pop axiom from the management books on the bestseller list. He insisted that all quarterly reports be presented on video with him as the star of the show.

During Dave's initial interview with Will, he had paced in front of Dave in his deep blue Egyptian cotton dress shirt with lapis cufflinks gesturing fanatically at the air.

"I tell my managers to break things and put them back together so that processes run more efficiently. You have to inspect what you expect. If we're not growing the business, we're going out of business. We need to build a company that will last, that cannot be duplicated because of our commitment," Will ranted on and on. "Our people have to subordinate their personal values to the core values of our company. The corporate identity is the priority. If we're not beating the competition every hour of every day, then we lose. And I hate to lose."

Dave watched in amazement thinking that Will wasn't interested in Dave's experience now that Will had an audience of one. Will talked until he was breathless, hoping that his motivational histrionics had left Dave breathless, too.

Eagleton was truly the product of the good old boy network. He had started with the company as a loan agent in the sixties and had worked his way up to branch manager. As the company grew, so did his responsibilities and span of control. Several of his long time associates had been placed in positions of senior management by no other merit than tenure. Will explained that the promotion from within was stagnating the company. Now they were trying to attract fresh talent from the outside, talent with experience in managing large mortgage operations.

David's first day on the job was quiet and uneventful, a good time to get organized. There was no one to meet with except his new boss. Initially Dave would be working for John Fremont, an experienced servicing executive for whom he had worked in the past. Not only were John and Dave old friends, John had recruited Dave for the servicing manager position. David would have to build his own servicing center from the ground up. He stood in the open expanse of twenty thousand square feet of office space trying to visualize the cubicles, the electronic bulletin boards and the numerous computer terminals and phones that would fill the empty space. He took a deep breath and stepped inside his small office.

He knew he was up to the task. He had brought copies of procedures and reports from previous jobs. He had several top priorities. He needed to recruit a management team, hire an administrative assistant, and build a time line for going operational in four months by the end of February. David could feel the excitement surge through him as he drafted his plan and made his recruiting phone calls. He was in his element.

By the end of the day he had momentum to his plans. He scheduled interviews both for his administrative assistant and management team members. Tomorrow he would tackle the initial meetings for phone systems and computer systems. David was gaining ground and feeling good about it. He was excited to be a member of an aggressive and entrepreneurial management team. In time he would discover how freewheeling they were. He would also realize that some senior managers didn't share his enthusiasm for change. Some didn't like the fact that he had been recruited.

Across town in the company headquarters near downtown Sacramento, David Jenkins, the new hire, was being discussed. Will Eagleton called the meeting with Bob Whiting, the chief credit officer, and Bruce Curly, chief operations officer. Both Bob and Bruce had been with the company as long as Will. All had been branch managers in the early days of the company. Bruce and Bob were at the opposite end of the physical fitness spectrum as if all the fat and flabbiness burned from Will stuck to them.

Eagleton sat at the head of the table with a bottle of water and repeatedly squeezed the grip strengthener that he carried around with him. He had a talent for wallowing in his own vanity while talking about the business.

"We can't continue to make these kinds of mistakes," he stated, raising his voice just below a shout. "HUD is going to lower sanctions on us, and probably fine us for not following their regulations."

"We pay the fine," Bob answered inspecting the gold bracelet on his plump wrist. "Then we tell them we hired David Jenkins to come in and straighten out the servicing business on their loans."

"Yeah, let this Jenkins come up with a response to HUD's audit," Curly joined in. "That shifts the focus away from us and on to him. His resume states that he handled one of the biggest servicing centers in the nation. And he had responsibility for all of the collection activity for all six of their servicing centers throughout the country."

"HUD probably knows this Jenkins. Let him deal with them. If he cleans up the mess, we can relax. If not, then we have a scapegoat." Bob Whiting sat back pleased with his strategy. The old senior management team would be safe from the potential fall out.

"Okay, that takes care of HUD," Will said. He relaxed slightly in his chair. "What about Freddie Mac's portfolio?" Freddie Mac, a quasi-government agency that invests in mortgage loans to provide liquidity for primary lenders such as National Assets, owned a small portfolio of six hundred loans serviced by National Assets. The company had recently failed an audit performed by them.

"We're too late with Freddie Mac," Bob said. "They want their loans out of here and under the control of a more competent servicer."

"Shit!" Eagleton slammed his palm down on the conference table. "Why did Bud let this happen?"

"Bud Murphy is in over his head as a servicing manager," Bob said flatly. He enjoyed seeing Will get emotional over the issue of Bud's incompetence. "The size of our portfolio has outgrown his abilities. I thought that's why we brought David Jenkins on board. Our only task now is to diplomatically lift some of that burden off of Bud's shoulders and on to Dave Jenkins."

"Bud's been with us for nineteen years," Will said. "Maybe he screwed things up. But I want him taken care of. I want things handled carefully. He's already called me questioning why we brought Dave Jenkins on. I think he knows that the job is too big for him. But he's worried that we are going to abandon him. And we can't do that. He's saved our bacon more than once."

"And he knows a lot," Bob added. He saw the fear flicker across Will's face. "He could hurt us if he feels unloved all of a sudden."

"So do we continue to let his incompetence hurt us, or his retaliation?" Curly asked. He was tiring of Bob's sadistic ploys and tried to get the conversation focused on a reasonable solution.

"Neither," Will answered. "Get this thing fixed and keep Bud happy."

Both Bob and Curly nodded obsequiously and gathered up their papers and notepads. Neither had an idea what they were supposed to do based on Will's last remark. As usual they would come up with some ideas and talk with Will about them. Both knew that the discussion was over and it was time to go to work. They had a lot of damage control to do. And Jenkins was in the spotlight. There was too much at stake to see this fail.

Dave tried to spend a portion of each afternoon looking for a house. He and his wife had contacted a California realtor while they were still in Des Moines. The realtor had narrowed down the list based on Dave's specifications. Now it was his job to condense their choices into a short list of five or six houses. Then his wife, Ann, could come out and decide on the final house.

Oddly enough, the realtor had found the perfect house for them the first day. Dave just wanted to make sure he wasn't rushing into a transaction without seeing other homes that were on the market. Ann had seen pictures of the house. It reminded them of the house they were selling in Des Moines, a one and a half story stucco with four thousand square feet in a deed-restricted community. Dave knew that Ann would love it. But he just wanted to make sure. So he kept looking in different neighborhoods.

He finally called Ann and asked her to come out to California. When Ann saw the house, they immediately put in an offer to buy. The offer was accepted and the closing date set. Now they just had to move.

2

Dave looked up from the work on his desk when he heard the knock at the door. He smiled and stood when he saw John Fremont standing in the doorway. John's six-feet, five-inch frame filled the doorway. He was in his mid-fifties and sported a neatly trimmed mustache. His features were striking. Dave thought that John could have been in movies had he chosen to do so with his good looks. But John had decided to go into the business world. And Dave knew that he was like a heat-seeking missile when it came to ferreting out problems in a mortgage operation. He was like a long piece of litmus paper always testing the strength of an organization with probing questions and watchful eyes.

"How's it going?" John reached out to shake David's hand. John and David had worked together in past years. David had worked as one of John's direct reports. Dave knew that one of the deciding factors for his taking this job was that he would get to work with John again. Working with John had been one of his most important learning experiences. John had started with the company about five months earlier and had been influential in recruiting David for this job.

"Pretty well, thanks," David answered. "It's nice to see a familiar face."

"It's nice to see any face judging from your surroundings." John laughed as he gestured toward the twenty thousand square feet of open space outside the door.

"The solitude will be gone soon enough," Dave joked. "Right now it's good for my concentration."

"And how about the weather?" John joked. "Autumn in Iowa or autumn in California. Which do you prefer?"

"No contest." Dave raised his hands in surrender. "I'm glad to be here.

Ann is ecstatic over the move."

"Any plans for lunch?" John asked. "There's a great little cafeteria in the corner of the Wards store. They serve a good hotcake breakfast for lunch."

"Sounds good," Dave answered. "Let's go." He flipped his pen on to the desk and forwarded his calls to his voice mail.

As they walked out into the midday sunshine, both Dave and John lit cigarettes. Dave let the warm air wash over him. The change in climate renewed his spirits as he looked out at the palm trees growing at intervals in the parking lot of the shopping center.

"This company must really be growing for them to rent second floor space over a shopping mall," Dave said.

"It's a good location for a back office operation," John answered. "If you have to be away from the main operations, it's nice to have access to all of these stores. Gives you something to do if you want to forget about the work for a little while. Campus settings are nice, but I like the privacy this location provides. At least the president won't be walking in our offices every hour."

"I didn't think about that," Dave said. "You've got a good point about the privacy and the distractions."

They stopped in front of Wards and both crushed out their cigarettes. Dave could smell the bacon and hamburgers cooking on the grill. The aroma of grilled onions made its way out to them and he realized how hungry he was.

The cafeteria was nothing more than a limited hot buffet and a short order grill with a counter between the cook and the customers. Dave grabbed an orange plastic tray still wet from the dishwasher and slid it down the stainless steel runners in front of the cook. He ordered a breakfast of pancakes and bacon. The cook told him that she would bring it out to their table when it was ready. Dave poured himself a cup of coffee and headed for one of the dozen tables around the counter. John duplicated Dave's order and sat down across from Dave.

"So what have you got going this afternoon?" John asked.

"I thought I'd call some job applicants and a couple of recruiters. You know, start building my management team," Dave said.

"I may be able to help a little," John said. "I've got a resume on a woman who used to work for me at American. She's a good default manager. May be a little pricey, but worth it."

"Hey, that's fine. Just think of the money we'll save on recruiting and relocation costs, not to mention time. I have a resume on someone who worked with me in Des Moines. She's acquired an impressive background in customer service. If I can get these two lined up, I'm halfway there." Dave reached into his pocket and pulled out a pencil draft of the organization chart he had building. "This is what it's going to look like by function."

John and Dave worked on the chart in between bites of pancakes and syrup. Dave glanced from the chart to John. He knew this job was going to work. John was going to be a sponsor and a mentor. Dave understood the importance of his efforts reflecting well on John. He knew that a manager was only as good as the people surrounding the manager. Dave considered it one of the basics to a professionally run organization. He knew the critical difference it makes when a manager has the full support of his boss. This was going to be a piece of cake, he thought.

3

The most important meeting that Dave had scheduled dealt with the systems issues for the accounts. Only three years ago the company had kept their books and serviced all their loans manually. Since that time they had designed their own homegrown accounting system that tracked the payments and other cash movements of the business. Later they added on some loan servicing enhancements such as default reporting, tracking escrow accounts and late charges. To someone who had come from a state-of-the-art mortgage center with fully integrated systems that tracked all the mortgage functions from the time the loan was put on the books to the servicing of the payments, escrow accounts, investor reporting and losses, it was frightening. The system looked like a patchwork quilt of manual interfaces and spreadsheet mentality that was vulnerable to mistakes and mismanagement. In Dave's mind it invited outright fraud.

National Assets must have worried about the same thing, Dave thought. Within the past year the company had converted to a national brand computer servicing system. Although they had loaded the loans onto the system through an exercise called a conversion, much of the data surrounding the loans did not make it onto the system. Dave figured that they had cut a lot of corners and done a stripped down conversion. That would make the conversion go faster and leave less room for balancing errors. In the wake of this type of conversion a lot of the processes would still be performed manually because the information just wasn't there to service the loans properly.

There were two hundred fifty thousand loans in the system. Dave had to find a way to extract the fifty thousand home improvement loans out of the portfolio and service them on a separate accounting and servicing platform. To his amazement he discovered in conversations with employees that no balancing had been attempted after the conversion. And there was no way to identify all of the fifty thousand loans that comprised the home improvement portfolio. One of the omissions in the conversion was giving each loan source and product codes. Without these two codes no one could tell what type of loan it was, or where it had originated, without manually researching the loan file.

In addition the old manual account numbers on the loans were thirteen digits long. The new system would only accommodate a seven-digit account number. That meant that the loans had to be manually mapped to the new system with no cross-reference mapping back to the old loan number.

Once Dave moved his fifty thousand loans onto a separate system there would be no automated cross-reference to the previous loan number. And there would be no escaping a manual research in order to look at loan records and payment histories. Dave wondered if this was all planned to leave a difficult trail back to the original loan, or if they were just that sloppy in installing a new system. He had been around long enough to know that the portfolio was ripe for fraudulent activity. He only hoped that he was not walking into a maze of fraud.

4

His meeting with Susan Orwell, the head of systems was at two o'clock. Dave thought that he would arrive early just to visit with Susan for a few minutes before the meeting. He knew that a lot could be accomplished before the meeting actually started if he asked the right questions. He had worked with Susan in past years at another company. She had been in charge of the customer service department at Fordham Bank. Dave knew that she was a bright person, well-experienced in the servicing of mortgages.

With the help of a few directions from the receptionist he finally found Susan's office in the back corner of a large room filled with cubicles. He stood at the door of her office and knocked softly. Susan sat at her desk trying to eat a sandwich while reading some email.

"Come in, Dave," she said motioning with a handful of chicken salad sandwich. "Welcome to National Assets."

"Thanks," Dave replied with a smile. "It's good to be here."

"You have no idea how badly we need your help," Susan continued with a mouthful of food. "These records are a mess. And I can't seem to get anyone to understand how tough this is going to be until we can get the fifty thousand home improvement loans identified."

"So I've heard," Dave replied. "I've got a couple of ideas that may help us out. I wanted to get your opinion before everyone else got here."

"Good. Let's hear them. I'll take all the ideas I can get at this point."

"As far as the system goes I understand that you're already at capacity because of the missing information in the original records."

"You've heard that correctly," Susan agreed. "In order to load the loans onto the new system, we needed two hundred seventy fields of information. You know, the usual customer information, type of loan, source of the loan, who owns the loan, social security numbers, that kind of information. We shaved that down to thirty fields of information and still couldn't get what we needed. The data input people just made up things to put into the fields so that the system would take them. Now we're paying for that. Because there's so much bogus information in critical data fields, very few of the interfaces work properly. We have very little processing capacity left on the new system."

Susan shook her head in amazement every time she had to tell the story. She came from a banking background where data fields were sacred territory. Nothing was put into a system unless it had a high degree of accuracy and had been double-checked.

"Why don't we make a copy of the servicing software?" Dave offered. "Then it will be like starting over with my fifty thousand loans. I can scrub the data in the original loan files. Take my time to get accurate information and lighten the processing load on your current portfolio. In addition I can use a separate set of flags and codes independent of what you are using. I think it will run more efficiently rather than perpetuating the mistakes that have already been made."

"That sounds like it would work," Susan thought about the idea. "Kind of create a hard wall between the two portfolios, but still use the same software."

"You've got it," Dave agreed.

"Sounds good," she finally said after some thought. "Let's run it by the others once they get here. Keep in mind that you'll have to load all the home improvement loans that paid off last year. Otherwise you won't be able to report the tax information."

"Good point," Dave answered. "I can assemble a team of temporary workers to get going on the project. What is the target date for the conversion?"

"Senior management wants you to be up and running with your own portfolio by the end of January," she said. "We'll perform the year end balancing and then you're free to run with it."

"January?" David asked startled at the short time frame. "That only gives me two months to scrub all the data in fifty thousand loan files, not to mention all the paid files, test the system, write procedures and load the loans in a weekend conversion."

"Welcome to National Assets," Susan said dryly and took the last bite of her sandwich. She tossed the lunch bag into her trashcan and rubbed the crumbs off of her hands. Next she tore open the wrapper to a dark chocolate candy bar. Dave smiled as he remembered that these were her favorite candy bars. She ate them constantly at Fordham Bank. Employees would offer them as bribes when they needed her help on projects. And it always seemed to work. Susan had a weak spot for dark chocolate candy bars. Dave made a mental note to get some for her. He thought he might need a few in coming days.

Soon the others began to arrive at her office for the meeting. Among them was Bud Murphy. When he stood in the doorway of Susan's office, he filled it. He stood six feet five inches tall and judging from his distended belly, Dave could tell that he liked his daily lunch of hamburgers and french fries. His face flushed a constant red, a sign of high blood pressure and stress Dave deduced. His hair was white and thinning.

Dave was good at reading people and he could tell that Bud was someone who liked to be in charge. His size and constant scowl would intimidate most employees. He had been with National Assets for nineteen years. During that time he had seen the company grow from a small loan operation in Chicago to the giant it was today. It looked as if Bud had expanded proportionately, Dave mused. The meeting had not gone ten minutes before Dave realized that Bud relied more on bluster and intimidation than he did on good business sense.

Bud categorically opposed Dave's plan. His reason was that the portfolios would be going in two different directions. Nothing would look the same and consolidated reporting would be impossible. Underneath his comments Dave read Bud's fear of losing control of part of the business he had helped build but could no longer oversee.

The meeting ended on the agreement that they would hold two more meetings. The first meeting would be scheduled with the managers who could identify some of the home improvement loans. The second meeting would be held with the systems staff to review the possibility of isolating the accounts on to a separate database. Everyone's calendars were marked with the dates of the meetings and the attendees drifted out of the room.

Dave looked over at Bud and decided that this would be as good a time to confront him on some issues.

"Do you have a few minutes I could spend with you, Bud?" Dave asked.

"Yeah, sure," Bud said with some reluctance in his voice. Dave thought that Bud probably wanted to have this initial confrontation out of the way too. At least they could size each other up, maybe reach some understanding or common ground. If they didn't, then Dave would know what direction some of his activities would have to take. He needed to know if Bud was on board with this split of the portfolio, or not.

"Let's go over to my office," Bud said. "It's right across the way."

The aisles were too narrow for Dave to walk alongside Bud. Dave walked behind him through the cubicles and followed him into his office. Bud's office was furnished with a large, aged mahogany desk, with two credenzas placed so that when Bud sat behind his desk he was completely surrounded by wood. It looked to Dave like a fort that one would hide behind.

Bud sighed deeply and plopped down in his chair. The office had a faint smell of methane and stale french fries. He picked up a handful of phone messages written on pink slips by his assistant. He mumbled the names just loud enough for Dave to hear.

"Will Eagleton, Bob Whiting, Bruce Curley...I wonder what they want now," Bud sighed to himself. Dave guessed that he said the names loudly enough to impress him. It appeared to Dave that Bud had momentarily forgotten about Dave's presence in his office. Dave suspected that Bud was surreptitiously sizing Dave up. Dave decided to break the silence.

"Well, Bud, at least we have the first meeting out of the way," Dave began.

"Yeah, but we got a long way to go before I'm comfortable with all of this," Bud said in one exaggerated exhalation while avoiding any eye contact.

"I thought that's what the meetings are for. So we get it right," Dave answered.

"If you're going to get it right, you're not going to be able to get it done by the end of January," Bud said, more of a threat than an observation. "It has to be built to last."

"From hearing how bad the data is, I think that the best we can hope for is to get a high level of comfort," Dave said patiently. "While we may never be one hundred per cent accurate, we'll be close enough."

"I...don't know," Bud said. "I want this done right."

"Look at it this way, Bud," Dave answered. "The accuracy will be a lot better than it is today." He was getting tired of hearing Bud parrot the same platitudes he had heard from Iron Will.

Bud couldn't hide the red flush of anger that covered his face. He put the pink messages aside and looked squarely at Dave.

"Just because the records are full of inaccuracies now, doesn't mean that we have to continue the error. We were under the gun to get all these loans converted onto a new system. We had to cut corners."

Dave wanted to say that's why it would be better to split the portfolio. He wanted to say that's why they were going to pull all of the files and scrub the data on fifty thousand loans. That's why the company was going to such great expense to fix the mistakes that had occurred while Bud was at the helm. But Dave knew that winning this argument wouldn't win Bud's cooperation. Dave decided to wait a moment before saying anything.

"Well, either way it's going to happen," Bud finally said. "I guess that's what Will wants to do." Bud looked out the window past Dave. "I don't agree with the decision. You may as well know that. But I'll do what I'm told."

"That's why I'm in here talking with you," Dave said. "I want this to go smoothly. And it will go a lot better if we cooperate."

Bud looked from the window to Dave as if sizing him up. "I know what has to be done. And you can count on me to do my part," Bud said evenly.

"I'm depending on that," Dave said. He knew that the lines were drawn. Dave saw the look of hostile compliance in Bud's eyes and heard it in his voice. He knew he would have to watch every step he took around Bud. Bud would love to see him fail, to tell Will that he had made the wrong decision. But Dave also thought that he had everyone in senior management on his side. Otherwise they wouldn't have hired him. They wouldn't have commissioned him to build a servicing center for the home improvement division.

"When can we talk about the budget and staff allocations?" Dave pressed. "It's my understanding that for next year's budget I get thirty percent of your expense budget and thirty percent of the staff to start out this operation."

Bud shot him a look of annoyance. "We don't need to meet. I know what you're supposed to get. I'll have my financial analyst send you some spreadsheets on the budget allocation for you to look over."

"Good. What about staff?" Dave continued. He knew that this was going to be like pulling teeth out of a grizzly bear. He also guessed that Bud was going to reallocate personnel so that Dave would end up with problem employees and poor performers. It was just the way things like this worked. The new kid on the block always got the garbage.

"I'm working on the staffing," Bud replied. "I'll get a list of employees and their job descriptions up to you within the next couple of days."

"Fine," Dave replied. "By the way I understand that any employee who had been written up with a performance or an attendance problem is ineligible for transfer. Is that how you understand things, Bud?"

Bud's face turned a darker shade of red and he made no effort to hide the anger in his eyes. He looked down at his desk in frustration and spoke.

"Technically that's correct," he said. "But some of these people would look at a transfer as a second chance. You could be doing the company a favor by looking at some of the problem employees."

"Okay," Dave replied magnanimously. "Subject to interviews with me and my approval, I'll look at some of them." Dave stood up to signal the end of the meeting. He had won that round. They had inflicted some pain on each other, but Dave thought it was unavoidable. He wanted to stay in control by being the one to end the meeting.

"Thanks for your time, Bud," he said as he walked toward the door.

"Yeah," Bud mumbled as he resumed staring at the pink slips of phone messages in his hand.

5

Over the next few weeks Dave immersed himself in hiring his management team. They, in turn, recruited supervisors and assistants. The organization was quickly taking shape. Dave knew that the next task was to have his managers write the procedures necessary for running their sections of the business. The major sections were comprised of customer service, default administration, systems, compliance and quality control, and cash processing. He agreed to use Susan Orwell as a shared resource for the systems issues. It would take too long to bring a newly hired person up to speed on the systems issues. Dave decided to wait until after the conversion to hire his own systems manager. Secondly, Susan had unique knowledge of the history of the prior conversion at National Assets. That knowledge would be critical for a successful split of the loan portfolio.

While all these initiatives were underway Dave and his management team designed and purchased the phone system and the software necessary to distribute incoming phone calls. They designed the monthly billing statements and programmed reporting formats that would transmit credit histories to the three major credit bureaus monthly.

In reviewing some of the management information from the current servicing business, it was clear to Dave that many unnecessary phone calls were coming in from customers who just wanted to know what their loan balance was. After consulting with his newly hired managers Dave decided that the new statements would take care of that issue. Then the inbound calls would drop off significantly.

His management team studied the available information and found similar opportunities for redesigning processes that would result in improved efficiencies. Dave shared some of these recommendations with Bud Murphy's servicing group where they were met with constant resistance. Dave's management team found that some processes critical to running the servicing operation were missing entirely from the servicing operation under Bud Murphy's management.

One of the processes that concerned Dave was the handling of insurance cancellations. When the National Assets servicing unit received a notice that insurance coverage on a customer's home had been cancelled, they threw the notice away. Their reasoning was that they could deny ever receiving such notice in the event of a loss covered by insurance. The practice accepted by the mortgage industry is to contact a borrower immediately after receiving a cancellation notice to see if the borrower had changed insurance companies. The customer usually had thirty days to correct the situation by either reinstating their old coverage or buying a new hazard insurance policy with another insurer. If the customer just let the coverage lapse neglecting any attempt to correct the situation, then the mortgage company was entitled to purchase insurance for the property and pass the cost on to the customer. The provision was covered in the deed of trust under a paragraph called "non monetary default" and allowed a mortgage company to force place hazard insurance coverage on a loan.

Dave was concerned about the liability associated with neglecting these generally accepted business practices. He decided to question Bud about it. The response he received was that if you didn't track something, then you couldn't be held liable for it. Besides, they had a blanket liability policy that could pay the losses. Bud continually threw out the term "plausible deniability" and ended the conversation abruptly. Dave's frustration was mitigated by the belief that this was exactly the reason that the senior management of National Assets had brought him on board. As a precaution he gave weekly updates to John Fremont and to Bruce Curley. In that way Dave wouldn't be accused of withholding process improvement proposals from Bud Murphy.

As the weeks wore on Dave was convinced that he was better off just getting his servicing operation running and leaving the home equity division to Bud Murphy's substandard practices. Bud's defensiveness and inflexibility were beginning to wear Dave down. He knew he had to stay positive for the sake of his operation. He wanted to keep enthusiasm high.

By mid-November Dave and Ann moved into their new home. They fell in love with it immediately. The rooms appeared spacious and comfortable to Dave even after the furniture was moved in. He especially liked the covered back patio that wrapped around two sides of the house. The yard was professionally landscaped. To Dave's delight the previous owner had planted eighteen rose bushes around the backyard. The Sacramento climate was good to roses. Dave decided that these roses would be his hobby, his diversion from the mounting pressures at the office.

Ann was busily redecorating and painting. She wanted the house to have her influence on it. She claimed that once the redecorating was finished, the house would feel more like her own home.

Armed with rolls of wallpaper and buckets of paint Ann went to work transforming a beautiful house into a stunning showplace. Professional carpet and mini blind cleaners paraded through the house for a day. Ann was in her element losing herself to the transformation of a newly purchased house into a comfortable home with her signature on it.

Behind the kitchen was a cluster of rooms called a mother-in-law quarters. Dave decided that the bedroom would make a good home office. He moved several bookcases along with his desk into the room. Since the room was away from the main traffic of the house, he knew that he would enjoy the privacy he wanted for the work he inevitably had to bring home.

The house was a sign of assurance to Dave and Ann that their move was going to be a good one. Before long they felt at home and Des Moines slowly faded to a memory of cold winters and cornfields.

Every December National Assets scheduled a meeting for all employees. It was presented as an annual sales convention in appreciation for all of the hard work and accomplishments of the prior year. The meeting was also a chance to discuss the coming year's strategies and themes. Dave had been hired in time to get reservations for the annual convention. It was to be held in San Francisco. The company had grown so much over the past year that they had to schedule two sessions in order to include all employees. Each session lasted a week. The employees were pampered with five star services at a major hotel. They were gifted with green tee shirts and brief cases and all types of motivational trinkets designed to foster loyalty and customer service.

When Dave checked in to the hotel he was greeted with music from a live band. He was photographed for the company album and given the brochure with all of the meeting schedules, dinners and social outings sponsored by the company. The first evening of the convention included a large formal dinner in an auditorium the size of a football field. There were speeches and award presentations. By the time the dinner was over some people had drunk too much. The tables were pushed back for dancing. The gala festivities lasted long into the night.

The next morning the meetings started promptly at eight thirty. After attending a couple of the sessions Dave noticed the theatrical religious fervor surrounding the presentations of some of the managers. It was the largest sales convention he had ever seen. Will Eagleton was in his element. To Dave he came off as part evangelist and part movie star. Iron Will did not believe in body fat. He stood on stage in jeans and a leather vest, bare chested and bare armed. Dave had an unsettling feeling when he first saw Will on stage. But his shock grew when he saw the rest of the senior management team join Will on stage dressed in similar attire. They looked like a rock band, or a bunch of bikers. Dave couldn't decide.

The color theme was a deep, vibrant green. National Assets adopted the color green as their company color. After all, green is the color of money, the color of growth, spring like and fertile. There were green banners in the auditorium. The tables were covered with green. The National Assets sign was green in its trademark form. Everyone wore the green company issued tee shirts. Will required employees to wear these to the informal functions at the convention. Dave remembered reading in a book on dressing for success that a financial person should never wear the color green. Oddly enough, a green suit did not evoke trust from customers.

On the last night of the meeting a few National Assets employees were drinking in a hotel bar. The group discussion deteriorated into a drunken brawl. A sales manager from Denver started making insulting remarks about the company. One of the other employees took offense to his remarks and the fists started flying. Will Eagleton sat in the bar at the time observing the whole scene. After the fight calmed down, Will pulled the Denver sales manager aside and told him that if he felt that way about the company, he should pack up his belongings once he returned to Denver and look for another job. So that there was no misunderstanding, Will fired him on the spot.

As the weeklong pep rally came to an end, Dave was thankful to be retuning to the office where he could wear a suit and get on with opening his operation. He was thankful for the insight into the culture of the company he observed during the convention. This was definitely an unconventional management team. They migrated from Chicago and held tightly together. And he noticed that Bud Murphy was considered one of the good old boys. Dave considered that if he made an enemy out of Bud, he made other enemies as well.

The more Dave considered this, the more uncomfortable he became. He wondered how serious the company really was in improving its processes. He wondered if he had been hired just to placate a regulatory agency or two. He decided to share his concerns with John Fremont.

Fortunately John Fremont had driven his car to San Francisco instead of taking the buses offered to the employees. Dave arranged to ride back with John so that he could discuss his concerns and observations. Dave was glad that John decided to check out of the hotel early so that they could get a head start on the bay area traffic.

They were on the road by noon and across the bay bridge by one o'clock. The hard part of the traffic was over. Now there was just the leisurely ride on the interstate back to Sacramento.

Somewhere near Vallejo Dave began to share his observations with John. He was grateful that he had someone he could trust, someone with whom he had worked in years past. Dave knew how valuable that is in the mortgage banking business.

"You know, it's funny, John," Dave mused. "The enthusiasm is palpable in this company. But, at the same time Bud is so resistant to change. It's like he doesn't realize all of this celebration is going to come to an end if he doesn't do something to turn his business around."

"That's where our opportunity exists," John answered. "That's exactly why we were hired."

"I don't know. I can feel a little distance and discomfort growing among the management ranks over this delinquency issue. I hope it all isn't just lip service."

"You aren't getting cynical on me already?" John looked over at Dave.

"No. I'm just getting cautious. I want it to work more than ever. It's seldom that you see so many employees so concerned about the success of their company. It's quite an opportunity."

After Dave shared his thoughts, they rode for a few miles in silence. Dave looked out at the factory outlet stores near Vacaville. Their parking lots were filled with holiday shoppers. John finally broke the silence.

"You know," John started. "I'm sure that you will be evaluated on your ability to get along with Bud, in addition to starting up your servicing operation."

"I thought about that," Dave replied. "But what if one goal excludes the other. I can get this operation running much more easily that I can get along

THE COLOR OF FRAUD

with Bud. I have the feeling that I would have to drop my professional integrity in order to get along."

"I'm sure you'll find a way to manage both," John said. He smiled and looked out the windshield down the highway. "I'll tell you what. I'll get involved. Bruce Curley has asked me to oversee both your and Bud's operation. Maybe together we can find some middle ground."

"Thanks," Dave said. "That will make a big difference." He relaxed in his seat and stared out the car window at the long rows of pink and white oleander that filled the highway median. He wondered if Bud would take John's direction. He hated to think what would happen if he didn't.

6

A few days after the conference ended Iron Will sat at his conference table listening to Bruce Curley and Bob Whiting sharing their observations of the convention. Once they were past the self-serving praise for a well-focused and thorough coverage of all the business plans and presentations, they discussed more pressing issues of the meeting. The discussion was a scripted format used out of habit because they had met so many times over the years. It was a ritual they were all comfortable with. Eventually the discussion arrived at their thoughts about the newly hired managers.

"Dave Jenkins and John Fremont participated well in the meeting," Will started off. "I'm glad that they felt comfortable with everything. Especially since they've been on board such a short time." He looked at Bruce with an expectant stare.

"I had a chance to visit with them informally one night at dinner," Bruce said. "My impression is that they are excited about being here and looking forward to the coming year."

"Yeah, but I talked to Bud," Bob joined in. "He's already having problems with Dave."

"What kind?" Will asked.

"Well, they mostly seem to be territorial issues. Dave wants to do things one way and Bud wants to leave things as they are," Bob said. "I hope they're just getting used to each other and that the problem will go away."

"I thought we hired Jenkins for his experience and new ideas," Will said. "He's got a good reputation with big companies. I was hoping for some fresh ideas to handle our business growth in servicing."

"Well, I am too," Bob replied. "But Jenkins has written some procedures and policies that could be difficult to comply with."

"In what way?" Now Will was leaning into table with his hands folded.

"I've seen a draft of a revised charge off policy. It's pretty rigid on the time frames as to when an account should be taken as a loss," Bob began. "And it's the standard accounting practice policy for most mortgage companies. But a lot of our business is consumer loan and revolving lines of credit secured by junior mortgages."

"I've seen his drafts of loss policies on every product," Bruce joined in. "As a matter of fact he sent them to me for my approval. He has a specific policy for each loan product complete with time frames for the losses and parameters to recognize early losses. This guy is thorough. And his policies make sense."

"What did you do with the policies?" Will asked.

"I passed them on to accounting to have them look at them and determine what the impact would be on our portfolio," Bruce answered. "I think we may be in for a large write-off of several million dollars if we were to implement those policies."

"We just went public a few months ago. Won't we have to abide by standard accounting, or generally accepted accounting principles?" Will asked.

"Well, yes," Bob hedged. "But we need some time to get there. So there isn't a strain on earnings. We need to prolong our transition period."

Will looked at them both for a moment. He had heard enough and cautiously moved off the subject of earnings and losses. He stood up abruptly from the table and flicked some lint off of his suit coat.

"I want you guys to see that this gets handled," he said. "We've got to find the middle ground where we can use Jenkins's fresh ideas while keeping Bud happy. I know that's a tall order, but it's just for a little while." He started to smile but caught himself. He couldn't talk about the future. The less said the better.

"I've already put John Fremont in as a sort of referee and mentor for both of them," Bruce offered. "That gives us some cushion and gives Bud Murphy and Dave Jenkins an outlet for their frustration."

"We can't afford any blow ups," Will warned. "Keep them happy. Keep them working on the business issues. Disgruntled employees retaliate. Bud knows a lot. And Bud has pulled off some miracles on stemming losses and keeping delinquency down. We owe him that much. And as for Jenkins, his resume makes the company look better. It convinces investors that were trying to do the right thing to handle the growth. But each day he's here, he learns more, gets smarter. He's no dummy, so watch yourselves."

Both Bruce Curley and Bob Whiting stood at the conference table nodding in the direction of the door where Will had just exited. They looked across the table at each other conspiratorially and walked back to their individual offices.

The executive offices were located near the downtown area, about five miles away from the loan servicing center where both Bud and Dave worked. Bud had the first floor of a partly vacated shopping center. Dave was building out the second floor for his operation. John Fremont had his office on the second floor of the servicing center close to Dave's office.

Bruce was grateful for the distance. He could feel the friction build between Bud and Dave. Bruce was an attorney by education, but had found the business world more profitable. He had started in commercial banking with business loans and floor planning financing for automobile dealers and boat dealers. After his foray into banking he went to work for the Small Business Administration, and eventually was recruited for the senior management team at National Assets.

He kept a low profile. It had become his trademark. He held more titles than any other officer in the company, yet he had no management staff reporting directly to him. They called him the stealth guy. He was always around but the radar of an organization chart would only pick him up as operating officer. And those charts were scarce. He made sure of that.

Bruce considered himself the voice of reason that intervened between the impetuous nature of Will and the devious moves of Bob. Although both Will and Bob were more outspoken, Bruce effectively made his point in meetings. He would listen, let them vent, and then give his thoughtful answers. It was a good combination in his opinion. He didn't have to compete by yelling more loudly than the other two. He had convinced the owners to go public with their stock.

A few months before Dave started with National Assets the company decided to go public. They were now listed on the lesser national stock exchange. Will, Mort, and other executives received the time-honored privilege of getting a private tour and ringing the closing bell on the exchange. The strategic move allowed them access to a larger source of funding during their time of high growth. Secondly, the move enhanced their reputation as a prominent financial institution among their competitors in a fast-growing market. Their securitization of loans gave them the opportunity to remove the loans from their balance sheet.

The process of securitization involves converting loans with similar interest rates and maturities into an investment that can be sold to investors. The ownership of the loans transfers to the investor while the servicing of the loan usually remains with the institution in exchange for a small fee. National Assets could free up their money by selling the loans. In turn they could use the proceeds of the sale of securities for new loans.

The accounting process behind these transactions usually brought large profits to the selling company at the time of the sale. Although some of the profits on the sale of these loans had to be taken in installments in proportion to the expected life of the loans, the transaction was more profitable than retaining ownership of the loans.

The result was that National Assets made money on the sale of the loans and on the servicing of the loans that they sold. In addition they found a less expensive way of funding their tremendous growth.

7

For the next four months David Jenkins built his servicing center for the home improvement loans, now sixty thousand loans and growing rapidly. The originations had increased the loan count dramatically. And the one servicing center that was operational struggled to keep up with the volume. As Dave's managers hired staff they put them to work on the servicing of loans downstairs in Bud Murphy's operation so that the transition would go smoothly when the work force came upstairs to their new cubicles and started working the separate portfolio.

By the end of April everyone was seated in cubicles ready for the launch of the new servicing center. With the endless problems that cropped up on systems and cash management, Dave had to delay the opening of his operation until May 5th. That was the "go live" date. When everyone walked into the center on that date, the new software platform would hold the sixty thousand loans. And Bud Murphy's operation would be sixty thousand loans lighter.

The opening day went off without a hitch. Dave had a breakfast catered in for his new employees. Every available section of floor space was lined with tables full of breakfast foods. Trays of scrambled eggs and sausage and bacon filled to overflowing. There was a whole table full of breakfast pastries and breads. Coffee, tea and an assortment of juices lined another table. Once again there were shirts. These were short-sleeved knit shirts with a logo adopted by Dave as the new home improvement logo. In deference to the company color Dave had part of the logo stitched in green thread on the white shirts. Everyone stood around in their new white short sleeve shirts devouring breakfast foods and talking excitedly. The festive atmosphere filled the workstations along with the rich smells of a hot breakfast. He, along with John Fremont gave the usual pep rally speeches on serving the customer's needs and the necessity for an efficient operation. Morale was high and a sense of pride surged through the work force. They knew that they were starting something historic and that they were at the center of it.

Downstairs Bob Whiting walked into Bud Murphy's office and patiently waited for Bud to get off the phone.

"Well, it looks like Jenkins made it," Bob said. He was dressed in his usual dark suit with cufflinks peeking out against the white shirt. Bob was an impeccable dresser but had a flair for gaudy neckties splashed with pink or yellow. He liked to mix the traditional dark suit with a tie splashed with loud colors. It was his statement of power and independence. He had been with the company for thirty years and still loved to tell the stories of lending money in the early days. He would start with the story that he would run the newly closed loans down to the local bank to offer them as security to fund the loans that they had made that day. They operated on a shoestring and Bob was proud the fact that he had been one of the pioneers in this behemoth company. And he didn't trust newcomers. He knew that he could stoke Bud's jealousy and fan the fire of mischievous behavior in Bud.

"Yeah," Bud said rolling his eyes toward the ceiling of his office. "Let's just wait and see if it blows. I doubt if Dave thought of everything. Something's liable to blow. Since their customer service number isn't that well known, I'll probably get a lot of the complaints. It will be my way of tracking their problems." Bud smiled at his own imaginings of a disaster on the horizon for the new servicing center.

"And Susan Orwell has made it possible so that I can track their delinquency performance," Bud added. He slapped a stack of computer reports on his desk. "I know where delinquency is today. If the rate goes up, all I have to do is start shouting about how they've screwed up my wonderful efforts over the past years."

"I hear he's asking a lot of questions that could embarrass you," Bob said dramatically. "I'm not saying that he's asking the questions to purposely embarrass you. It's just that they could cause you some inconvenience and explanation." Bob could see the dark look flash across Bud's eyes. "How can he match your delinquency statistics if he closes out the books on the last day of the month?"

"I still have control on what gets reported to the home office," Bud said. He had raised his voice more than he meant to. "I'll keep the books open as long as it takes after month end to get the delinquency rates down."

"What will keep him from eventually feeding his reports directly to home office?" Bob taunted. "What if he raises the protest that you are not cutting off the business at month end?"

"Look, if you guys want to keep some flexibility, some maneuvering room at month end, you better help me make sure that doesn't happen," Bud said coldly. "If we just cut off the month end without adding in straggling mail payments, we could be in a lot of trouble on our delinquency rates."

"Only for one month," Bob teased him relentlessly. "After that first month, the delinquency should trend down again. Besides, it's the way business is done in the real world. Now that we're publicly traded, someone's going to raise the question."

"That's not the way it's done in the real world," Bud snapped. "We're the real world. Why do we have to have some asshole come in here and tell us that we've been doing it wrong all these years? I've done what you asked me. I don't ask a lot of stupid questions. I've made us look good. You let this happen and you're making me look bad. You're hanging me out to dry." Bud's face flushed a deep shade of purple.

Bob smiled in satisfaction. He had Bud confused and angry, just where he wanted him. He didn't want Dave and Bud to ever get along. He didn't want Bud sharing old secrets. There was too much at stake he thought to himself. There were things that Bud couldn't know about yet. Yet Bob needed all of the players to make this work. Will had told him that.

"Well, I'd try to get along with him," Bob said in a conciliatory manner, "but at a distance." He stood to leave. As he readjusted his coat, he brushed the wrinkles out of his trousers and admired himself in the full-length mirror behind Bud's office door. "Keep me posted on how things go." Bob turned toward Bud one more time as he stepped into the doorway. "By the way, I'm on my way up to congratulate Dave on getting his shop open. Want to come along?"

Bud stared at Bob for a minute. He couldn't decide whether Bob was taunting him or not. After a moment he just shook his head. He wasn't about to go upstairs. He swore that it would be a long time before he ever set foot on Dave's turf. *He can come down here if he wants to see me,* Bud thought.

After a while Bud realized he had been staring into the open doorway of his office. Bob had left. Bud didn't even know if he said good-bye, he had been so lost in his anger. He picked up a pencil off of his desk and forcefully stabbed the sharp point into the computer print out on his desk.

8

The success of the new servicing center exceeded Dave's expectations. The mammoth operation had lifted itself off of the paper plans and organization charts into a smoothly functioning machine with a life of its own. There was one exception. The delinquency rates continued to rise steadily week after week. And the month end reports showed that the number of customers who had not paid on their accounts during the previous month was growing at a surprising pace. Other than that issue the phone system worked efficiently. The automated call distribution system could read the delinquent status of the loan and route the call to the collection department. This eliminated a lot of transferring that usually takes place in large operations with heavy incoming phone volume. The large electronic displays flashed information on how many incoming calls were taken, how many customers were on hold, and how long they had waiting for a customer service representative.

At a glance to another board Dave could see how many outbound collection calls were being made, how many staff were talking to customers and how many staff were off the phones. He brought his knowledge of phone and system technology from larger operations and put them to use in his new servicing center. The effect this had on the productivity of both the staff and the supervision was impressive. Executive management was impressed with the efficiency of the operation. And so was Dave.

Dave called his default manager, Eldora Redding, and asked her to look into the rising delinquency rates. He couldn't understand how he could be improving the coverage on delinquent loans, yet tracking a bigger delinquency number than Bud Murphy had before the split. Dave set a meeting for later in the week to review the findings with Eldora. He was starting to hear some of the indirect criticism on their handling of the delinquency. Any further increases in the delinquency rate would attract the attention of senior management as well as the investors on the loans. Dave knew he had to be ready with some explanations on the trend. He would also have to offer a plan on what he was doing to address the alarming rise in delinquency.

As a starting point he had accumulated several of the month end reports published by Bud Murphy's group. He studied the delinquency trends for the most recent months leading up to May. All of the reports showed the delinquency on the home improvement portfolio remaining static until May. The range of delinquency held steadily between 4.5% and 4.7% over a four-month period. This range of delinquency rate was an impressive show of control. Dave couldn't understand why the increase was happening so suddenly just as he had taken over the accounts.

He had taken special care to hire an experienced management team for the default unit. And the group of phone collectors had received extensive training before they had gone live with the operation. Trainers drilled the collection staff in state laws and negotiation techniques. They were tested on investor guidelines and dispute resolution guidelines. Each collector had at least forty hours of computer systems training and knew the federal Fair Debt Collection Practices Act verbatim. Dave knew that something was seriously wrong. It was just a matter of time before he discovered the cause.

On Friday afternoon Eldora knocked on the door of Dave's office. Eldora was in her mid forties. She was small and dressed professionally. Her hair was dyed blond with subtle streaks of gray. Her eyes and mouth looked like they had been pinched together by years of staring at delinquency reports. Her face fell naturally into a thoughtful frown. Years of smoking had left her voice deep and rough sounding. She had been recruited and recommended by John Fremont. She had managed delinquency operations for fifteen years. She knew what she was doing and gave a sense of confidence that Dave found comforting in light of this problem.

She walked over to Dave's desk and placed a stack of loan files on the corner of his desk. In addition she had several computer generated delinquency reports tucked under her arm. Without invitation she sat across from Dave and removed a pencil from her hair.

"You're never going to believe what I'm finding out about these accounts," she began. She smoothed out her business suit and took a sip of her coffee. She drank it all day long. Dave was surprised that she wasn't more excitable with all of the coffee she consumed throughout the day. Eldora also had a habit of sticking two or three pencils in her hair and then forgetting about them. Although she denied forgetting about them, her staff constantly removed them before she went into a meeting or left the building.

"I just hope it's something we can understand and fix quickly," Dave said. He looked over the stack of reports and file folders in front of him.

"Well, yes and no," Eldora answered. "Why don't I start with my conclusions and we can work backward for a little while."

"Fine," Dave said. "Just tell me when you change directions." Dave and Eldora liked each other. They respected each other's experience. Both had extensive experience in delinquency management. They talked the same language. Eldora earlier commented that it was gratifying to work for someone who understood the world of delinquency management. Both of them knew from experience that a delinquency manager could spend the majority of one's time educating a superior on the complexities of default management. And after that extensive education of a superior, there was no meaningful direction given. A delinquency manager usually found one's self alone, constantly defending one's actions and relying on initiative. It was a lonely job. If the delinquency rates rose, a delinquency manger was placed under an immense amount of criticism. If the results for the month were good, then everyone had the impression that the management team was only doing what was expected of them. A delinquency manager never succeeds, only survives. Dave knew that from his own experience.

"The core of our problem is in our conversion work," Eldora began. "We did such a good job of researching the data on these accounts that we put more delinquent loans into the portfolio than Bud Murphy's group was carrying."

"In other words he wasn't counting all the delinquent loans in his report?" Dave asked.

"That's right," Eldora smiled. She sipped her coffee carefully. "Now whether he or his staff knew what they were doing is something we will never be able to establish. But no matter how we bring this to the company's attention, it will embarrass Bud."

"So we lose no matter how we handle this," Dave said.

"There's more." Eldora slid the thick report to the side and pulled a single sheet of paper out of her folder and handed it to Dave. "These are the charge off reports for the preceding four months. I asked my staff to go back and research the loan type even though these loans didn't come over to our operation. If you'll read the summary of loan types, you notice that almost seven hundred thousand dollars worth of home improvement loans were written off as losses each month for the preceding four months."

"They just wrote off loans to loss in order to keep down the delinquency level." Understanding flashed across Dave's eyes. Eldora smiled.

"I'm so glad you understand delinquency," she said. "You're right. Bud's group was not collecting payments any better than we are. He just reduced delinquency rates by writing off loans to loss whenever he felt like it and was within the budgeted amount. Or he simply didn't count the loans as delinquent. And it gets more interesting. Prior to four moths ago, he didn't charge off one home improvement loan. He knew you were coming. It is a perfect way to hide delinquency, especially before he hands it off to someone else."

"Maybe he thought that we would never find out about it," Dave said.

"It gets more interesting," Eldora said. "Bud still has control over all charge off. No account gets written off to loss unless he approves it. Remember I told you that the home office wanted the charge off report centralized under Bud so that they could get the numbers from one source."

"But we send him a list of loss accounts every month to be charged off," Dave said.

"And not one of our accounts has been written off in the last few months, since we went live with our operation," Eldora said. She saw anger and frustration flush across Dave's face. It was the same wave of emotion that had swept over her yesterday when she was putting all of this together with her staff.

"What else have you found out?" Dave fought to control his anger and to keep focused until he had all of the information. He knew he already had enough to cause Bud a lot of embarrassment, but he needed to follow this to the end.

"Well, just as a precaution I had a couple of my mangers comb through all of the delinquent accounts for the following summaries." She held up a bundle of reports. "I wanted to know which accounts haven't paid in the past six months. I also inquired how many account balances were deficiency balances where we have settled the account and have no expectation of additional cash flow. Then I had them comb through those accounts that were in bankruptcy proceedings. The total of these non-performing accounts comes to seven million dollars. Seven million dollars of dead accounts that never should have been brought over to us as performing receivables are on the books. For months Bud has been understating the delinquency problem, understating the losses and hiding the real value of the servicing assets. The performing loans are a lot less than senior management thinks."

"Holy shit," Dave said. "I can't believe this." He saw the disappointment in Eldora's eyes. He could read her disillusionment about taking this assignment. Dave could read her suspicions that she was set up for this delinquency problem. He thought he saw the tears starting to form in her eyes.

"I wish we could have found this out the first month we were in business," Dave said.

"There was insufficient time to establish a trend," Eldora answered. "Besides how often do you expect someone to hide the losses when you take over an operation?"

"Well, time is still on our side as long as we surface this to the proper people." Dave picked up some of the reports and started thumbing through them.

"Who are the proper people?" Eldora asked. Her voice was full of skepticism. "Bud's got friends everywhere."

Dave leaned back in his chair and rubbed his face with his hands. He needed a plan. He had to act quickly before someone else discovered the problem. If that happened they would put the blame squarely on his shoulders. He knew that.

"How soon can you write this up for me in a summary memo?" Dave asked.

"How about first thing Monday?" Eldora said. "What are you going to do with it?"

"I'm going to request a meeting with the credit policy committee," Dave said. "That's my best chance to have the chief credit officer along with John Fremont sitting at the same table with Eagleton, Brice Curley and Bob Whiting. Then it should be a lot more difficult for anyone to hide it."

"We'll see," Eldora said. "I'll get you what you need on the memo with plenty of summary back up."

"Thanks, I think I'm going to need it," Dave said.

Eldora stood to leave and gathered up her reports. She looked at Dave for a moment trying to sense whether Dave was angry with her for bringing all this up. As if reading her thoughts Dave smiled at her.

"By the way, good job," he said warmly. "Not too many people could have uncovered all of this on their first look into it."

Eldora returned his smile and strode out of the office. Both of them wondered if they really had all of the answers that quickly. If all of this information had come on the first look, how much more lay hidden in the historical reports of the company. Dave suspected that the search was just beginning.

After Eldora left Dave stepped into the doorway of his office and looked out at the two hundred cubicles that filled the main floor of the office. He looked around proudly at the electronic bulletin boards that flashed information about the customer service phone traffic. Ninety percent of the incoming calls were getting answered in the first thirty seconds and there were no calls on hold. He glanced at the fax machines as they busily produce papers and intermittent beeps. He caught fragments of phone conversations from the collectors as they talked to delinquent customers. The servicing processes were all working, he thought to himself proudly. He had brought the operation up without a hitch.

But now he wondered where it all was heading. He hoped he had built it strong enough to last. He hoped that it would withstand the path he was about to take it on by bringing all of this delinquency and charge off information to the attention of senior management. Dave was fearful of the accusations senior management may try to deflect to deficiencies in his operation. He hoped that his servicing center could keep control through the inevitable scrutiny it would have to undergo.

He decided that his first step was to talk to John Fremont. Then he would put his plan together. Always have a plan, he remembered John saying. It will give you something to fall back on when the going gets tough. He turned around and picked up the phone receiver and called John.

John agreed to meet Dave outside the building. There was a smoking area at one corner of the shopping center where they occasionally met for a cigarette break. Friday afternoon was turning warm. The weekend traffic was already getting heavy on the nearby streets. Dave noticed that a lot of Bud Murphy's employees were leaving early.

After Dave had informed John of the discoveries on losses and delinquency, they were both quiet for a few moments.

"What's you're next step?" John asked.

"I plan on getting a time slot at the next credit policy meeting and bringing this to everyone's attention," Dave answered.

"You're kind of painting yourself into a corner," John said. "Once you do that, a lot of information may disappear or, at least, become inaccessible."

"I'm afraid that may happen anyway if we continue to dig. Someone's going to notice," Dave said. "Besides, if I bring it up at the meeting, I'm in the clear. I've surfaced a problem. You know how much weight that carries if the regulators get wind of it."

"By putting yourself in the clear, you might be putting yourself at risk," John said. "You'll publicly give Bud and any of his friends a good reason to go after you."

"They're not exactly my friends now," Dave quipped.

"Okay," John agreed. "But before you go into that meeting, I suggest you get your hands on the operational summaries for the last year. That way you'll have the raw data for your research once this is out in the open." John jabbed his cigarette into the ashtray. "Are you inviting me to this meeting?"

"Of course," Dave said and smiled. "You're supposed to be overseeing these two servicing operations."

John returned his smile. "This is going to get interesting. By the way, Gil Sheets, the new comptroller called and wanted to meet us. It's going to be a week before I can schedule anything. Why don't you give him a call and fill him in on some of this. It might be a good idea to make a friend of him and let him hear this story firsthand as part of his orientation."

"Good idea," Dave said. "Thanks for the tip."

Both walked back upstairs to their offices. Dave picked up his phone messages and started returning calls. Then he was going home for a quiet weekend. He knew it might be the last restful weekend for a long time if things didn't go well at the credit policy committee meeting.

9

Gil Sheets, the new comptroller, picked up the phone in his office. He was getting ready to fly back to Texas for the weekend to be with his family. His position in the company was a result of the rapid growth. National Assets had vigorously recruited Gil for the comptroller's position. They knew of his reputation in Texas as a cautious and thorough financial analyst. In his previous job he had restructured the assets of the company in a way that gave them major tax and borrowing advantages. His efforts produced several million dollars in a combination of savings and revenues for the organization.

He would report to the chief financial officer for the present. The goal was to take some of the financial reporting responsibilities off the chief financial officer's shoulders while the company reorganized into a more effective management team, one that could respond quickly to the needs of the developing business lines. The growth and expansion spread into more parts of the country due to successful marketing campaigns. Someone had to help control the flow of funds.

"Good afternoon, Gil," Dave said. "Welcome to National Assets. I thought I'd take a minute to let you know who I am and what I hope to do for the company. Sometimes it sticks better than just reading the organization chart."

"I've heard your name," Gil said. "And I appreciate the call. You know how quiet the phone is for the first few weeks on a new job. It's getting a little tedious reading all these reports and sitting in meetings trying to get oriented."

"I can appreciate that," Dave laughed. "I'm fairly new here myself. If you have a few minutes I thought we could talk or maybe set up a meeting over a cup of coffee early next week."

"Why don't we talk now," Gil answered. "I've got a little time before I have to head to the airport. I'm going to be in Texas next week getting ready for the move. You know, moving vans and motels?"

"I know exactly," Dave laughed again. He knew he was going to like working with Gil. He wasn't yet part of the network of cronies and had no history with the company. Gil would be a good objective listener for what Dave was about to say.

Dave briefly took Gil through the first months of his preparatory work on the new home improvement servicing center. Dave toned down some of the conflict that had arisen between Bud Murphy and him. Then Dave began outlining his findings on the delinquency rates and the loss issues over the last few months leading up to the opening of the servicing center. He carefully left any of his personal speculations out and hoped that the facts would paint a clear picture. Judging from Gil's responses, it worked.

"I appreciate your bringing this to my attention. I can look into some of this when I get back from Texas. And judging from what you've said, I'll take care to be discreet about it until you've had your say in the credit policy meeting."

"Is there any way I could get a look at the investor accounting reconciliation reports for the last few months?" Dave pressed. "That would give me information on how much money flowed to certain investors."

"You're asking for something I haven't been able to look at yet, Dave," he answered. "Let me see what I can do. I don't even know if those accounting reports are on the system or still completed manually. I'll call you when I get back and let you know."

"While you're at it maybe we could look at some of the bank statements for the investor accounts?" Dave continued to press.

"Let me see what I can get," Gil answered. Exasperation crept into his voice.

After the perfunctory goodbyes Dave hung up the phone and looked out his office window. The streets were full of evening rush hour traffic. Lines of cars sat in the hot sun waiting for their turn to get through the intersections. Friday evenings in California rush hour traffic were always a challenge to Dave's patience. He wondered if he would ever get used to the traffic. Tonight he knew he would be able to sit in the traffic and spend time thinking about next week. He could momentarily escape from the increasing pressure of his job.

He walked out the side door at the bottom of the stairs to the servicing center and let the hot evening air wash over him. His weekend was beginning. And he knew he would need his rest for the week ahead.

10

During the early weeks of operation in Dave's new servicing center John Fremont convinced National Assets to open an expansion operation in Albuquerque, New Mexico. The fledgling operation had the responsibility of disposing of properties that the company had acquired through foreclosure.

National Assets had about three hundred loans in their foreclosure inventory. The company was trying to sell them. They assigned a tenured National Assets employee who had worked most of his career in delinquency operations. Unfortunately he was in a bigger job than he could handle. His way of coping with the stress had been to ignore the details of property disposal and to accept gratuities from vendors who were hungry for business. His method of operation cost National Assets tens of thousands of dollars in unnecessary interest costs and selling expenses. His dishonesty slowly surfaced and the company had to take action. The company fired him within thirty days of finding out about his self-enriching activities. Bud Murphy protested vigorously over the firing of his long time friend.

John Fremont knew that the management position in New Mexico would take someone with experience in repairing and marketing properties throughout the United States. They needed someone with an extensive record in the disposition of real estate. They needed someone who could diplomatically fend off the offers of bribes for business. The industry called these foreclosed properties REO's, which stood for real estate owned.

John recruited an associate of his for the job. Buster Burns lived in Albuquerque and managed an REO disposition operation for a national bank for over ten years. The bank recently sold the operation and Buster was looking for another job at the time John called him.

Buster was in his late forties, bald and wore thick glasses. The years of office work had softened and fattened him. He looked like he was made out of dough with a noticeable lack of wrinkles in his face. He dressed professionally in expensive suits and still practiced the time honored fashion of wearing cufflinks in his dress shirts. He was friendly and intelligent. After a few minutes of discussion with him, it was apparent that not many people knew the foreclosure, reo disposition and eviction business better than Buster.

Buster was well known in the mortgage banking industry as a no nonsense manager who could sell properties quickly while keeping the losses to a minimum on each account. It was an art that few default managers mastered as well as he. It was more like running a real estate brokerage and a property preservation business. Buster could quickly spot the houses that were going to be problems. He aggressively marketed these and surprised a lot of people at his quick and economical sales of these distressed homes.

Buster was about three months behind Dave in getting his operation started. At John Fremont's suggestion, Buster decided to spend a couple of weeks in Sacramento talking with Dave about his experience in getting an operation started with National Assets. They liked each other immediately. Both Buster and Dave were veterans of large companies. They knew each other by reputation and found they had a lot of common ground in the business.

Dave gave Buster full access to his organization charts, policies and procedures manuals, and his project charts. Buster found the information invaluable in getting the names and numbers of key people from Dave's notes. He saw where he could take short cuts and he understood who the decision makers were in the critical departments of telecommunications and systems.

Like Dave, Buster had also served on fraud prevention committees within the business. Both had a deep appreciation for fraud detection procedures. They could spot fraud very quickly based on their experience and their research. And they knew how to follow the trail to the perpetrators of fraud within the mortgage business. Sometimes fraud tracked back to an employee. Employees had to have cooperation from other employees or from outside vendors. The separation of duties built into most operations required collusion between employees in order to perpetrate fraud.

At other times there was a ring of criminals operating from city to city. They posed as customers. Some within the fraud ring posed as realtors, employers, appraisers and sellers. An unwitting lender could lose millions of dollars in a few days on only three or four transactions. Then the ring would dissolve and leave town, leaving the lender with devastating losses and a confusing trail.

Both Dave and Buster had seen variations of fraud in their years of mortgage banking. But Buster was the expert. John Fremont hired him with that talent in mind. National Assets, an aggressive lender in new markets, was especially vulnerable to fraud. And John knew that fraud rings looked for lenders like National Assets who didn't have the resources or the experience to guard against fraud loans.

During one of their lunches together John and Dave brought up the subject of fraud loans within the company to Buster. Buster listened to them intently. Without ever looking at the loans Buster recognized the red flags, the warning indicators of fraud. Within a week of that conversation, Buster had tracked some of the fraud back to the manager who had previously managed the REO, real estate owned, assets. He found fake invoices from companies that had never performed work on the foreclosed homes. The charges were exorbitant. Yet no one had noticed. When the audit department confronted the long time employee, he admitted to some of his dealings, enough to get him fired.

That event proved to be a turning point in Buster's fledgling career at National Assets. Somehow he had managed to incur the anger of a group of senior managers in the home office. The event also forged a close bond among Dave, John and Buster. They had become the change agents that the company was looking for. Their resumes made the company look more attractive, gave it more credibility within the mortgage banking industry. But they were gradually becoming a thorn in the side of a lot of the entrenched managers who were embarrassed at the mistakes that these three were continually finding within the company.

Even with John and Dave's help, Buster had an unusually difficult time getting his operation running in New Mexico. He had made enemies and he was paying for it. John counseled him that he was just going to have to go a little slower. John told him that eventually they would have the operation in place. And John slowly built his empire within the empire of National Assets. He built it quietly and steadily. He knew that eventually he would have the leverage he needed to make the company run the way a mortgage business was meant to run. It was just going to take a little time.

11

The following Wednesday Dave walked into the credit policy committee meeting. The committee was comprised of the senior management team of Will Eagleton, Bruce Curley, Bob Whiting and the chief legal counsel for the company, Wilma Maloney. They met once a month in the plush executive conference room near Will's office.

Dave walked into the executive building and made his way through the lush tropical plants and soft green walls that gave the appearance of a rain forest. The overabundance of vegetation gave a wild and ominous appearance to the lobby. Dave had the feeling that a leopard was going to leap from the bushes and pounce at his throat before he reached the meeting. As he entered the conference room he noticed that John Fremont was already sitting at the long table. To Dave's surprise Bud Murphy was also sitting at the table next to Will. The corners and the ends of the table were occupied leaving Dave a chair near the center. Although Dave was not surprised to see that all the power positions at the table were taken, he was concerned that Bud Murphy was there. He figured that Bud would eventually find out about the meeting. But Dave knew that now he faced a potential confrontation with Bud. He knew that what he was about to reveal would make Bud defensive and confrontational.

Dave nodded his good morning and took his seat at the table. He was pulling his chair up to the table when Will started the meeting.

"I think that the first thing on our agenda is to hear what Dave Jenkins wants to discuss," Will said evenly. "Then we can let him get back to work." The message was clear that Dave was not invited to attend the entire meeting. "Dave, why don't you go ahead and get started?"

"Thank you, Will," Dave said as he passed out the small folders of information. "The issue I want to bring to everyone's attention deals with delinquent loans and losses. What I've found warrants your attention and ideas for handling this issue. If you'll look at the first page you'll find a summary of my findings and my concerns about the home improvement portfolio," he began briskly. "My primary concern is that the delinquency rates appear to be increasing over the last three months. However, if you take into consideration the way that we are classifying the delinquent accounts in comparison to the way they were grouped before the accounts were handed off to me, you'll see that the delinquency hasn't really gone up that much."

"Then why is it higher on your reports?" Bob Whiting asked.

"Because not all of the delinquent accounts were counted in the rates prior to three months ago," Dave answered. Eyes turned to Bud for some kind of response. But, Bud remained silent. "Why that is, I don't know. The attached reports show that this is true. In addition, there was an inordinate amount of loans written off to loss the month before I took over the home improvement portfolio. This would artificially lower the delinquency rate and understate the growing delinquency problem that this company has been experiencing over the past year."

"That's quite an accusation," Will said. "Are you sure you can back that up?" The room was quiet.

"I already have," Dave said calmly. He noticed that Will had not touched the packet in front of him. Dave was sure it had something to do with "deniable plausibility" if the issue ever ended up in court, or in front of a regulator. Will had the option of conveniently denying ever hearing about this problem. "If you'll turn to the appendix, I've restated the delinquency figures for every month end for the past year without taking into consideration the charge off figures. That gives us a more accurate depiction of the growing delinquency problem."

"Is that it?" Will said curtly. He shot an angry glance toward Bud.

"Actually there's more," Dave continued. "There's another seven million dollars in non-performing loans in the portfolio that should have been charged off a long time ago."

"Seven million dollars?" Bruce spoke up. Dave could hear the alarm in his voice. "We don't have seven million dollars budgeted for charge off this early in the year."

"Based on the migration analysis, the flow of loans from one stage of delinquency to a more serious stage of delinquency, the problem will only continue to grow. I project that it will increase to at least thirteen million by the end of the year." Dave noticed that no one, not even the corporate counsel, was taking notes. Will turned to Bud and spoke.

"What's your read on this, Bud?" Will asked. Bud was visibly flustered at being put on the spot.

"Well, I, ah," he stammered, "my guess would be that these accounts could use some more collection activity before we charge them off. Otherwise I would have charged them off when the loans were under my control."

"You better reconsider that answer," Dave snapped. "These accounts don't need more work. They're uncollectable. Some of the customers have died. Some are bankrupts with no collateral on the loans to go after. Some are accounts that were settled for a portion of the balance over a year ago and should have been charged off to loss then." Dave noticed his voice had risen more than he had wanted it to.

"Now wait," Will interrupted. "This bickering is getting us nowhere. We have to remember we're all on the same team here." Everyone's expressions relaxed a little. "Are you sure you're not overreacting to this issue, Dave?" Will said in more amicable tone of voice.

"I don't think so," Dave said with conviction. "Based on the incidents of fraud that my staff discovered and brought to my attention, and based on the sanctions imposed on us by HUD after their last audit citing of our servicing deficiencies, I think that we have a serious problem on our hands. And if I'm going to fix it I need everyone's concurrence that we have a problem and that we need to restate our delinquency. We also need to take more losses until we whittle down this seven million dollar block of non-performing loans, before the number grows."

There was silence among the group for a few moments. Dave wondered why John hadn't said anything. It was apparent that he was comfortable being an observer on this controversial issue for the present. Finally Will broke the silence.

"Why don't we put this on hold right now and give it some consideration," Will began. "In the meantime Bud can review this list of non-performing loans and see if any of them do need more collection work. We don't want to run out and tell our investors about a seven million dollar special charge off, unless we absolutely have to."

Bruce Curley turned to Dave and said, "Dave, why don't you give us a charge off projection, month by month, for the rest of the year. In your forecast why don't you build in an incremental amount of charge off that will eliminate the seven million dollars over the months remaining in the year? In that way we can quietly and gradually address this issue if we do have to charge these loans off."

"Good idea," Will said. "In the meantime this issue is not to be discussed outside this conference room." Will looked directly at Dave. "I know that you will need to involve some of your staff to work on parts of this project. But they don't need to know the whole picture. And we don't need to enter any discussions about this issue." Will stood up. "Is everyone clear on that?" he asked.

Everyone nodded their assent and gathered up their papers to leave. Dave noticed that Will still hadn't touched the folder placed in front of him. He left it on the table as he stepped out of the conference room.

Bud was the next to leave. He gathered his papers, shoved them into a folder and left the room staring down at the floor all the way out. John Fremont stood and looked at Dave.

"Why don't you send me a list of those loans," John said. "I'll make sure that Bud gets a copy. That will give me a chance to discuss it with him."

"Fine," Dave said. "I appreciate the help."

The remaining officers smiled curtly and nodded toward Dave as they left the room. Dave suddenly realized that the meeting had broken up before they had planned to break it up. He wondered if the bombshell he dropped on them was enough bad news for one morning. He also wondered if they had only met to discuss this issue. In any event Dave had an uneasy feeling as he left the building. He wondered if he had any support left after his presentation. He wondered if his career move to National Assets had been a mistake.

All he knew in the final analysis was that he had no choice but to surface his findings. He was here and couldn't second guess his career move. He would have to play this out as best he could. He took a deep breath as he headed for the parking lot.

12

As soon as the meeting had ended, Will Eagleton, Bruce Curley and Bob Whiting refilled their coffee cups and gathered in Will's office. Will invited them to sit around the small round mahogany table. The office walls were fifteen feet high and covered with Egyptian art. There were paintings of Set and Ra. Many of the prints resembled the paintings seen on the inner walls of the pyramids. A bust of Nefertiti stood on a small end table near Will's oversized desk.

Once they were all seated around the table, Bob Whiting started the conversation.

"We've got to find a way to put a stop to Dave Jenkins digging around and announcing his findings," Bob said.

"That's why we hired him," Bruce answered. "He's obviously good at what he does if he discovered all of this in his first few weeks of running the operation."

"Yeah, but Bob's right," Will added. "We don't need him to go out and talk about this to anyone. Frankly I'm pleased that he brought it to our attention first. That's a good indication of his loyalty."

"I don't trust him or the situation he's creating," Bob said. "I think we ought to get rid of him before he finds out anything else."

"He already knows too much," Bruce said. "Besides, he didn't create the situation. He brought it to our attention. Like Will said he came to us with his findings."

"I know that," Bob said impatiently. "But he's in such an adversarial relationship with Bud, there's no telling what he'll do next."

"What makes you think he won't work out his differences with Bud?" Will asked.

"Because Bud's an asshole," Bob quickly replied. "We all know that. He's impossible to get along with once he loses his temper."

"We owe Bud," Will said. "He's pulled us out of some tough situations on delinquency. And he's done it without home office and our investors finding out about it."

"It's too volatile a situation," Bob said. "We need to cut our losses. Who's going to be interested in buying the company if they're buying into a big fight among the management?"

"I don't want to hear any more talk about selling the company," Will said. His voice rose sharply. "We don't even think about that plan right now." He looked directly at Bob to make sure he understood the warning. "I'll have a talk with Bud," Will said in a calmer voice. "We have everything to gain if we can win Dave's loyalty and if we can get Bud and Dave to get along. Let's work that angle for now." Will turned to Bruce.

"Bruce, I want you to work with John Fremont," Will said. "Make sure he acts as a go between for Bud and Dave. We need to keep an eye on him, too. He's new and he knows a lot."

"I'll get to work on it right away," Bruce said. He decided not to tell Will that he had already started on that plan.

"We need to keep a lid on all of this. We have to give the appearance that we're addressing and correcting our deficiencies caused by our rapid growth. Perception, gentlemen, is everything. Remember that and we'll all be rich someday soon."

All three smiled conspiratorially and stood. Will walked back to his desk and retrieved a bottle of spring water from his private refrigerator. Bruce and Bob walked back to their respective offices down the hall.

The lunch hour was approaching and Will Eagleton grabbed his green nylon gym bag and headed out the door. He spent at least three lunch hours a week at the fitness center four blocks from the office. After buying a bottle of water at the front counter of the gym, Will headed into the locker and changed out of his suit.

Armed with a towel and water bottle Will stepped onto one of the treadmills and started jogging. He gradually increased the speed until he was running at a good clip. The treadmill motor whirred as Will drove himself for twenty minutes running toward something only he could see in his mind. When he shut the treadmill off, he was drenched in his own sweat, gasping for air and staring in the mirror with a determination that draws curious looks from the casual athletes.

After catching his breath he approached the free weight room as if preparing for a fight. He grabbed a set of dumbbells and started pumping away. He growled with determination and muttered curses at himself in the mirror. A couple of body builders thinking that he might be mentally unstable gave him a wide berth. They found other machines to use while Will was cursing and growling. Soon the veins on his arms looked as if they would burst. He paused long enough to admire his physique in the full-length mirrors before he moved on to the next set of free weight exercises.

He strode to the counter twice for fresh towels. He prowled through the gym attacking weight machines like a wild animal on the prowl for its first meal in days. Finally he finished his workout with countless sit-ups on an incline board. Forty-five minutes from the time he entered the locker room he left. Other members of the gym relaxed once again into their workouts when they saw him leave.

13

Dave thought that it was strange that he hadn't heard from Gil Sheets. It had been almost a week since they had talked. Even though Gil was in the process of moving from Texas, he had promised to call Dave earlier in the week. Maybe he just got busy with the move, Dave thought. Maybe he hasn't had time to look at the material on losses and delinquency.

Dave drove in the traffic near the state fairgrounds thinking about the comments in the meeting. He knew that he had scraped some raw nerves. And his findings were treated with a lot less urgency than he thought they would be treated. He wondered if they knew about this problem all along. He wondered if it was some kind of test to see if he would find problems on his own. He had the uneasy feeling that his presentation had been perceived as an attack on Bud. And if they perceived it that way, then they would all stick together a little more closely. Dave had an uneasy feeling about taking the job, moving to California, and leaving a respectable company. He resolved to have an exit plan for himself by the end of the week.

He mentally made a checklist of things he would do. First, he would update his resume. Then he would make some calls to friends in the industry, do a little networking in case they knew of any openings. Also his friends would make good character references as long as he stayed in touch with them. He needed to make sure that he had been reimbursed on all of his business expenses, so that he wouldn't be leaving any money on the table if he did have to leave in a hurry.

As he pulled into the parking lot of the old shopping center he felt better just thinking about an exit plan. The exercise always alleviated some of the stress he was feeling. He learned long ago that the worst thing he could do is to allow himself to feel trapped in a job. Then all kinds of bad things seem to happen.

He smiled at his administrative assistant as he passed her cubicle on his way to his office. He hired Marilee from another department within the company and she had done a good job of keeping Dave organized. She took the initiative in deflecting much of the unnecessary details away from Dave and into the hands of the appropriate managers. She kept all the details of phone calls and meetings. And she managed many of the projects necessary to bring the operation up and running on schedule. Dave felt fortunate to find such a capable assistant.

"Hi Marilee, any messages?" he asked cheerfully.

"Couple of voice mails for you," Marilee answered returning his smile. "One from a Gil Sheets, and the other from Bruce Curley. Mr. Curley wants you to call him back."

"Thanks," Dave replied. He stepped into his office with a handful of mail that Marilee had given him as he passed by. He dropped his briefcase next to his chair and hit the message button on his phone. After he had navigated through the password and menu selections he finally listened to his two messages. Bruce Curley wanted to talk to him as soon as possible and Gil Sheets said that he was sorry he missed Dave and that he would try to call back tomorrow. Dave wondered why Gil hadn't left a number. Then he realized that he was either on the road, or was too busy to be near a phone for very long. Dave carefully logged the calls in his appointment book.

Bruce Curley answered on the second ring. Dave had a feeling that Bruce was sitting by his phone waiting for his call.

"Thanks for returning my call so quickly, Dave," Bruce said in an amicable voice. "By the way that was an excellent job on the presentation earlier today."

"Thank you, Bruce," Dave said. He waited for Bruce to get to the point.

"I think that the next step would be to put together an action plan that addresses the incremental charge off of those non performing loans as well as looking at adopting a more explicit write off policy."

"I submitted a policy to you a couple of months ago, Bruce." Dave said.

"Yes, I know," Bruce replied. "But what I need you to do is to sit down with Bud and agree on a policy that will fit both servicing centers so that we have some consistency to the loans we are writing off to loss. We can also do some more accurate projections if we know what loans qualify for charge-off."

"I agree," Dave said carefully. "But I know that Bud prefers to have some flexibility on this issue. I think that we are going to have a little trouble agreeing on a universal write off policy."

"I'm hoping that you can use your interpersonal skills to overcome that, Dave," Bruce answered. "I know that you have a lot of experience at managing delinquency. And Bud, proud as he is, needs to benefit from that experience. It may take some effort on your part to arrive at an agreement on this policy, but I'm counting on it happening. As you said this morning, 'if we don't address this loss issue now, it's only going to get bigger.' I would take it as a great favor if you'll work with me on this one, Dave."

"Okay," Dave said. He ran his fingers through his hair and closed his eyes. "I'll give him a call and set up a meeting. I want to keep you informed by way of copies on everything so that you know what efforts I'm making on getting this resolved."

"Good idea," Bruce said. "And I know that you'll get it handled. We know that you can run circles around Bud in the servicing business, Dave. That's why we're paying you more than him. I also know that he's a senior vice president and that you're only a vice president. Maybe we can address that issue so that Bud's dealing with someone on his own level."

"That would be nice," Dave replied. He hoped that Bruce could hear the smile in his voice. "I would certainly appreciate that gesture."

"I'll see what I can do and call you back tomorrow."

"Thanks. Bruce," Dave said. "Thanks a lot."

The conversation ended shortly after that. As Dave replaced the receiver on the phone he stared at the reports on his desk. He was stunned, but pleased. Maybe they were sending him a signal, he thought. Maybe he had done the right thing in surfacing the loss issue this morning.

"You're going to be late for your own meeting," Marilee's voice interrupted his thoughts. She was standing in the doorway with a copy of his calendar feigning exasperation.

"Oh, where is it?" Dave asked. He looked down at his own calendar.

"Conference room 210," she answered. "Just follow me. I've got the copies of the agenda. After all you invited me to this meeting."

"Right," Dave said. "Let's get going."

Dave walked down the hallway beside Marilee. He was thankful for her thoroughness, especially when he had so much to distract him right now. He smiled at the thought of his forthcoming promotion as he entered the conference room.

Later that day while Dave was sitting at his desk he received a call from Buster Burns. Buster had returned to New Mexico and was glad to be out of

Sacramento.

"Dave, have you heard the news?" Buster began excitedly.

"No. What news?" Dave asked.

"About Gil Sheets, the new financial guy they just hired." Buster paused for effect. "He resigned. He went back to Texas and resigned."

"I thought he was in the middle of the move to California?" Dave asked.

"He was," Buster answered. "The word is that he had seen enough to know that this wasn't a move he wanted to make. So he quit."

"Wow." Dave was at a loss for words. He had been waiting to hear from Gil. Now he doubted that he ever would. "I wonder what he saw?"

"My guess is that he saw something in the numbers that scared him away. John Fremont called and told me about your meeting with the big wigs. Sounds like you really stirred them up."

"That wasn't my intent. I just felt that I had an obligation to bring some irregularities to their attention," Dave said evenly. "I didn't know that it was going to go so badly. I wonder if Gil just didn't like California."

"That's doubtful," Buster answered. "He worked out there once before. He loved it. I think he found out something."

Immediately Dave thought about the information he had shared with Gil just before Gil had left for Texas. He wondered if that influenced his resignation. He gripped the phone willing Gil to return his call.

"Look, Buster, I've got to get going. Let me make some calls around here. I can sound innocent enough, since no one here told me that Gil is gone yet. I'll let you know what I find out."

"Okay, buddy," Buster said, "but watch your step. You may have stumbled onto something they didn't think that you would find out so quickly. I'm starting to do some analysis on the losses myself, on the foreclosed properties. You wouldn't believe what I'm finding out."

"Look," Dave said cautiously, "Maybe we better call each other at home tonight. These lines may not be safe, even though I just had them installed. Besides, I gave Gil the information on the irregularities on delinquency and write offs before he left for Texas."

"I'd keep that to yourself, my friend," Buster said. "How about sending me a copy?"

"What are you going to do with it?"

"Just look it over. See if there are any patterns to what I'm finding on the foreclosures. I'd love to help get Bud in trouble."

"I don't think we can," Dave said. "He's too well entrenched."

"We'll see," Buster said calmly. "They eventually will need a scapegoat for all of this. Call me tonight when you get home."

"Okay. I'll talk to you later," Dave said and hung up the phone. He stared straight ahead at the wall of his office. It was an empty wall, freshly painted. He had ordered a print for the wall, but it would be four more weeks before it would be up there. He wondered if he would last long enough to see the painting. He gripped his desk to hold off the wave of panic that swept through him.

An uneasy feeling gradually took hold of him as he thought about the events of the past few days. He reached for the phone and called Ann at home. Although he called her during the day occasionally, Ann could tell that something was troubling Dave. He explained what had happened with the meeting. He described some of the managers whom Ann had never met.

"So what does all of this tell you?" she asked when Dave had finished his update.

"I'm beginning to wonder if the promotion is an attempt to keep me quiet. Maybe they want me to be complicit until they find a way to fix the problem."

"Maybe you should wait until tonight so that we can talk about this without you using a company phone," she cautioned.

"Now who's paranoid?"

They laughed, said their goodbyes, and hung up. Dave knew that he would get a chance to explain everything to Ann during dinner. It was important for him to find out her reaction to all of this. Dave knew that she was a good sounding board in matters like this.

14

The founder of the company, Leo Pecunia, still occupied an office in Chicago and helped to oversee the Chicago operation even though he had turned control of the company over to his son in California. Here in Chicago stood the original building where the company had grown into the equity lending leader it was today. The offices still managed the accounting and secondary marketing functions. Also the chief legal counsel, Mort Smalley, kept his office next to Leo's. They were lifelong friends and Mort refused to leave the comfort of Chicago for the new offices in California.

Although the building in Chicago was old and simple by comparison to their new offices in California, the executive offices were the old style, too. The offices were plush. Thickly carpeted rooms lined with dark paneling and bookshelves and leather chairs still gave off the scent of cigar smoke from previous years. The artwork was original and oil based. Even the executives in California, the Chicago transplants, as they were known, still referred to the Chicago office as the home office. They all held great respect mixed with a healthy dose of fear for Mort Smalley.

Mort dressed in thousand dollar suits and liked to visit the best restaurants in the city. He tipped the waiters and the chef before he sat down at his table to order. That way there were no misunderstandings, no guessing, about the service he expected.

As generous as he was with tipping, he was as ruthless with anyone who crossed him. Many former employees attested to this as they made their way to other jobs within the industry. In some secret and powerful way Mort Smalley ruled National Assets. The managers who knew him were thankful that he chose to stay in Chicago. But his reach was limitless when something went wrong in the company. He had heard about David Jenkins discovering the hidden losses. He had anticipated it. He had warned Will and Bruce that if they went around the country looking for talent, not to be surprised when this new talent started discovering the true condition of the company.

But he had a different approach to keeping the secrets within the company. Pay them enough money, treat them well and they will reciprocate with loyalty and hard work for a while. Mort thought of them as he did the chefs and waiters that he tipped. Once the meal was over he had no use for them. But while they were working for you, in a sense, treat them well with money. He believed in setting the expectation with dollars. If that didn't work, Mort believed in the power of fear.

Mort sat at his polished mahogany desk and looked at the legal pad with his notes jotted in pencil. Classical music played softly in the background. His white brows furrowed and his manicured hand touched a button on his phone.

"Get me Will in Sacramento," he said in a soft, calm voice. In a few moments his secretary made the connection.

"Good morning, Will," Mort cloaked the iciness in his voice with feigned courtesy. "How are things in California?"

"We're going to have a record month, if that's what you mean," Will replied. "I get the idea that you've got something on your mind."

Mort laughed into the phone. He pulled the legal pad closer and put on a pair of reading glasses.

"I hear you've been talking about losses," he began. "Or more precisely that Mr. Jenkins, our new hire, has found new interest in loan accounting practices that were conducted before his time."

"You heard right," Will answered. "How did it get back to you already Mort?"

"He's been asking for reports. He's been asking for historical reports. He's been asking about the funding processes. He's been asking about investors and if these investors have published any guidelines. He's asking for old audits. He's questioning why we don't report account balances to the credit bureau. In other words he's asking all the right questions, Will. Or should I say he's asking the wrong ones." Mort's voice wasn't as friendly now. He waited silently for Will's response.

"He's running a servicing operation, Mort. What guy worth his salt wouldn't want to look at some history?" Will said. "Besides, he's been good about bringing any concerns to the credit policy committee meeting. I've got more problems with Bud Murphy getting along with him than I have anything else."

"Good. Good," Mort answered thoughtfully. "I want those two to keep their distance from each other. I don't want them to get close, you know, true confessions over a beer."

"That isn't going to happen," Will said with exaggerated assurance. "At least not this century."

"Good," Mort said again. His voice was calmer. "What's going on with this new guy in Albuquerque? I get this letter from an attorney we've been doing business with for thirty years. This attorney says that the new guy, Buster Burns, isn't going to send him any business. This upsets me, Will."

"I'll give him a call," Will said trying to placate him.

"No, I think I'll have a chat with Mr. Burns," Mort replied coldly. "I'm taking this personally." There was silence on the phone until Mort spoke again. "And this Mr. Jenkins? Keep him close and reward him for the fine work he's been doing. He needs to know that loyalty is rewarded, that it's one of our core values here at National Assets."

"I'm already doing that," Will answered evenly. "We're promoting him to First Vice President to put him on the same level as Bud Murphy. That will add a little fuel to the fire. Bud will be pissed over that for a couple of months, at least. We're also giving him a bigger share in the bonus pool and increasing his stock options."

"Nice," Mort commented. "Nothing like a few heavy chains to keep the good ones quiet."

"And loyal," Will added.

"We'll talk again on this next week, Will." It was more of a command than a suggestion. Mort hung up the phone without saying good-bye. After he inspected his polished fingernails, he tore the sheet of notes from his legal pad and placed it through the shredder. He stood up and walked to his window that overlooked the small commercial area surrounding the building. The trees were still bare from the winter cold. The sky was the usual gray overcast that preceded a good snowfall in the area. Mort smiled coldly at everything and at nothing in particular.

15

The morning traffic seemed heavier than usual to Dave as he made his way to the office. There was a slight chill in the air, a chill he knew would disappear when the warm California sun made its way up off the horizon. He loved the weather in California. Every day that it wasn't raining held the promise of warm afternoons. About a mile from the office Dave liked to stop at a coffee shop and get a cup of coffee and a roll.

Today he stopped and decided to drink his coffee at one of the outside tables and watch some of the traffic make its way down the streets. He sat and mulled over the events from last week. Since his meeting with the credit policy committee, he had made little progress with Bud Murphy. Dave found out about his promotion and took it as a sign of good faith on the part of the company. He promised himself to acknowledge that gesture by keeping his servicing operation running flawlessly and by finding a way to restate the delinquency figures more accurately. That, he thought, should please everyone. He had even received approval to hire additional staff to work the delinquent accounts. Money seemed to be no object. Or else they just weren't that strict with the budget. In any event Dave was feeling energized about his job. But the self-imposed stress was on.

The disappearance of Gil Sheets still puzzled him. Gil had never returned his call. Dave eventually found out that Gil decided to stay in Texas. The company had given no official explanation for the resignation. To most of the employees it was a non-event. But to the management team there was an air of unresolved mystery around the resignation, more so for Dave since he thought he might have been one of the last people to talk to Gil before he resigned.

When Dave arrived at his office he saw the messages that had come in already this morning. John Fremont wanted to meet him for lunch. Buster Burns wanted him to call. And a couple of angry customers who were unhappy with the way they had been treated by the customer service staff wanted personal conversations with Dave. At the bottom of the pile was a message from Bud Murphy. Dave was surprised because it was the first time that Bud had taken the initiative to call him. Dave decided to call Bud first.

"Good morning, Bud," Dave greeted him after getting through the secretary's screening.

"Morning, Dave," Bud said gruffly. "Listen, I was wondering if you were free for lunch some time this week." Dave could hear the effort in Bud's voice.

"Sure. How about tomorrow?" Dave said cheerily. "Anything special you wanted to talk about?" Dave thought he would press his good fortune.

"Yeah," Bud started. "There are a couple of things on delinquency. I thought we should begin talking about these non performing loans as well." Bud paused momentarily. "And I thought since we're going to be working together, I ought to iron out a few wrinkles I put in the way."

"I'm looking forward to it," Dave answered. "How about 11:30 tomorrow?"

"Let's make it 12:30," Bud said. "I've been working late lately. Too early a lunch makes for a long afternoon. Why don't we just walk down to a restaurant in the mall to avoid traffic time?"

"Sounds good," Dave said. "I'll stop by your office just before 12:30 and we can go from there. And thanks for the call, Bud."

"Yeah, sure." Bud said a quick good bye and hung up.

Dave sat at his desk stunned by Bud's gesture. He thought that somebody, maybe Bruce or Bob, had talked to him. Perhaps John Fremont had convinced him to work cooperatively. In any case, Dave was pleased that another obstacle seemed to be dissolving before his eyes. He clapped his hands in excitement and smiled at his phone.

"Must be good news," John Fremont said from the doorway. Dave hadn't seen him approach his office. John's height combined with his deep voice demanded attention and usually startled the unsuspecting target of his greetings. Dave was no exception.

"I think it is," Dave said thoughtfully. "How are you this morning, John?"

"I've got some interesting news," he said. John stepped into Dave's office and closed the door. He sat down across from Dave. "I've got a story that's kind of interesting. Thought you might like to hear it. And I'd like to get your thoughts on it."

"Let's hear it," Dave said. He leaned across his desk toward John.

"Remember the convention last January?" John began. "Remember that sales manager from Denver who got in a fight at the bar?"

"I heard about it," Dave said. He leaned back in his chair. He knew John well enough to know that he was going to tell this story at his own careful pace. Dave knew that it was John's way of thinking something through for the last time before he sent it out in words. He was a careful man and Dave had learned that lesson well from John.

"Well, he was fired for getting into the fight," John continued. "As soon as he returned to Denver they let him go because of his behavior at the convention." John paused for dramatic effect. "Guess where he's working now?"

"I have no idea," Dave answered. His curiosity was growing.

"He went to work in Florida for a company called Property Disposition Professionals, known as PDP. It turns out that PDP is owned by National Assets. And PDP is a large institutional stockholder in National Assets."

"Why would the company that fired him be interested in hiring him at a subsidiary company?" Dave asked. "Unless they were protecting him."

"Or protecting themselves from him," John smiled excitedly.

"Well, we can talk more at lunch," John continued. "In the meantime ask yourself this question." John paused dramatically. "Why did the company choose to go public and list themselves on the exchange, just within the last few months?" With that question hanging in the air, John smiled and walked out the door.

Dave pushed aside all of John's questions and observations and dug into the day's reports. He had designed a set of daily flash reports that told him where the delinquency was, what the customer service rates were, and other daily productivity benchmarks that would let him know if some part of his operation was deficient. He knew that one day's results did not necessarily indicate an operational deficiency, but he wanted to catch things, ask questions early on. He could usually find deficiencies before they blossomed into full-blown problems that took time and money to fix.

As he looked at the reports he could tell that the operation was going well, except for the delinquency. The payment rate, the cash flow was sluggish. A lower percentage of the portfolio had paid than at this time last month. Unless he did something to speed up the collection of payments, he was in for another bad delinquency month. It was time for an impromptu meeting with his default manager, Eldora Redding. He figured that she was probably already doing something about the issue. He just wanted to make sure that she was doing enough. He also wanted to hear her plan.

At lunch Dave and John huddled over plates of pancakes and bacon. The breakfast special had become their lunch of choice. It was quick, inexpensive and very unhealthy. But Dave's food preferences ran along the same lines as John's. As they drenched their pancakes in syrup John continued where he left off that morning.

"Don't you find it interesting that after thirty years a company like this decides to go public?" John began.

"Not if they're in a rapid expansion period, John."

"Look at the profit margin," John continued. "They're getting at least four percentage points of spread between their cost of borrowing and their yields. They can pay all the bills take a mountain of charge off and still have ample money to grow."

"So you must have some theory on this," Dave said. "Let's hear it."

"Well keep in mind I'm just speculating," John said. "But what if the funding was from a questionable source. I asked myself that. So then I looked at the annual report to find out who the major stockholders are. This gets very interesting." John took a forkful of pancakes and put it in his mouth. Dave watched patiently.

"Okay," Dave said. "Now I'm curious. Who owns the stock?"

"I thought you might ask that," John said smiling. "Outside of the Pecunia family there are no major individual stockholders. However there are a few companies that own big chunks of stock. One of these companies is PDP, Property Disposition Professionals, the safety net for our fired employee. Don't you find that interesting?"

"Who are the other companies?" Dave asked.

"From what I can tell one is an investment firm," John answered. "Why would an investment firm buy a large portion of stock in a company like this? There are better investments. The other ones are home improvement businesses out east."

Dave took a few moments to word his answer carefully. He moved his plate aside and looked directly at John.

"Yes, I find it interesting. But if there were any truth to what you're hinting at, it would be very dangerous to talk about it to anyone. And if it isn't true, the speculation would be very damaging to the company." Dave shoved his plate aside. "So if it's true it could be hazardous to your health. And if it isn't, it could be hazardous to your financial well being, not to mention your reputation." Dave knew that John had the best instincts for trouble of anyone he had ever met in banking. And if John thought something was wrong, he was usually right.

"It's too good not to pursue," John protested. "Besides, think what it could do to your professional reputation if there is something bad going on and we don't surface it to the authorities."

"Just so we understand each other," Dave said, "let's put a name on it. What exactly do you think they are doing?"

"Laundering money," John said simply after he looked around to make sure no one was within earshot. "They're laundering money. And National Assets is their washing machine."

"So why would they go public and put themselves under so much regulatory scrutiny?" Dave asked.

"Sometimes it's better to hide something out in the open. Maybe they were starting to get looked at anyway. Going public would make it appear they had nothing to hide, especially if they are growing. Since their stock doesn't seem to appeal to anyone but institutional investors, they can continue their illegal activities. The process is in place. And it allows them to cash in on stock increases. And it could make the company more attractive in an acquisition."

"You think they're getting ready to cash out?" Dave asked. He knew that John must have stumbled on to some information that he wasn't sharing.

"Well, funny you should ask that," John said. "What if they decided to sell? What if they decided to bring in some legitimate employees like us to add credibility to the company? They are always bragging about the fact that they have some experienced mortgage industry professionals on the payroll. I've seen and heard them discussing our resumes with the investors and the correspondent bankers. I'm sure that they are putting all of their secondary marketing customers at ease for a reason."

Dave could sense that John's tenacity was taking over. He knew that John wasn't going to let go of this. He saw his promotion and stock options evaporating as illusive carrots that would never be cashed. He couldn't leave the company now. If what John was saying was true, his reputation was already damaged. He would have a lot of explaining to do to his next prospective employer, if another employer would even look at him.

"I think we better leave this alone," Dave warned.

"I can't," John said. He took another bite of his syrup-drenched pancakes.

"Either way, it's too dangerous."

"If you don't want in on it, I'll take it up with Buster Burns. He's already looking in the same direction," John said.

"I think I'd rather stay out of it for now," Dave answered. He knew that would be impossible if John were right. But he was too busy with his servicing operation to spend much time looking around. John was in a better position to do some investigating.

16

It was late afternoon when Buster Burns, sitting at his desk in Albuquerque, received the call from Mort Smalley. Buster had leased the entire second floor of a new commercial building for his operation to dispose of real estate that was foreclosed on. Only a fourth of the floor had been finished for his fledgling operation. He had hired an attorney, a few processors and a management team to receive the first shipment of seven hundred accounts that were in some stage of foreclosure or eviction.

Buster had undertaken the job of personally inspecting the loan files. He was surprised to find the rampant abuse of lending policies and possible fraud. Some of the customers had not even made their first payment on their account. In the mortgage industry first payment defaults are an indication of fraudulent lending activity.

"Good afternoon, Mr. Smalley," Buster said when he picked up the call. "Or should I say 'good evening' with the time difference in Chicago."

"Let's cut the formalities and just get to the reason for my call," Mort said abruptly.

"What's on your mind?" Buster asked slightly surprised.

"I understand that you've chosen not to use some of the law firms that National Assets has used over the past years. Do you mind telling me why?"

Buster had defended this complaint wherever he had worked. He had his own group of law firms throughout the United States that had performed well for him over the years. And his list was always changing. Whenever he would find attorneys eager for business and willing to move the foreclosure actions along in the courts as quickly as possible, he used them. In turn he fired the law firms that proved to be slower and less responsive. Every foreclosure manager had his own set of attorneys.

"I'm comfortable with the ones I've been using over the years," Buster answered. "Besides, I've looked at the performance timelines of some of the attorneys that National Assets has been using. They aren't very efficient. We can save a lot of money in terms of cost of funds if we get through the foreclosure process as quickly as possible."

"Save your little public relations education speech for someone who cares," Mort interrupted. "These attorneys have stayed with us for many years. They've proven themselves to be valuable contractors for our company. And we don't need you to come along and destroy relationships that took years to build up. You've destroyed more loyalty among them in a few weeks than I can possibly repair."

"I'd be glad to take another look at them if they want to match the timelines I expect for legal action, Mort," Buster said.

"No, you don't understand," Mort said. "You're going to use them all. I don't know why you didn't consult with someone before you dumped all these attorneys. Some of them are stockholders in our company."

"I didn't dump them. This is a new operation. I just chose not to use them," Buster answered. He knew his voice was rising. "Sacramento can use them. But I'm using the attorneys I know will deliver."

"What's with you?" Mort snapped. "Are these guys giving you a kickback on the business? Are you afraid you won't get nice Christmas gifts from them?"

"You're out of line, Mr. Smalley," Buster shot back.

"I don't think so. I think the company has a right to know why you have such an irrational loyalty to these law firms."

"I could ask you the same question," Buster said. There was a moment of silence.

"You've just stepped over a line you're going to regret crossing," Mort said evenly. "I don't know who the hell you think you are talking to me like that, but you're about to find out."

Buster felt a wave of panic course through his body. He admitted to himself that he didn't know how powerful Mort was. He knew he didn't need any enemies that high up. But now he had to play this out. He knew that if he backed down now, he wouldn't have a chance.

"You do what you have to, Mr. Smalley," Buster said calmly. "As long as I am in charge of this operation, I'm going to use the law firms and any other vendor that I deem appropriate to my success. If you request otherwise, put it in a memo and I'll give it the consideration I would any other issue that comes before me. And that means that I'll consider it with the best interests of the stockholders in mind."

"We'll see about that," Mort said. There was another moment of silence on the line. Then Mort decided to hang up the phone.

Buster sat back in his chair and exhaled loudly.

"What a jerk," he said to himself. He stood up from his chair and paced around his office trying to sort out his conversation with Mort. He knew that two things had to be done quickly. He needed to get in touch with John Fremont and let him know what had just happened. John had hired him and he didn't want John to get blindsided by this issue. Secondly, he knew he had to complete an analysis on the incoming loan files to validate his suspicions of fraud. It might be his only leverage if he needed some protection. He knew that even in the tough political corners of a company friends could desert one quickly. And he didn't want to put John in that position.

He called two of his managers into his office and outlined their special project that would last over the weekend. The managers were glad to help. They knew that getting the analysis on paper was going to take a lot of research, the kind of research that only an experienced person could do. They needed to look for trends, patterns in the loans. They had to document the payment of fees to vendors. Build the spreadsheets that would show the patterns of abuse and imprudent lending.

One group would track appraisers and recipients of loan disbursement checks. Another group would reverify employment records of some of the applicants. Some would have to perform telephone interviews with a sampling of the customers, if they would be willing to talk. And they would have to track where the loans were sold. How the money moved through the transactions would be critical to his investigation.

This was a road that Buster had been down before. He knew it well. Once they started the pieces would fall into place. Now it was just a matter of time. And time might be in short supply for Buster after his talk with Mort.

17

Dave stood in the doorway to Bud's office and waited for Bud to end his phone call. Bud looked up without smiling and waved him into a chair. It was time for their scheduled lunch. Dave sat in a chair near a conference table and looked around the office. Bud had collected some beautiful prints for his office over the years. Most were landscapes of the western United States, open and peaceful settings. Dave let himself get lost in the artwork while Bud argued with someone on the phone.

Dave looked over at Bud to see him roll his eyes in frustration. He also noticed the shade of red that crept up Bud's neck as he became more agitated on the phone. Dave wondered if Bud wasn't on the verge of a stroke. It appeared to him that Bud at the least had a problem with high blood pressure. Some ailments were common to managers in the financial world, he thought.

Bud finally ended his call and started rummaging through some papers on his desk. He finally pulled out a packet of papers and slapped it down toward the edge of his desk.

"Here," Bud said. "I had my staff work some new charge off policies that I thought we both could use. I know that you were going to work on them too. I figured you had more important things on your mind with getting your operation up and running."

Dave took the package to hide his surprise. He couldn't tell if Bud's actions were a friendly gesture or an attempt to railroad him into using something other than what he had wanted.

"Thanks," Dave said calmly. "I'll look at them later."

"Let's take them to lunch with us," Bud suggested. "Maybe we can talk about them while we're waiting for our food."

"Fine with me," Dave said. He figured that this issue was headed in a direction he didn't want to go. Bud was pushing too hard. They walked down the mall sidewalk to a corner cafeteria where Dave usually had lunch with John Fremont. After they had ordered their lunch both sat at a table. Bud started in on small talk telling about his family and his move to Sacramento a few years earlier.

Bud grew up in Chicago. He had been the manager of a branch office for National Assets. When the company moved to Sacramento, Bud was asked to run the servicing operations in addition to his duties as a credit officer. He had no formal training for the job. His responsibilities grew along with the company. And before he knew it he was responsible for more than he cared to be. Like most managers of the company, he thought that the more autocratic style he adopted, the more effective he was. Sometime before his transfer he divorced and remarried. His two daughters by his first marriage were in college. And he had three children at home. Two of them came with his second wife. And the third was born after they moved to Sacramento.

"So the kids take all my money for school. The ex-wife gets her share and my current wife spends the rest," Bud quipped. "And the company gets my time. So my time and my money are pretty well used up." Bud shrugged innocently. "That's life, I guess."

Bud seemed like a decent person when he was away from the office, Dave thought. He was probably someone Dave could eventually like. But there was the business wariness, the edge, the Chicago edge that Dave didn't quite trust after his dealings with Bud and his friends in senior management. He had no doubts that anything he said would find its way back to Will Eagleton's office. Dave suspected that Bud was on a search and destroy mission. Bud would search for information now and try to destroy Dave later. Dave thought it best to treat the conversation appropriately just in case he was right.

"I've been in this business all my career in one form or another," Dave began. "I've been fortunate to land some jobs with big companies. It taught me a lot about business practices and getting along with people." Dave waited until the waitress had served the food and left. "I see a lot of opportunity with National Assets. My hat is off to you for staying with them for nineteen years and building the company into the giant it is today."

Bud flushed with embarrassment. The last thing he expected was a compliment from Dave. Dave noticed the reaction and knew that Bud was keeping his guard up as well. Both took a break from the conversation and spent the next few minutes eating. After they were through Bud pushed his plate aside and slid his coffee cup in front of him.

"Why don't we go over that charge off policy that my people have been working on," Bud suggested.

Dave picked up the packet of papers and started scanning the policy. Even though he read it quickly he could tell that the policy was ambiguous and left a lot of arbitrary escapes for not writing off accounts after a fixed period of non-payment or reasonable circumstances of uncollectabiltiy. Dave finally put the papers aside and looked at Bud.

"This is a good start," Dave said. "But it needs some work. It needs more specific criteria so that anyone can come in and audit against the policy. It can't leave any room for subjectivity."

Bud held his gaze. His neck flushed red. He looked down at his coffee and took a sip.

"I think it serves the purpose adequately," Bud said casually. "We don't want a policy that's so inflexible that we hang ourselves with it."

"How would we hang ourselves with it, if we comply with the policy?" Dave asked.

"Sometimes you need a little room to maneuver around the auditors." Bud said. "Besides, if we make it too restrictive, we're looking at taking huge losses in a short period of time. That could really scare the investors."

"The losses are already there, Bud," Dave pressed. "We need to deal with them. All I'm suggesting is that we deal with them according to standard practices in the industry. We get this loss issue behind us and we can use our resources for more productive things."

Bud's face and neck flushed a deeper shade of red. Dave could tell that Bud had reached the end of his patience.

"You come in here and think you can turn everything upside down, don't you?" Bud said in a trembling voice. "I've done just fine controlling the delinquency and losses before you got here. Who the hell do you think you are to tell me how to do my job after I've been doing it for nineteen years?"

The waitress arrived and cleared the dishes away. She took her time refilling the coffee cups hoping that she could hear more of the argument. After she left Dave broke the strained silence.

"I'm not telling you how to do your job, Bud. I'm just trying to show you a better way of doing something. We need to take our losses and state our delinquency rates according to the standards set by the industry. If we don't change it, someone else will be in our offices changing it for us. And it won't be over an informal lunch."

Bud calmed down and saw the logic of what Dave was telling him. He looked at his coffee cup as if the answers were in there.

"I don't like change," Bud said. "I'm comfortable running things the way I've been doing." He looked up at Dave. "But I see what you're saying. It's probably got to change. Otherwise they wouldn't have hired you." He looked away from the table. He sighed deeply and stood up from the table.

"Why don't you go ahead and keep those," Bud said. "You can make the changes that you think are necessary. Then we can get together and talk about them. If you don't mind, I'm going to leave you here and go for a little walk. I need to do some thinking."

"Thanks for meeting me for lunch," Dave said. "I really appreciate the gesture."

"No problem," Bud said and walked away.

Dave slumped in his chair and looked at his coffee. He could tell how hard this was on Bud. And he knew that Bud wanted to make this thing work. But the struggle for control was waging inside Bud. And Dave knew that he had to win Bud over in order to be successful himself. Dave knew that if someone mandated that Bud follow Dave's direction, Bud would probably do everything in his power to sabotage the efforts. He had to win Bud over completely.

Dave stood from the table, laid a tip next to his plate and picked up the papers that Bud had given him earlier. He decided to walk around the stores of the mall before returning to work. He needed the distraction of the shoppers and the crowded aisles of merchandise before he went back to his office. He knew that other battles were waiting there to be fought. And for the first time he was getting tired of it.

As he approached the door to the servicing center Dave noticed John Fremont standing a few feet away from the entrance finishing a cigarette. He decided to walk over and tell John about his lunch with Bud.

"I just had an interesting lunch," Dave stated as he approached the alcove where John was standing.

"With Bud?" John asked.

"Yeah. How did you know?" Dave didn't bother to hide the surprise on his face.

"I just saw him walk by when I came downstairs," John said and smiled. "He was walking fast with a frown on his face. He looked upset. Then I saw you coming down the sidewalk a few minutes later. I just put it all together," John explained.

"I thought you were getting psychic on me," Dave said. "Yeah, we had a chat about charge off policies. It didn't go well."

"Watch yourself," John warned.

"What does that mean?" Dave asked. "I think we finally came to an agreement on the fact that the policy had to be changed. He wasn't happy about it, but he saw my reasoning."

"Don't get defensive," John said. "I think that there's a big gap in getting Bud to agree to something and to his actual compliance. I'm just warning you to be careful."

"What brought this sudden concern on?" Dave asked. "Come on. Out with it. I know you're holding something back."

"You didn't hear about Buster Burns?" John said mysteriously.

"I heard he got sideways with someone in Chicago," Dave said carefully. "I think it was over some vendor issues, attorneys."

"Really?" John said. "I didn't hear about that."

"Well, what did you hear about Buster that you're trying tell me?" Dave pressed.

"He was in a serious car accident last night. Police said it looks like someone may have run him off the road." John flipped his cigarette into the ashtray stand next to him.

"Wow, I just talked to him yesterday," Dave said. "He told me about his conversation with Mort Smalley. It sounded like it really got heated on Mort's end." Dave froze with a realization. Before he could dismiss it, John read his expression. Dave looked at John but didn't say anything.

"That's why I'm saying it," John finally said. "Be very careful."

"You're not saying…"

"No, I'm not," John said. "But I don't believe in coincidences either. So be careful."

"Is Buster going to be okay?" Dave asked.

"From what I heard, he'll survive. But he won't be back to work for a while. The company has decided to suspend the transfer of additional files to Albuquerque. They have enough to keep them busy. And the operation is not going to add any additional people pending a review of the viability of that operation."

"They're thinking about closing it?" Dave asked in disbelief.

"Buster made a lot of waves," John said quietly. "And his complaints didn't always go to Will Eagleton." John paused a moment as if collecting his thoughts. "You and I both know that the fewer people involved in fraud, the easier it is to pull off. But you need some third parties, some intermediaries to make it look less suspicious if there is a lot of fraud going on."

"I'm following you," Dave said.

"Money laundering in this case is getting illegal money into the legitimate money supply. That's why any cash transaction of ten thousand dollars or more has to be reported to the government on a Currency Transaction Report. And amounts under ten thousand dollars would take too many transactions. What if illegal money is funded into National Assets through shell corporations owned by National Assets? The shell companies pose as investors."

"How do they get their money back?" Dave asked.

"In one scenario National Assets sets up fraudulent home improvement dealers who submit contracts to be purchased. National Assets pays these dealers with their own laundered money. They make a few payments on the loans and eventually let them go delinquent. The loans are finally written off to loss once a safe period of time has passed."

"Wouldn't the customers notice all of this?"

"Why do you think that the company doesn't disclose the balance owed on their statements?" John said. "And why do you think that you have so many loans with balances disputed by the customers? And why do you think that the company doesn't report monthly to the credit bureaus?"

John took a moment to let the information sink into Dave's thought process. Then he continued.

"Now just add in a few fraudulent vendors along the way and you've got a complete scenario for money laundering and fraud. Buster's actions may have disrupted that flow of money."

Dave looked at John and nodded. He needed to get away. He needed to think some of this through. What John was implying was too fantastic to believe. What kind of people was he working with? He walked to his office and closed the door. He needed a new plan. He quickly grabbed a legal pad and pencil and began to make a list.

He stared at his phone wondering if the line was tapped. He stared at the corners of his office looking for devices that could be picking up his actions or his conversations. He looked at the tangle of wires behind his computer and wondered if there were more connections than necessary. The paranoia began to feed on itself and Dave wondered who was listening or watching him. He struggled for control of his fear.

He quickly wadded up the paper he had been writing on. He took a deep breath and gave the office a final look. If it's true, I'll make it work for me, he thought.

He filled his briefcase with important papers and had his secretary order a shredder. He cleared the office of all personal belongings and put them in his car. On his way back up to his office he used a pay phone outside of the mall and called a security company to meet him in the morning. He would have his office swept for eavesdropping devices and pay for it himself. He knew at least four different ways home from work. He decided to take alternating routes every night.

It was time to put some distance around him. He didn't believe in coincidences any more than John did. After all it was John who had mentored him. And he had learned the job well. And if John said be careful, he knew to be very careful.

The following morning Dave met the security specialist at his office. The staff was not scheduled to arrive for another hour. The specialist inspected and probed looking in every corner with a small high-powered flashlight. Then he used a device that looked like a metal detector to sweep the walls and ceiling.

Underneath the bottom of the window frame he pulled out a wireless listening device no larger than a pen. A ten inch wire that served as an antenna protruded from one end. The specialist dropped it in a small can and screwed the lid on tightly. He looked up at Dave and spoke.

"This is all I can find," he said tapping the top of the can. "Do you want to keep it?"

"No get it out of here."

"You can use it to your advantage," the specialist added. "You can have them listen to what you want them to hear."

"But I don't know who is listening," Dave answered. "And it makes me nervous just to have it in here."

"Suit yourself," he said dropping the small canister into his briefcase. "Your office is clean for now. I would guess that someone is monitoring your text messages on your computer. But I can't do anything about that."

Dave handed him cash and thanked him as the specialist left the building. He sat at his desk trying to collect himself after the shock of finding a listening device in his office. He thought of a short list of people who would put the device in his office. He decided to quietly change the lock on his office door and to keep his office secured when he was out. He picked up the phone and made the call to the locksmith.

18

By mid-December nothing much had changed with Dave's attempts to get the delinquency accurately restated and a new charge-off policy implemented. At the end of each month he would send his delinquency figures to Bud. Bud was supposed to combine Dave's report with his own. Somehow Bud would always find a way to report a lower delinquency than the numbers that Dave had submitted. As a safety measure Dave would publish his own internal reports reflecting a higher delinquency rate, a more accurate rate. He also submitted large amounts of loans to be written off as losses. Again Bud would find a way to reduce the number of loans that were charged off every month.

Although Bud's tampering with the delinquency and losses was a source of frustration with Dave, he bided his time. Senior management seemed confused over the conflicting reports, but appeared to look the other way when Dave brought it to their attention.

Dave pressed the company to take several million dollars in losses before the year-end so that he could start off the New Year with a clean slate. The business could show a lot more profitability if they put this problem behind them. But no one wanted to resolve the issue. As a last resort Dave decided to publish a report listing all of the non-performing loans along with the implications to his operation if the problem wasn't resolved by the end of the year. He also let the credit policy committee know that he would find it difficult to sign the year-end reports needed for an independent audit. The independent audit was needed since they were now a publicly traded company.

The report had its desired effect. Dave was scheduled to address the credit policy committee later in the week. He hoped this would be his opportunity to resolve the write-off issue once and for all. He worked hard on a presentation and gathered every piece of supporting information that he could find. He knew he couldn't leave that meeting without an approval to write off the loans. It would mean a difficult road over the next year if he carried all the bad loans on the books into the coming year.

He looked at his calendar and knew that time was running short for getting his Christmas shopping done. He hadn't had time to prepare for the holidays because of his long work hours. He felt a twinge of guilt. Yet he knew that this had to be taken care of. He thought about all the years he had sacrificed time away from home in order to do his job. He wondered if there would ever be a year when he wasn't pressed for time over the holidays. The children were coming in from out of town. Ann had to make the arrangements for transportation from the airport and for a lot of the Christmas shopping.

There were cards to send out and presents to wrap. Dave regretted missing out on a lot of the preparations. He knew that those preparations were what usually put him in the mood for the holiday celebrations. But he couldn't afford the time this year. There was too much riding on his presentation. And if he lost his loan policy argument, he was really going to feel the let down in January. He silently cursed Bud and the company for putting him into this situation. He knew that he had to take responsibility for a lot of his frustration. He also knew that he had never felt so frustrated about a job as he did this one. Maybe he had made a poor choice. Maybe he had been deluding himself all this time, he thought. Maybe the credit policy committee had no intention of listening to his recommendations.

He finally slammed his hand down over his calendar and looked at his watch. It was time for lunch. Lately he had taken up the habit of going for walks on his lunch hour. There was a subdivision of old homes bordering the shopping center. He usually walked across the parking lot to a large discount department store. Behind the store was a private gate that allowed him access to the neighborhood. He walked the streets of the neighborhood and admired the well-kept lawns and beautiful trees imagining what Sacramento must have looked like twenty years ago when these houses were new and the landscaping was small.

A few blocks into the subdivision was a park with a stream running through it. The park was usually quiet and unused. The large oak trees cast a beautiful patchwork of shade over the grounds. Picnic tables were interspersed throughout the park. Dave would find one in the shade and sit on top of the table. He would sit and think, relax, let his mind wander around the park and process the events of his day. It was his way of taking mini-vacations relieving the stress he felt from his mornings in the office. It was his way of recharging himself before he had to face the grueling afternoons.

The temperature was warm enough in the park today for Dave to shed his suit coat. He walked to a table and climbed to sit on the top. He looked around for ants that might pose a problem. Satisfied that he had the table to himself, he took a deep breath and looked out at the park through his squinting eyes.

A soft breeze warmed the surface of his skin. An occasional jogger moved through the park. Dave could hear the jogging shoes slapping along the asphalt path. A couple of children played under the watchful eyes of their mother. Dave took it all in and let the tension of the morning flow out of him. He thought of parks like this that he had stopped at on vacations. He would pull off the highway and eat sandwiches at a picnic table while looking at a map wondering where their next stop would be. The carefree feeling of traveling came back to him and transported him to the small towns in Colorado that had roadside parks.

The small towns usually had a billboard welcoming road weary travelers. Signs boasted of the Lions Club and the Sertoma Club. The chamber of commerce had a list of the fine hotels in the area. There was usually a small visitor's center nestled in among some towering oak trees whose shade beckoned the hot, dusty vacationers to park and rest, get out of the car and stretch. And when he did, he could see snow capped mountains in every direction. He could smell the pine mixed with icy mountain air. He would take his family to sit at a grouping of nearby picnic tables where they would talk about what they wanted to do that afternoon and where they would eat.

He wished he were on vacation and started thinking about the coming summer vacation and where he and Ann would go. Now that the children were grown and out of the house, they had more flexibility in their travel. They could go where they wanted and not make so many stops that the children had demanded out of boredom or need to use the rest areas. But it was all part of the memories. It was all part of the getting away from the pressures that built up over the year from days like this.

A butterfly landed at the other end of table and Dave idly watched as it made its way from one end of the table. Dave pulled out a cigarette and lit it as he watched the butterfly slowly move its wings back and forth on the table. It seemed content to just enjoy the sunlight and to stay in Dave's company for a while. Finally the butterfly rose in the warm air and flew off to investigate other things. Dave leaned back on his elbow and looked up at the sky. He wished he could stay out here and just soak up the atmosphere of the park with all its warmth and serenity.

He thought about work. He wondered why the senior management of the company was so reluctant to acknowledge the losses it had on the books. Why were they in denial over non-performing loans? Why didn't they just write them off and get on with business. There had to be more to it than Dave was seeing. Why would they risk censure from the Securities and Exchange Commission. Why would they risk lawsuits from the investors if the truth ever came out about the false reports that were being filed? He needed to put the pieces together. And now it would be harder for him to do that. Buster was in the hospital and Gil Sheets had resigned. He had lost two of his three staunchest supporters. These were the two that had been interested and concerned about the condition of the company. What had they discovered, he wondered. And what had they talked about?

Dave sat up and crushed the ash from his cigarette. He tossed the butt into a nearby trashcan and rested back on his elbow. He felt as if he was on a roller coaster headed for a collision and there was nothing he could do to stop it. He just had to sit there in horror and watch it crash. He knew that he couldn't let that happen. He thought about the two hundred people that he had hired for his operation. They were depending on him for good leadership. He didn't want to let them down. But it seemed inevitable.

He kept coming back to the fact that there was little he could do but document the irregularities and keep bringing it to management's attention. If they chose not to do anything about it, then he would have to either go along for the ride, or resign. He knew that his resignation would be tainted with the opinion that he just couldn't adapt to the National Assets culture. He just couldn't make it in the world of home improvement equity lending.

He sighed and stood up off of the picnic table. He thought he saw someone standing near the trees at the entrance to the park. He looked more closely and saw a young man in a pair of khaki slacks and blue shirt. The sun reflected off of his long, blond hair. Dave thought he had seen him around National Assets. Maybe he was an employee. He had never seen any other employees at the park. He dismissed his paranoia and started walking toward the young man.

To his surprise the young man didn't move. He seemed to be waiting for Dave to approach.

"Nice day out, isn't it?" Dave greeted him with a smile. He was now within a few feet of the man.

"It sure is," he answered. "You're Mr. Jenkins, aren't you?"

"Call me Dave," I'm more comfortable with that. "You have me at a disadvantage. Do I know you?"

"I'm Shane Davis. I work in the information technology department." Shane held out his hand and Dave shook it.

"I'm pleased to meet you," Dave said automatically. "Do you come to the park often?"

"Actually, no," Shane said nervously. His eyes darted around the park as if to see if they were being observed. "I just needed to talk to you."

"About what?" Dave asked. He felt his stomach tighten. He read the nervousness in Shane's face.

"Well, I've only been with the company for about a month now," Shane began. "And yesterday I was given a work order to install a line that would track all of your emails and computer transactions. It seemed to me to be an invasion of your privacy and I just thought you would like to know."

"I appreciate that," Dave said evenly. "Who gave you the order?"

"My department head. But it came from somewhere else. And I don't really know where it originated."

"Who can monitor my computer?" Dave asked.

"Anyone with the software to access the server can go in and watch your activity on the computer, even if you don't send anything out. They would be able to go in at night and look at all of your files." Shane took a breath and continued. "Everything I've heard indicates that you are a decent person. So I thought it was a little unfair that someone would do this to you. Most of your employees speak highly of you. I hope I haven't made a mistake telling you about this," Shane said nervously.

"If there are any repercussions, you are always welcome to come and work for me," Dave said. "As a matter of fact we are looking for systems people. And I appreciate loyalty in a person. It tells me a lot about them."

"Maybe I'll take you up on that," Shane answered. He sounded more relieved.

"Before you do," Dave continued, "you may be able to perform an invaluable service to me from where you are working now."

"You want me to try to find out who is at the other end of this monitoring request?" Shane asked.

"You're smart as well as loyal," Dave commented with a smile. "Why don't you walk back to my office with me and we can talk. At least we can walk to the parking lot and split up then."

As Dave walked back to the office and talked to Shane he knew that he was in a war now. He even had a spy. He was saddened that his job had come to this. But he was ready for the challenge. He had learned the ropes of corporate infighting long ago. And he felt good that he would be able to put his skills to use, dangerous as it may prove to be.

Candi Combs, a prostitute by profession, smiled to herself as she filled out the application for employment at National Assets. She was tall and thin, a real beauty. And she capitalized on her natural assets every day by turning heads in her direction. She wondered how she was going to pull off working as a customer service representative in the new servicing center.

"There's a space here for previous employment," she joked. "What am I going to put in there?"

"Just write down that you worked for a temporary agency in Chicago, mostly as a customer service representative," Will coached her. "I'll give you a number to write down. They'll back you up on it."

"Are you sure about this?" Candi asked. She had her doubts even though Will was going to pay her a bonus every week for the next two months in addition to her hourly wage. He also promised to pay a large bonus at the end of the assignment. She knew that she could probably make as much money on the street. But she was ready for a break. The National Assets executives had been a good source of income so far. They were big tippers, she thought. Besides, this might be fun.

"All you have to do is get close to this guy and let me know what he's doing. Two months at most," Will assured her.

"What's his name?"

"Davis, Shane Davis. He works in the systems department. But he spends a lot of time over at this operation where you will be working. He's young and single. He'll notice you right away. The rest is up to you."

Will looked her over appraisingly. He thought that Shane would have to be blind not to notice her. Her light brown hair fell straight down to the middle of her back. He could picture Shane drooling over her the first time he saw her. He rocked back in his chair and smiled in satisfaction of his idea.

After Candi finished filling out the application, Will gave her the Chicago number. He rehearsed the high points of the interview telling her what to say and what to avoid.

"What if they don't hire me?" Candi asked.

"Then we'll put you to work over here in the headquarters building. But it will work better if you get the job over there. The labor pool in Sacramento is thin right now. Odds are that you won't have a problem getting hired. Just call me every day to let me know what's going on. Can you do that?"

"I'm a quick study," she said seductively. "I think I can handle it."

Her movements were deliberate and slow. She stood up and reached for the application. She folded the paper never taking her eyes off of Will. He watched as her slender fingers and long pink nails ran repeatedly down the crease in the application. Will swallowed hard.

"Keep in touch," he said as he picked up his phone as if he were going to make a call.

"You can count on it." Candi understood that she was being dismissed. She smiled at Will, slowly turned and walked out of his office.

19

During the Christmas holidays Dave decided to turn one of the spare bedrooms in his home into an office. Under the guise of working at home he had requested remote access to the proprietary servicing system on his home computer. He had invited Shane out to his house for dinner in order to have the connection made. Shane had given him some written instructions on how to access some portions of the system without detection. Shane said that he would show Dave how it all worked when he came out to the house. The company would not be able to tell if Dave had accessed information from his home or from the office. And the transactions weren't time stamped so that no one could tell when Dave had accessed the system unless they were on line with him watching his every move.

One Saturday evening before Christmas, Ann was in the kitchen preparing dinner for four. Shane had accepted Dave's invitation to dinner in conjunction with his work on Dave's home computer. Dave was in his home office when he heard the doorbell ring.

"Hi Shane," Dave greeted him warmly at the front door. "Thanks for coming over tonight."

"Thanks for the invitation," Shane replied. He was smiling proudly as he introduced Candi to Dave and Ann. "And thanks for letting me bring Candi along."

"You're one of the new hires in the customer service department?" Dave asked.

Candi nodded shyly and cleared her throat. "We just finished our training week. Next week we get to take phone calls from real customers. But we have to sit with an experienced customer service rep so that they can listen in and critique us after each call."

"How do you like it so far?" Dave asked out of politeness. He was wary about talking business away from the office with someone he didn't know.

"I like it so far," Candi said cautiously. She smiled warmly into Shane's eyes. "And it's led me to Shane. I'm happy about that."

"We can tell," Ann laughed. "Let's go eat before everything gets cold. Who wants wine with dinner?"

"None for me," Shane said quickly. "I don't drink. But I know that Candi enjoys a glass of wine."

"Then three wines and an iced tea?" Ann asked as she made her way back to the kitchen.

"Sounds good," Shane replied.

After dinner Shane sat at Dave's home office computer and worked his magic. His fingers flew across the keyboard while he explained to Dave what he was doing. The end result was that Dave would not only have access to the system just as he would if were at work, but he could also access certain files that dealt with the financial history of the company provided that they had converted on to the system.

"There's a lot more information on the system than they would lead you to believe," Shane said as he worked furiously to get into the databases.

Shane wrote down some access codes and instructions for Dave to follow. Shane mentioned the optimum times for accessing the files. Soon Dave gave up trying to follow the commands and the computer screens that Shane summoned and dismissed in seconds. He wished he had a video camera or a tape recorder to get all of this down. He feared getting stuck and having to call Shane to get him out of a jam.

"In the event you have any questions or get stuck on this home networking, just give me a call at one of these two numbers," Shane said as he finished. "One number is my cell phone. The other is my pager."

"I can't tell you how much I appreciate your help," Dave said as Candi walked in on them.

"What are you two up to?" Candi asked. She stood in the doorway of Dave's office.

Dave's instincts told him to be cautious. He hoped that Shane would be discreet about what he shared with Candi. In any event Candi didn't appear to be that interested in computers, Dave thought.

"Oh, Shane was just helping me with a computer glitch," Dave said evenly.

About an hour later Shane and Candi left. The evening was a success for Dave. He couldn't wait to get started on the research. He hoped that he understood Shane's directions clearly enough to get the information he wanted.

Dave had papered the walls of his home office with rolls of brown wrapping paper tacked to the walls. On the large sheets of paper he diagramed the history of the company over the last two years. He also charted out the organizations in both Sacramento and Chicago. He carefully documented the timeline of events since his arrival at National Assets. On a long folding table he had stacks of recent audits performed by regulatory agencies and internal departments.

He also had stacks of investor agreements and loan servicing agreements. He outlined the agreements and put together a chronology of the loan sales. He accumulated a list of active vendors that National Assets had paid large sums of money to over the last few years. He compared it to the 1099M's that reported the disbursements to the internal revenue service at the end of the year. Slowly he was building the picture of the company that he needed to see. He was sure that all of this information would lead him to the answers he needed to have.

He also drew timelines that tracked the careers of the senior management team. He had included Bud Murphy's career in this exercise just to see if there was some kind of pattern he didn't know about. He worked feverishly on the project. He started getting home at an earlier hour. After dinner he would go into his home office and work on his project.

His final piece of the puzzle was to build a chronology of the growth in assets and the cash flows of the company. Next he built a chart showing the allocation of the stock, who owned how much and when they had acquired the stock.

Dave worked relentlessly on the project, never stopping to draw any conclusions until he had all the information he wanted on the wall charts. After he was finished, he stepped back and began to take it all in. He would sit in his chair staring at the diagrams and timelines. He rearranged information. He asked himself questions. He would log on to the system to get more information. Gradually the picture was taking shape. Slowly the facts were leading him to the answers he was searching for.

He hadn't told anyone about his project. He went to work every morning and took care of the daily business. He attended meetings and put forth his ideas and recommendations on projects. As far as he could determine, no one discovered his home project.

And now he could ask pointed and seemingly unrelated questions after meetings or at a lunch counter without arousing undue suspicion. He was enjoying the project. It gave him some diversion from the daily routine. It was apparent to Dave that the more he saw of the regulatory criticism, the more Bud had done to evade the proposed solutions. Dave discovered a long trail of cover up and sloppy activities that could cast enough doubt on whether the company could be held liable for their neglect. But at best, Dave knew it was just a word game that most regulators could see through. And in the final analysis, the company would have inflicted irreparable damage on its own operation exposing itself to losses larger than the ones they had now. It would be hard to explain to someone who didn't have a substantial understanding of servicing operations.

The question that Dave kept coming back to was why. Why did the company choose to cloak itself in sloppy practices and denial, he wondered. It was clear that the audits clearly outlined the deficiencies and what corrective actions needed to be taken. No one had ever acted on them. And the reason why still went unanswered.

Dave decided that the best way to answer that question was to run some theories by John Fremont. He could use him as a sounding board and maybe John could shed a new perspective on all of this information.

A few days after the Christmas holidays Dave invited John for a mid morning coffee break. They walked over to a donut shop close to the mall. The holidays had not relaxed John. He seemed tense and preoccupied to Dave. And at first Dave thought that John was too distracted to take all of this information in. Dave proceeded to outline his findings to John. The more Dave talked, the more interested John became. They ordered a second cup of coffee and walked outside so that they could have a cigarette and a little more privacy.

"I think you ought to run all of this by Bruce Curley," John said.

"What if he already knows this?" Dave asked. "He's a smart guy. And I've noticed that he was copied on a lot of this correspondence. He has to know all about the problem. Or else he doesn't read his mail."

"Bruce supported the hiring of new talent," John said. "He wouldn't want to keep staffing in the midst of a big cover up. I think he wants to fix the problems."

"I don't," Dave said. "I think that he's discovered the cost of fixing the problems and he's looking for some less expensive compromise."

"Maybe he just trusted Bud to start fixing the problems," John suggested.

"Maybe he just wants to give the appearance that the problems are getting fixed," Dave said. He put his cigarette out in the bottom of his coffee cup and threw it in a nearby trashcan. He walked back over to John and looked out at the parking lot.

"Let me run a theory by you and see if it hits any nerve with you," Dave began.

"Okay. Let's hear it," John said.

"Just suppose for a minute that they are running a money laundering operation. Maybe the money laundering started in Chicago. After it grew they decided that it was something that they should move out of state so that it would be harder to track." Dave pulled a small pocket memo out of his suit coat and looked at his notes.

"How would the dirty money come in?" John asked.

"Through fake investors and phantom institutions," Dave answered. "The money collected on the loans would be passed through to the investors on an actual accounting basis. Only the money collected would be passed on net of the servicing fee. If the losses on the loans are not taken, then the company doesn't have to fund the losses. They just pass the loss on to the investor through a diminished yield. Before they went on to an automated system, the sloppy accounting would sufficiently hide the money trail. Eventually the company had to go to automation because of high growth and increased loan volume. Their lending programs are so liberal that they start getting more market share than they had anticipated. They grew too quickly for their own good. The combination of automated subsystems and hiring more experienced managers left them nowhere to hide. Some of the big national banks want some of the business and start buying blocks of loans from National Assets. That creates more revenue. Management overreaches. Greed takes hold. The money keeps getting laundered. But now they no longer have to rely solely on bogus institutions."

John stared at Dave for a moment. He pulled another cigarette out and lit it. He thoughtfully exhaled the smoke and drew the conclusion that Dave hoped he would come to.

"That would be a scam that would eventually have to end. A national bank would eventually find out that they had been taken. They would want National Assets to repurchase the bad loans. Or, out of embarrassment, the bank might attempt to cover their mistakes somehow. National Assets would have to find a buyer for the company, possibly one of the participating national banks," John said slowly.

Dave smiled and clapped his hands.

"Exactly," Dave said enthusiastically. "They hire us. Have us clean up a few things. Our resumes add credibility to the company. We write a few procedures. We lay out some well written corrective action plans. Enough things change to get them through a due diligence visit. And they're home safe."

"That's unbelievable," John whispered. "It's too fantastic, too genius. If it's true, somebody put a lot of time and thought into this and wouldn't want anyone upsetting the plan."

"What length would they go to?" Dave asked.

"Enough to put Buster Burns in the hospital," John said without hesitation. "Enough to put us in the same danger if they thought we would make any waves about it."

"I think we need to step back and think about this," Dave suggested. "I need to know if you think that there could be any truth to that. Maybe you could test this theory in a couple of ways I haven't thought of. Then we get back together and talk."

"Let's meet for lunch tomorrow," John said excitedly. "We'll meet at a restaurant a few miles from here."

"Just be careful," Dave said. "I don't want you ending up like Buster."

"The same goes for you," John warned.

They walked back to their offices with their heads down as if they were reading the sidewalks for answers. Occasionally Dave would look around to see if anyone was following them. He scolded himself for being so paranoid. Yet, after the incident with his computer, he knew that many things were possible if the company wanted to spy on him. And he also knew that many things were probable if the stakes were as high as he thought they were.

20

Over the next week Dave was called to an unscheduled credit policy committee meeting. He was surprised to hear that he didn't have to prepare a presentation. He was even more surprised to find out that the committee approved the write off of three million dollars immediately. In addition they wanted from Dave a forecast of his write off's for the first six moths of the year. To those monthly forecasts they wanted him to add an incremental two million dollars in write offs until the all of the non-performing loans had been written off by July. After July the loss forecast was to include only the loans that would normally fall into the loss category from the normal course of business.

Dave excitedly left the building before the committee had a chance to change their minds. He couldn't believe that they were finally letting him go ahead with the request he had been making for months now. He was going to get to unload the non-performing loans. His business could run at a profit. By the time he was back in his office he had been through the forecast numbers in his head. All he had to do was write them down, have the delinquency manager validate them, and get them sent to Bruce Curley. He wondered now if there was hope for his operation.

When he returned to his office he found a note from Marilee indicating that company auditors planned on auditing his operation next week. They wanted Dave to call them. Dave thought that the timing of the audit was strange for a couple of reasons.

The first reason was that his operation was less than a year old. That wasn't time to implement all of the processes and work out all of the deficiencies. Usually a department was given enough time to get their business operational and self critique the daily activities. That apparently wasn't going to happen here.

The second reason was that external auditors usually came in at this time of year. They tested for good procedures and sound business practices as well as compliance to their regulations. Then, in about ninety days following the external audit, the internal auditors came in for a follow up visit to see if the deficiencies had been corrected.

Dave grabbed the phone and dialed. He didn't need this much disruption right now. The audit department answered on the first ring.

"I had a message to call you regarding an audit scheduled for next week," Dave said impatiently.

"Oh, yes, let me see" the receptionist answered in a cordial voice. "You want to talk to Paul Frank. If you'll hold a minute, I'll get him on the line."

Dave waited listening to the torturous elevator music that played in his ear and made the seconds seem like an eternity. When he heard his pencil snap in his hand, he made an effort to relax. As he took a deep breath, Paul Frank, the senior auditor, came on the line.

"Thanks for calling so quickly," Paul said. "We wanted to let you know that you are scheduled for your first internal audit, Dave."

"Thanks for letting me know ahead of time," Dave answered. "I thought that your visits were usually a surprise."

"They are," Paul said. "But we let the senior manager know. There may be something that you want us to focus on. So we usually have a discussion with you first."

"Oh, I didn't know that," Dave said. He relaxed a little. "Our operation is so new I'm sure that there is a lot you could look at. But I'm interested in your opinion as to whether my collection department is following the procedures that we've set down for them."

"Good. We'll be sure to take a look at that," Paul said in a matter of fact voice. "Anything else?"

"No, not really." Dave hesitated. "It seems unusual to me that you would be scheduling an audit so soon after we have the operation up and running. With the start up curve that comes with a new operation I would think that an audit would be more beneficial in a few months."

"Yes, I know it seems a little soon. But we're starting on a new schedule so that we can audit each business once a year. Since you're part of the home improvement division, you get audited along with them."

"Oh, I see," Dave answered. He was unconvinced, suspicious that someone was trying to distract him. But he knew that further arguing would just make it look like he was trying to hide something.

"I'll send over the questionnaire that we need filled out," Paul continued. "If you could have that filled out for us by the time we arrive, I'd appreciate it."

"No problem," Dave said. "We'll see you next week."

Dave hung up the phone and wrote the event in his calendar. He still thought that the timing was onerous and disruptive. But he knew it was inevitable. Maybe he could find out if someone was throwing out distractions in his search for the truth.

21

After Dave had left the credit policy meeting Bruce Curley, Will Eagleton, and Bob Whiting huddled around the conference table. They were all looking at the speakerphone as Mort Smalley began to talk.

"That should keep Dave quiet for a little while," he said. "But we need Bud to continue to do what he's doing."

"You want him to keep doctoring the figures," Bob clarified. He wanted to make sure that everyone was thinking the same.

"Watch what you say on the phone," Mort said curtly. "We've got to get the company looking attractive for a possible sale. If a prospective buyer comes in and sees that we have a plan to address the backlog of losses, they look upon us more favorably."

"We need to keep a gag on Buster, John Fremont and Dave Jenkins," Will offered. He didn't give out any information about Candi and Shane. He thought it better to keep control of that situation. Besides, it was Dave that they were focusing on. Shane was just an inconvenience right now. Will could take care of that situation when the need arose.

"Buster should be out of commission for awhile," Mort said. "I leave it up to you how you handle John and Dave. We can show them off, but don't let them speak to any prospective buyer."

"I think what we need to do is to undermine their credibility a little," Bob Whiting said. "We could probably start by reducing their visibility at meetings. You know, don't inform them of meetings. Not tell them about the rallies we hold for the employees by not inviting their departments. And I've ordered an audit on Dave's new operation. That ought to keep him busy."

"That's a little harsh," Will said. He flushed angrily as he thought of Bob taking such a step without consulting him.

"Yes, but it will be effective and will sow the seeds of discontent among some of the employees," Bob offered. "Maybe we can find some initiatives that Dave and John have implemented and haven't gone well. We can focus on those for some criticism, just enough to throw them off balance," Bob continued.

"Don't get them too discouraged," Mort warned. "They may be more motivated to speak to someone outside the company."

"That's why we have to destroy their credibility," Bob said emphatically. "So if they do talk, they won't be as credible as they are now. People will just think that they are disgruntled employees."

Bruce sat at the table observing the conversation. He fidgeted in his chair uncomfortably. He watched Bob become more animated as he put his ideas out for discussion. These ideas could destroy the careers of two good employees who had accepted jobs with the company in good faith. Now they were the targets of a campaign that could damage their careers. He tried thinking of ways to get Dave and John out of the way without all of this intrigue. Mort's voice interrupted his thoughts.

"Bruce," Mort said, "you've been awfully quiet. What do you think about all of this?"

"Frankly, I'm trying to think of an alternative solution for dealing with John and Dave," Bruce said. "I have a feeling that if we go after them, they are very capable of rising to the challenge. These guys know corporate infighting better than we do. They've been raised on it." He paused to gather his thoughts. "It wouldn't surprise me if they didn't already have enough documented information about the company to make us a red herring on the market. If we kick these guys, they're going to kick back hard."

There was silence for a few moments while everyone digested what Bruce had just said.

"You bring up some good points, Bruce," Mort finally said. "We can't have too many accidents. That would look bad, too. Do you have any ideas, Bruce?"

"I'm thinking why not bring them in? Put them under contract with big incentives pending the successful sale of the company. That way we put their talents and loyalty to work for us," Bruce suggested.

Will and Bob looked across the table at Bruce in shock. They couldn't believe that Bruce could even consider that idea. Mort broke the silence.

"I like it," Mort said chuckling on the phone. The facial expressions around the conference table relaxed. "Money's a powerful incentive. And it usually dulls the edge of righteousness," Mort quipped. "Bob, I want you to get with legal and draw up some golden handcuffs for these two. I also want you, Bob, to call Dave into your office and let him in on the potential sale of the company once you have him sign the confidentiality agreement."

Bob sat up straight in his chair and frowned. He disliked the thought of having to deal with Dave in a cordial way.

"Will, you take John Fremont," Mort said. "Warn those two that they can't discuss it even with each other. Maybe it will do some good."

"I think we have a lot to gain by bringing these two under the umbrella of confidentiality," Bruce said. "In any event, they will be easier to deal with and they will incur some liability if they decide to talk."

"Good," Mort said. "Let's get this underway. Can you have them both under the umbrella by Monday?"

"We'll take care of it," Will said.

Bob slammed his notebook in frustration and stood up from the conference table. Bruce stood up and put his papers in his briefcase. Will, as usual, had no papers to put away. They all said their goodbyes and hung up. Will sent Bob and Bruce out with a final warning.

"The sale of the company may depend on how successful we are in getting these two guys on our side," he said carefully. "Let's make sure we don't forget what's at stake here. Our stock is falling and we'll be hard pressed to meet our operating expenses for the remainder of this year unless we find a buyer."

Bob and Bruce nodded and walked out of the conference room. For the first time in thirty years they were looking at a major change in their company. And they weren't accustomed to walking into uncertainty. Each walked away in silence wondering what this new year would bring. Bob entertained thoughts of secretly destroying the credibility of John and Dave. He entered his office with greed in his heart and a devious smile on his face.

22

The following Monday morning was a typical mid-January foggy morning. Traffic moved slowly through the streets of Sacramento. Dave wondered if he was going to make it to Bob Whiting's office downtown for a nine o'clock meeting. Dave didn't let the bad traffic dampen his mood. He was still excited about his success in getting the company to take some action on the non-performing loans. He could operate with a clear conscience. He could also foresee his operation coming into profitability once the losses were behind him. As he approached the downtown area the sun pierced through the fog. Dave squinted to adjust his eyes to the sudden brightness.

He pulled into the headquarters parking lot at ten minutes until nine. He watched as staff walked from the parking lot to their buildings. He waved at some of the people he recognized. He stepped out onto the parking lot and locked his car. He smiled as he looked toward the east and saw the sunlight outlining the Sierra mountain range. The tops of the mountains were capped in snow and reflected the morning sun in a white luminescent glow against the brilliant blue sky. He took a deep breath and strode toward Bob Whiting's office.

"Good morning, Dave," Bob greeted him warmly. "How do you like your coffee?"

"Black is fine," Dave said. He was surprised at Bob's cordiality and wondered what was behind it. He knew that Bob kept his distance from him. And he knew that Bob was a close friend of Bud Murphy's. Dave had heard from others that Bob had hired Bud twenty years ago to work at National Assets. Once they were seated in Bob's office, Bob placed a document on his desk and looked at Dave. The desk was empty of any other papers. Dave noticed that the office was immaculate, one that reflected the business environment of a retiring person with not much left to do. On the credenza behind his desk was an old desktop manual typewriter with black keys trimmed in chrome. It looked like something that may have been used thirty years ago when the company was starting up. Bob noticed that Dave was looking at the typewriter.

"That was my first typewriter," Bob said proudly. "I used it during my first years with the company. I've typed many loan disbursement checks on that machine back when I had to do everything for myself." Bob stared at the typewriter as if it were an old friend who could sit and talk about the good old days with him. "If these damn computers ever go down, I'll be ready to keep the business going with that old typewriter."

Dave didn't know if he was joking. He smiled politely at Bob.

"I guess you've seen it all change before your eyes," Dave said.

"Yes, too many changes," he said nostalgically. "Those were exciting times when you could sit and type the loan documents and proceeds checks right at your desk." His head nodded like a puppet. His gaze time traveled back twenty years. "Things were a lot simpler. We could really get to know the customers."

Dave knew too well the conundrum that every company faced in trying to grow while providing good customer service. He knew that customers yearned for those good old days as much as Bob did. Yet every company kept right on growing or they went out of business. Lending regulations had stifled all spontaneity between a customer and a financial institution. Dave knew that. And he also knew that it was companies like National Assets that had prompted regulation because they didn't police their own businesses.

"Let me tell you why I called you into this meeting today," Bob began. He ceremoniously picked up the document from his desk. "I am going to disclose some information to you. It's proprietary information, very confidential. I need you to agree in writing that you will not discuss this information with anyone, not even your spouse. You are only at liberty to discuss this information with other employees who are also informed of this issue, and only to the extent necessary. Is that clear?"

"So far it is," Dave said hesitantly.

"I'll need you to sign the confidentiality agreement now so that we can discuss this." Bob handed Dave the top sheet from the packet. Dave looked it over and wrote his name at the bottom of the page. He handed it back to Bob.

"You'll be getting a copy of this before you leave here today," Bob said answering the question that must have shown on Dave's face. He put the paper aside and folded his hands on the polished surface of his desk.

"Now for the important part," Bob began slowly. "National Assets has decided to go out into the market and attempt to find a buyer. In order to continue this vigorous pace of growth, we find it necessary to find another way of funding that growth. After a lot of discussion, we have decided that selling the company, rather aligning or merging ourselves with a large, national institution would give us access to the financial resources we need to meet our goals set forth in our strategic plan."

Dave sat back and wondered how long Bob had practiced this speech. He wondered if he wasn't reading it from a page on his desk. The language was precise, yet ambiguous. It was safe, yet potentially dangerous if the market were to hear about it.

"As a matter of fact," Bob continued, "Mr. Pecunia has talked to several institutions with the thought in mind to only invite companies that met our parameters. Those parameters are that the acquiring institution reflects the core values and growth strategies that we have espoused for so long. Secondly, that they had a high regard for the human resource in a company, as we do. We want them to know that we consider our people as a company's most valuable asset."

Dave had to stifle a laugh. After what the company had put him through the last few months, he was outraged at Bob's hypocrisy. Maybe they're just all in denial, he thought. No wonder they want to sell the company. They don't know what's going on. He tried to hold a neutral expression so that Bob wouldn't pick up on any of his reactions.

"Mr. Pecunia has narrowed the bidders down to three possible choices," Bob droned on. "Over the next two months these three companies will send due diligence teams into our operations to perform their inspections and to refine their bids. We will be giving a series of presentations to these companies off campus, so to speak." Bob paused for effect. "It is critical that the names of these companies not be disclosed to anyone."

Dave knew the drill better than Bob. He had been involved in more acquisitions in his career than most people. And he was usually in the position of the acquirer. He decided not to offer that piece of information to Bob.

"We will set up an information center in San Francisco," Bob continued. "We want the majority of the presentations and the due diligence work to be done there so as not to disrupt the day-to-day activity of the company. We'll have the interested members of the due diligence teams come out for a tour of the facilities under very controlled circumstances. Even when they come out for the tours, we are not to disclose the names of the companies involved. If the employees figure it out for themselves, we are not to respond in any fashion. Is that clear?"

"I understand completely," Dave said. "What part of the presentations do you want me to be involved in?"

"I think we'll have Bud present the loan servicing operations," Bob said indifferently. "You can attend as a subject matter expert in the event there are questions directed at your business operation."

Dave stiffened in his chair. "Why wouldn't Bud and I be given equal time?"

"Because once they hear about one servicing operation, they aren't going to want to sit through the same thing again," Bob said in an exasperated tone. "Besides, we just want to give them an overview on how the business works. We want to be careful that we don't compromise what I would consider trade secrets," Bob said with an air of importance.

Dave just shook his head and looked away from Bob.

"Do you have a problem with that approach?" Bob asked pointedly.

"Would it matter?" Dave answered. He was starting to lose patience.

In a conciliatory gesture Bob got out of his chair and walked to the side of his desk and sat down on the edge. He folded his hands on his lap.

"I've known Bud for years," Bob said in a friendlier voice. "And I know what he is going to say and how he is going to react. I don't have that level of comfort with you." Bob inspected his cufflinks for a moment. "I know that Bud probably won't present his material as well as you could, but I will know where and when to help him. His stage fright may turn into an asset."

Bob rose from the edge of his desk and returned to his chair. He handed the five-page contract to Dave.

"You'll need to read and sign this before you leave my office," Bob said. "It assures you two years of salary and the acceleration of your stock options. When the sale goes through, you will be much better off financially than you are today. You are still entitled to all performance bonuses and incentives. Take a few minutes and look it over. Mr. Pecunia is being very generous to his management team regardless of their tenure."

Dave took the contract and read through it quickly. He realized that it was a generous incentive, probably worth a half a million dollars depending on the stock value at the time of the sale. All he had to do was cooperate with what his employer asked of him, he thought. He leaned forward, placed the contract on Bob's desk and stood up.

"I'll have to think about it," Dave said calmly.

Bob's face flushed red immediately. He almost jumped out of his chair. It was clear that he hadn't anticipated any problem with an offer this generous for an employee's loyalty.

"What do mean 'you'll have to think about it'?"

"Just what I said," Dave said evenly. "It's a lot of money, but I'm not sure that it matches my earnings potential in the industry. If something were to go wrong with the sale that would endanger my reputation, I might have a hard time finding another job." Dave was starting to enjoy the trouble he was causing Bob. He knew he was on dangerous ground once this incident made it back to Will Eagleton. He decided to hold his ground.

"Look," Dave said calmly, "you've got my signed confidentiality agreement. I know better than to discuss an impending sale with anyone. I'm just not accustomed to anyone putting a contract under my nose and telling me to sign it. I want to give the matter some deliberation."

Dave thanked Bob for his time and walked out of his office. He remembered Bob standing behind his desk, shocked at Dave's response. On his way back to his office Dave pulled off at a coffee shop and went in. He needed some time to think before he went back to the office.

He decided to get the coffee to go. He walked back out to his car and lit a cigarette. He removed the plastic lid from the cup and watched the steam rise to the top of his car. He sat and stared out the windshield while he replayed the events of the morning. He decided that he needed to contact an attorney, someone he had known a long time. He could decide what to do with the contract and talk through his concerns about the due diligence. He didn't want to get caught in the company lies and get himself in trouble with the authorities. And he didn't want to end up blowing a good deal for the company.

What if the National Assets cash position was so low that they would have trouble meeting their payroll in a few months, he thought. What if his honesty put the company in bankruptcy? Would keeping quiet be a lesser evil? It was becoming clear to him that he was about to become a party to some type of negligence. He felt the pull of the half million dollars and the stock options. He knew that the company was counting on his greed. He knew that he was in a dangerous situation until he gave National Assets an indication of where he stood. He crushed out his cigarette and started for the office.

As he drove the last mile to the servicing center he could only think that his efforts over the last year were in vain. If the company sold, all his work wouldn't make a bit of difference. He consoled himself in the fact that he had learned a lot, had accomplished many things, and put together a very good staff. Maybe he could take his experience to another job. That is if he didn't lose their trust, he thought.

Dave walked up the stairs two at a time and strode through the reception area of his servicing operation. He had all the doors fitted with security access badge scanners so that no unauthorized people could walk into the servicing center offices. He did it mostly for the safety of his employees. One of the additional benefits of having a security system that only the employees could access is that it kept out uninvited sales people. No one could walk into an office and make a sales call without an appointment. The problem was growing in the industry because the number of companies in the mortgage business was diminishing while the survivors grew in size and market share. That left fewer targets for the sales forces of computer systems, stationary and office supplies.

Dave noticed a man in a blue suit sitting in the lobby as he walked across the reception area. He nodded and kept walking to his office. When he entered his office, the receptionist called him on the intercom.

"Mr. Jenkins," she said, "this gentleman is waiting to see you. He said he didn't have an appointment."

"I'm sorry, Gina, you'll have to tell him that I have a prior commitment and can't see him right now," Dave stammered. He wanted some time to himself to digest the morning meeting with Bob. "If he wants to leave a message, I'll return his call this afternoon."

"I'll take care of it, Mr. Jenkins," Gina said.

Dave spent the next two hours reading mail, signing documents, reviewing the daily reports and answering his email. He was thankful that he decided to look at the email. Will Eagleton and Bob Whiting were on their way over to see him. He wondered why they hadn't called. Dave flipped through his messages distractedly. He quickly walked out to Marilee's desk to see if there were any undelivered messages. She had put her screen saver on indicating she was out to lunch. Dave scanned her desk and found the slip of paper marked urgent. He wondered why she hadn't put it on his desk. Then he remembered telling her once that any urgent messages should be delivered in person. She was probably planning on doing it as soon as she returned.

When Dave walked back into his office, Will and Bob were walking down the aisle of cubicles toward Dave. Dave noticed that both had big smiles and were carrying their brief cases. This was going to take awhile, he thought.

"Dave, good to see you," Will said warmly. He shook his hand and turned to Bob. Bob Whiting just nodded his hello and didn't offer his hand to Dave.

"Come into my office," Dave said. "This is an unexpected surprise. What brings you two over to my office?" Dave knew that the protocol at National Assets, much like at other large companies, dictated that the employee go to the senior manager's office. It was unusual to have a senior manager come to a subordinate's office, especially when it meant a drive across town in the middle of the day.

"I understand that you left Bob's office without signing your employment contract," Will said. He stated his concern simply and went right to the point. "We are offering you a substantial amount of money just for doing your job. We're only asking you to do what you would have been doing if we weren't putting the company on the market."

"That's just my point," Dave said. "You are putting the company on the market. If I sign that agreement, you would expect my full attention to my work, when it could be better use of my time to find a job with more of a future."

"Whoever buys us will leave us alone to operate as we always have done."

Dave stifled a grin. He didn't know if Will was that naïve about acquisitions, or if he was just trying to lie his way through this conversation. He had been through enough acquisitions to know that companies didn't spend millions to acquire other companies just to leave them alone.

"They could always change their minds about that," Dave said. He didn't want to sound argumentative. He looked at Will and smiled.

"Sometimes companies like to bring in their own management," Dave said.

"Part of our agreement is that we will only let companies bid who intend to leave the National Assets operation intact," Will said.

"I'm sure that's the intent," Dave persisted, "but they can always change their minds. If a forecast gets missed, or if profits fall off, a parent company will be in here in a heartbeat. I know that from my own experience, Will." Dave looked from Will to Bob. Both were staring at him intently. Dave couldn't read what was going on. Maybe they just want his cooperation, he thought.

"Am I under some obligation to sign this?" Dave asked.

"No," Will said quickly. Bob shifted in his chair. "But why would you turn down all this money?" Will's voice sounded colder. "The company is holding out its hand in a gesture of goodwill. I'm curious why you wouldn't accept that, unless you have something else on your mind." Will jaw muscles flexed impatiently.

"No, not really," Dave said. It suddenly hit him that they wanted his silence. They needed his complicity. Even if he weren't called on to give a presentation, they wanted to show him off. And they didn't want him saying the wrong things to the right people.

"I'll tell you what," Dave said. "It's my understanding that some of the senior managers received a three-year contract. Make mine a three-year contract instead of the two. Put in a clause that says if my job responsibilities change more that twenty-five per cent, that I can exercise my option to leave with the full value of my contract in cash."

Bob froze in his chair. Will's face flushed a deep red. There was silence in the office for a moment. Dave chose to stretch his bet a little further.

"I'm not asking for more than anyone else. And I'm not asking for any safeguards other than the ones we've discussed here," Dave said in a neutral tone.

Will stood from his chair and held out his hand to Dave. "Okay, I'll have Bob run it over to legal and get the changes made. I'll have the document back to you before the end of the day. You can fax me a copy before you go home tonight...the signed copy."

"Sounds good," Dave said.

After they left Dave sunk back into his chair. He stared at the wall in front of his desk. He couldn't believe that he made it through the negotiation. And he felt a sense of pride. The receptionist, Gina, entered his doorway.

Mr. Jenkins?" she asked timidly. "The man who was here earlier to see you. He left a message for you." Gina handed him the envelope with his name handwritten on the outside. Dave could see that there was nothing more than a business card on the inside of the envelope. And some auditors are here asking for you."

"Thanks, Gina," Dave said.

He opened the envelope and took out the business card. It identified a Bert Gunderson, special agent with the Federal Bureau of Investigation. Dave flipped the card over and noticed a handwritten message that simply said, "Don't sign anything until we talk."

Dave sat in his chair puzzled by the message. What would the FBI want with him? And how did they know that he was about to sign an agreement, he wondered. Were they listening to his conversation somehow? The feeling

THE COLOR OF FRAUD

of victory he had been enjoying just a few moments before quickly evaporated. It was replaced by a feeling of foreboding. And there was no one else to talk to. He needed to make some quick decisions. He wondered if the five hundred thousand dollars the contract represented was just out of his reach.

He immersed himself into the daily work on his desk. He knew he had two meetings to attend this afternoon. He found an empty conference room for the auditors. Dave's impression was that the audit team seemed nice enough. They gave the impression that they were here to perform a good audit. Dave's feelings of paranoia were allayed by their sincerity. *Maybe this will be okay*, he thought.

Even though he wasn't chairing the afternoon meetings, he would be expected to make some decisions. He didn't want anyone to think that he was distracted. It was important not to get the staff nervous he thought. He resolved to maintain a professional approach to his job. He couldn't afford to start a panic even though he could feel the beginnings of one inside of him.

Shane Davis had spent the last three days in an unscheduled systems training seminar in Kansas City. It was getting late as he sat in front of the computer screen in the conference room rubbing his tired eyes. He had decided to stay late to work on some homework that was due by the start of class the next day. Other students had come and gone to complete their homework assignment in the hours following their group dinner.

Shane was the only attendee from National Assets. He knew that the company was counting on him to bring back some useful information for their computer system. And he wanted to get the most out of the seminar before heading back to California tomorrow afternoon.

Shane was surprised that his manager had allowed him to attend the seminar. He had a long list of deliverables on his desk and his availability to other projects and training seminars was scarce. But his boss had said that the need for this seminar had come from higher up. No one questioned the directive and Shane ended up in Kansas City.

He stood and stretched. He yawned loudly since he was the only one left in the room. He shut down his computer and turned out the lights in the conference room. Shane walked through the lobby of the motel and out the front door. He decided to walk over to his room and have a cigarette on the way. His walk took him by the pool that was closed for the winter. He noticed that the grounds were not very well lighted. He took a deep breath to dispel his nervousness at the darkness.

Even though the night air was chilled, Shane stood and finished his cigarette. He wished he had brought a jacket. He knew he would be warm and comfortable in his room in a few minutes. He could fall asleep thinking of Candi. He couldn't wait to get back to California and see her. He was confused that she hadn't shown up at work for the past two days. He tried to call on each of his breaks. And her home phone was disconnected. Maybe she was having money problems, Shane thought. He resolved to find out when he stepped off the jet tomorrow.

He looked ahead to the stairway that took him up to his room. Before he walked through the last of the bushes surrounding the pool he heard footsteps behind him. He didn't turn quickly enough. The next thing he felt was a strong forearm pull tightly against the front of his neck and the cold muzzle of a handgun pressed against the base of his neck. Somehow he knew that he would never make it to his room.

23

In his home office that night Dave looked around at the wall charts and the stacks of reports he had accumulated. He had taken the money laundering theory about as far as he could. He felt confident that he had enough information to either scare the senior management or to warrant the interest of a regulatory agency.

Dave knew from experience that outright fraud was difficult to prove. That's why so few cases actually get prosecuted. Unless someone confessed, the chances of a successful prosecution were slim. He knew that there was a fine distinction between sloppy business practices and outright fraud. And many individuals claimed sloppiness in their business practices as a defense for fraudulent activities. His foray into the money laundering scheme was his first. So he wasn't sure what he had. What he needed was corroborating evidence. He wished he could get videotapes, or a confession. And he also knew that those things were beyond his reach.

With Ann's help he consolidated his work into two large notebooks. In addition he made a copy of the study on to a diskette. Dave decided to put the diskette in his safe deposit box. He packaged the notebooks to be shipped to a close friend who lived out of state. He packed the original papers that he had used for research into his car. He decided that the he should return those documents to the office. In that way he would have them for easy reference. Also, he didn't want to be accused of storing sensitive documents in his house.

Dave sat back in his chair and looked around his home office. He was satisfied that the room was clean of any company documents. No one would find anything of interest here, he thought. His gaze fell on the business card of the FBI agent. On an impulse he picked up the phone and asked directory assistance for the number of the local FBI office. He noticed that it was different than the one on the agent's card. Even though he knew that it could be a cell phone number or a private line, Dave decided to call the number he obtained from directory assistance. He asked for Bert Gunderson. The receptionist responded after a few minutes of searching that there was no Bert Gunderson at the FBI. Dave's stomach began to tighten. He hung up the phone and walked out to his back patio.

The fresh night air carried a chill from the Sierra Mountains. Dave lit a cigarette and stared up at the sparkling sky. Suddenly he wished his life were as clear as the winter sky. He wished he were anywhere but in Sacramento. He wanted to be on vacation in the southwestern United States. He wanted to be out in the desert miles away from anyone connected with business.

He tried to recall the man who sat in the receptionist lobby. He claimed to be an FBI agent. Dave thought that maybe he was with the drug enforcement unit or the economic crimes unit. Perhaps he worked with an assistant US attorney's office. The possibilities fatigued Dave's already exhausted mind.

Dave wondered if he was part of an elaborate set up to see if he would talk to the government about what he knew. And why was the executive management team treating him so differently? He looked inside of his own house and saw the light of the television flashing across the walls of the darkened house. He knew he wouldn't sleep well with all of this on his mind. Maybe if he stretched out on the couch and made some plans for tomorrow, sleep would eventually come.

As he turned to go back in the house he noticed a car parked a couple of houses down the street. The orange yellow light from the streetlamp silhouetted the head and shoulders of a man sitting behind the wheel in the car. Dave's heart beat faster. Maybe he was imagining the person in the car, he thought. It looked like it may just be the back of the car seat and the headrest that looked like a person. He knew that the homeowners association didn't allow parking on the street. Dave felt a chill go up his spine. He backed into the house and set his home security alarm. He knew he would get very little sleep tonight.

The following morning Dave stopped by his favorite coffee shop for a large cup of french roast. Since he had an early start on the day, he decided to sit at one of the outside tables and drink his coffee. The cold morning air made the coffee steam wildly. Dave had the patio to himself until Bert Gunderson appeared.

"You're a hard man to catch up with," Bert said. "A good man is hard to find," he laughed at his own play on words. He sat down without waiting for an invitation that might never come. Dave recognized him immediately from yesterday.

"Not really," Dave said casually. "I just like to keep my appointments."

"Aren't you curious why I tried to talk to you?" Bert asked.

"I don't know whether I would use the word 'curious,'" Dave answered evasively. "I guess you could say that's a part of it. How would you know that I have documents to sign?"

"Let me start at the beginning," Bert said. "We've been investigating individuals with National Assets for some time now. We suspect that there is some racketeering and some money laundering going on under the legitimate business operations of the company. I collect pieces of information. I think that you may have some information that could be useful to us. And it's my understanding that you have tried to voice your concerns within the company about some of the delinquency and loss procedures that don't really comply with standard industry procedure."

Dave wondered if this was a trap or if this agent had a source within the company. He knew that he was in a very dangerous situation if he talked to this stranger.

"I've never worked in a company where there weren't a few deficiencies in their operation," Dave answered. "That's what my job is all about. I help to improve processes. I don't see where that could be construed as illegal."

"That's because you don't know the whole picture," Bert replied. "I've worked on this case for months and..."

"Evidently you haven't found much if you're asking a new guy like me to help you with something you don't even know is going on for sure," Dave interrupted. He stood up from the table. "What you're asking of me is to compromise the confidentiality that this company has entrusted to me. At this point in time I would find that highly unethical. And I'm sure you would agree that ethics come into play here somewhere."

"You need to be careful," Bert said. He was clearly losing his patience with Dave. "You don't want to be a party to these crimes. I know that you are trying to do the right thing, but you need to step back and look at things a little differently."

"No, I don't," Dave replied. "All I have to do is my job to the best of my ability. As long as the company doesn't ask me to do something illegal, I have every obligation to follow their business directives."

"If you sign that employment contract," Bert warned, "you lose a perfect chance to clear yourself of any association with this wrongdoing."

"Thanks anyway," Dave said, "but I like being able to feed my family, to make a living." He remembered the call he had made last night to the local FBI office. "I'm not interested in anything but doing my job. If I change my mind, I'll give you a call. If I lose your card, I'll look up the number in the phone book."

"I suggest you don't lose the card," Bert said calmly. "You'll want to talk to me eventually."

Dave watched Bert's face closely. But he didn't register any reaction to his last statement. In the moment of silence that followed Dave turned away from Bert and walked to his car. He felt a wave of relief wash over him as he pulled back into the mindless traffic that would carry him to his office.

"Good morning," Dave smiled as he walked by Marilee, his assistant. "Would you get me Shane Davis on the phone, please? He works in systems support."

Dave thought that the best way to isolate him from any outside interference was to find out from Shane what he could do to clean up his computer files. It was also time to disconnect the home access that Shane had set up. Dave started making a list of the things he needed to ask Shane. Maybe he would take him to lunch. Dave could thank him for his help and ask him all these questions away from the office.

"Dave?" His assistant stood in his doorway. Without invitation she came in and sat down in front of his desk. She looked upset. "I'm sorry to be the one to tell you this, but someone just told me that Shane died at a training seminar in Kansas City. I heard that he was drinking heavily one night after class and got himself in some kind of altercation with a police officer. I was lucky to get that information, you know the secretarial grapevine and all. Do you want me to find out more about it?"

"No. No, but thanks," Dave said absently. "I'm sorry that you had to hear the news that way. I really liked Shane." Dave looked down at his list to hide his shock. Now he would never get the answers to these questions. He looked up at his assistant. "You know, if you can find out anything, I would like to know about it. I would also like to know if there is going to be a funeral service here in town. You know somewhere to send flowers?"

"I'll see what I can find out." She walked out of his office and left a silence in her wake that Dave couldn't deal with. First Buster was injured, now Shane was dead. Then he thought about Gil Sheets whose career had come to an end before it really started. He needed to talk to John. He needed to go for a walk. He grabbed his calendar and looked at the day's meeting schedule. He was supposed to be in an all-afternoon meeting to work on the due diligence presentation. He decided to spend the rest of the morning reading the daily reports and talking to his managers. The business had to go on. He knew that was his first priority. Things had to go on as usual. Too many people were depending on that now. And he was thinking of the people that really counted in the equation, his staff and the customers. Those expectations had to be met first. Dave promised himself not to lose sight of the business demands.

The late morning sun heated the asphalt of the parking lot as Dave began his walk. Dave strode to the residential border and passed through the gate. He breathed deeply as he walked trying to calm himself. He couldn't let go of the fact that Shane was gone. He tried to convince himself that it was just coincidence. But it fit the pattern too well. First Buster, now Shane had been taken out of the picture. He had to get to John Fremont before something happened to one of them. He felt as if he was being carried by events in a swift current that would drown him if he tried to struggle. Yet he knew that the current would take him deeper into a world of lies and false reports that would eventually come back to haunt him.

Then he thought about his meeting with Bert Gunderson. Was he really an agent or just a test, he wondered? The thought occurred to him that maybe he was from another office that the local FBI office didn't know about. Dave was reluctant to call the office again for fear of arousing suspicion. He stopped walking and closed his eyes. He wanted to chase all of this from his thoughts. He wanted it all to leave his life. He knew his job shouldn't be this complicated. But, if he were going to simplify things, he needed to have a plan. He quickly turned and walked back toward his office.

Dave was halfway through the parking lot when he heard a car honk behind him. He turned just in time to see John Fremont waving from inside his car. Dave walked to the passenger side of the car and got in.

"I've been looking all over for you," John said as he accelerated and pulled out onto El Camino Avenue. "Did you hear about Shane?"

"Yeah, just this morning," Dave said. "I didn't hear the details. I only heard that he died. The police mistook him for a burglar."

"Yeah, and he was staying at the motel for a training class," John added. "I heard that he tried to grab the policeman's gun. I also heard that he had been drinking at the motel lounge. He might have been feeling kind of confused and resentful of the fact that he was mistaken for someone else. It's certainly no way to treat a guest," John said.

"I find it a little too coincidental with what happened to Buster," Dave said. "Besides, I know that Shane didn't drink."

John reacted visibly to that piece of information. He stared at Dave in surprise.

"I was thinking that we may be in immediate danger," John said. He drove up Watt Avenue until the traffic thinned out. John pulled his car into the entrance of a park and looked around for an inconspicuous place to park, a place where they could see the other cars that came into the park.

"We need a plan," John said. "I'm getting worried about my family."

"Not to mention our own safety," Dave answered. He loosened his tie and reached for his cigarettes. "You have any ideas?"

John sat for a minute staring out the windshield. He rolled his window down and shut the car off.

"I was thinking that sometimes it's better to stay out in the open rather than hiding," he finally said. "I think that the meetings and presentations with the prospective buyers might be a good time to let the buyers know what's going on. I don't think that anyone at National Assets is going to do anything if too many people are around."

"If we mess up their sale, they're going to be mad. They're certainly going to want to get even." Dave said. He told John about his meeting with Bert Gunderson and the efforts behind the employment contract.

"I signed mine this morning," John said. "I talked to my attorney last night and went over it with him. Basically he said I had nothing to lose by signing it."

"I think it puts us in a little deeper," Dave offered. "I'm sure that it would look better if we just walked away from the whole mess."

"No," John replied quickly. "You think they'll let you just walk away with all of that knowledge about the company?"

"I don't know. I was hoping that it was a possibility," Dave replied.

"It won't hurt to get paid some big money for the trouble they put you through," John answered. "If you walk away now, there's no money in it. And maybe there's still some risk."

"What are you going to do?" Dave asked. He watched John reach for the ignition key and start the car.

"I'm going to fight it," John said. "I'm going to make sure that everyone interested in buying National Assets knows what I know. They can draw their own conclusions. All I have to do is show a few reports that will make someone start asking questions. If they don't ask the right questions, then shame on them for not doing their homework. I'll just stay away from making any wild accusations."

Dave shifted in his seat and flipped his cigarette out the window. He didn't like where John was going with this.

"Are you with me?" John asked as if he were reading his thoughts.

"I don't know," Dave answered slowly. "I'm not that comfortable with that approach. It sounds dangerous."

"It's already dangerous," John said. "It's the one strategy that stands a chance. They don't want a fight. They don't want anyone to publicly step up and be honest about their concerns. That's why they're handing out promotions and incentives and employment contracts to those they think will be compliant."

"It didn't work for Buster or for Shane," Dave protested.

"Buster really got on the wrong side of Mort Smalley. We don't know all the facts about Shane. It could be just coincidence."

"There's always that possibility," John said. "But when did we start believing in coincidence?"

The internal audit was completed within two weeks. During the exit interview the audit team complimented Dave on his operation. Even though it was only a few months old it was already running better than some of the other, more established business. Dave was pleased with the feedback.

"It's not our job to put words of praise in an audit report," Paul Frank said. "But I think a few words would go a long way in offsetting the major deficiency we need to report."

"What major deficiency?" Dave asked.

"Well, Dave, frankly we see a lot of loans on the books that are most likely losses that should be recognized as losses. In addition, your delinquency numbers are understated. And, according to some of the investor guidelines, you are supposed to be reporting credit histories on some loans to the credit bureau."

Dave could hide his shocked expression. He fought to control himself before he spoke. "I don't want to sound defensive about this," he started, "but I've been surfacing these issues of delinquency and losses to executive management and the credit policy committee since I've discovered the irregularity." Dave turned to his credenza and pulled out a file of correspondence that validated his position.

After a few minutes of reading some of the memos, Paul looked up clearly puzzled.

"I would agree that you've done your part, Dave. This corroborating correspondence makes a difference. The fact remains that the deficiency exists. We'll still have to include it in the report." He sighed deeply. "But you can outline in your response all of the corrective action that you have taken to remedy this situation."

"That's fair enough," Dave agreed. "Just getting it on record with the audit department is a prudent action. Now, as far as the delinquency getting understated, what set of reports were you using?"

"Well, we went through Bud Murphy's financial analyst to get the month end delinquency numbers. That's what we started with. Then we pulled a comparison off of the system as a cross check. There were more accounts on the system than on the report."

"Exactly," Dave answered enthusiastically. He was enjoying this. Finally someone outside the servicing business was affirming what he had been saying all along. "Here are my month end reports." He handed a set to Paul. "You'll notice that my reports state a higher rate of delinquency than Bud Murphy's financial reports. And my reports match the system."

"I don't understand," Paul said. He looked puzzled as he studied the delinquency reports. "Why would Bud Murphy's group understate your delinquency?"

"Because he doesn't want anyone to know how bad the delinquency is," Dave answered satisfied that he could finally make his point. "Or else someone above him doesn't want the bad news published."

Paul Frank and his two assistant auditors were quiet for a few minutes. They looked over the reports and then at each other.

"We'll go ahead and send you the preliminary report on our findings, Dave. Answer them the best you can. And put a lot of this documentation to support your response. We'll take it from there." Paul stood and shook hands with Dave. The puzzled look hadn't completely vanished from Paul's face when he left.

One week later Dave received the preliminary audit report from the internal audit department. Dave submitted his response with plenty of documentation. A few days later he received the final report. The major deficiency of not taking losses in a timely manner and understating delinquency had been reduced to a minor deficiency. The audit department had inserted an explanation that they had researched the issue with the accounting department.

The report stated that Dave would work with the corporate finance department to come up with a solution. The item about not reporting credit histories to the credit bureau was missing from the final report.

Dave chuckled to himself when he reread the section. The only thing he could think of was that the executive team had counseled him on the best way to handle the issue. Dave guessed that some senior executive probably wanted the whole issue removed from the report. From what Dave knew about Paul Frank he doubted that would ever happen. Dave was happy just to get this issue published in a document outside of his organization. He knew how much that added to his credibility.

24

The city by the bay, the place of earthquakes, fog and Alcatraz had been chosen for the due diligence meetings that would result in the sale of National Assets. The late January weather in San Francisco usually brings an early morning fog to the city. The commuters accept the delays and the low visibility on the bridges and surrounding streets. Fog hides the bay until the mid morning sun is strong enough to burn the clinging gray clouds away. Sometimes the strong breezes chase it away and leave a chill in the city streets.

National Assets decided to hold the meetings for the due diligence in the President Hotel located on top of a steep street near the piers. The hotel was over a hundred years old and had housed many presidents and foreign dignitaries who had visited San Francisco on their travels. The registration counter was a sixty feet long wooden work of art complete with ornate wrought iron windows and a backdrop of mahogany letterboxes.

The lobby filled with guests and convention attendees. The area appeared more like a church or a public library with forty-foot ceilings and rich warm paneling from floor to ceiling. Plush couches and chairs were arranged in intimate circles and bordered with plants. Two pianos played softly at each end of the long lobby. The traditional gift shop was busy selling post cards and souvenirs of the bay area. The hotel gave an atmosphere of respectability to the negotiations that were taking place.

National Assets had reserved the penthouse floor and the two levels below the penthouse to house all of their employees and the employees of the company interested in buying them. The field of possible purchasers had been narrowed down to three major banks. Two of the banks were national banks and the other was a regional bank that had been on an acquisition spree for the last three years. Each bank would take turns spending a week at the hotel performing a due diligence inspection of the National Assets books.

The format was set uniformly for each of the banks. The week would begin with a hospitality dinner, an evening set aside to introduce the senior management of each organization. The following day was a series of concurrent presentations on the operations of National Assets. The accounting function would be giving a presentation in one conference room while down the hall, the sales department would be presenting their organization. At the same time another department of National Assets would be giving a presentation. The afternoons were open for the visiting bank to review loan records and various financial reports. The following day would start with another round of different presentations followed by an afternoon of looking at records. Thursday was set aside for an on-site tour of the buildings in Sacramento where the operations were going on as usual.

The following week the whole process started again with the second bank. After one bank spent a week with the National Assets group, the next bank came in the following week. After the three visits, the deadline would be established for the final bids. These offers would be taken to the board of directors for approval to sell the company. The estimate was that a bank interested in purchasing a company usually spent about three hundred thousand dollars in due diligence expenses on a business the size of National Assets before they submitted their final bid. And the banks were willing to spend the money because National Assets held a commanding market share of the businesses that they had tried to get into for the past two years. The cost of acquiring a company could be offset by the immediate gain in talent and plant operations for a bank. They wouldn't have to build anything. The market share was immediate. In addition they would have an instant revenue stream coming from a new business. This usually made good press at the next stockholders meeting.

Dave spent the weekend putting the final touches on his presentation. Even though he wasn't supposed to give a separate presentation on the home improvement servicing business, he wanted to be prepared. He also had to work with Bud on his presentation so that some of the reporting numbers were combined. Dave was there only to answer questions specific to the home improvement servicing operation and to present his organization chart to the inquiring banks.

Dave decided to ride with John Fremont from Sacramento to San Francisco. They arrived at the President Hotel about midnight on Sunday. When he checked into his room Dave received a call that an impromptu meeting was going to be held by Will Eagleton in thirty minutes. Iron Will wanted to review the strategy for the meeting one last time. He also wanted to assure his management team that they would be taken care of once the company sold. And he wanted to stress the confidentiality of the whole exercise one last time. The meeting lasted until two in the morning. Dave knew that it was going to be a grueling three weeks. At least it would keep his mind on the business and off of all the other imaginings, he thought.

After his talk with John on the way over to the bay area, Dave decided he would keep a low profile and let the due diligence meetings take their own course. He suspected that John was going to be more vocal about his concerns. This created some tension between them. Dave knew he would be wise to distance himself from John if he started to voice his concerns to the visiting bankers.

The group from National Assets met for breakfast and planned their day. They needed to set up the presentation rooms and the research library where all the company records would be temporarily housed. Dave noticed that his most recent internal audit was missing from the collection of audits performed within the last year. He was happy that he kept copies of both preliminary and final reports.

Each participant was issued security badges at the breakfast table. Dave soon discovered the reason for the elaborate security. The penthouse floor was heavily guarded and controlled by a security force. The security guards searched all brief cases and collected all tape recording devices and cameras while anyone was on the penthouse level. The only people who had free access were the National Assets executives from Chicago along with Will Eagleton. Dave had never seen such tight control over a due diligence exercise in his career.

By Monday afternoon all of the arrangements were in place. The first wave of bankers would be arriving that evening in time for the reception and dinner. Dave considered how to spend his free afternoon. He decided to get out of the hotel and walk around the downtown area. He could do a little sightseeing and pick up something for Ann since Valentine's Day was only a couple of weeks away. He stepped out of the front door of the hotel and lit a cigarette. He felt a sense of relief just standing away from all the preparations.

About a block from the hotel he spotted an old church that had been turned into a museum. He headed up the street in the direction of the church. As he walked along he noticed how heavy the traffic was in the early afternoon. It never appeared to let up. He realized why some residents didn't own cars in San Francisco. The access to public transportation and the constant heavy traffic was a persuasive incentive to get rid of one's car. It appeared to Dave that parking presented a major problem as well. Cars were constantly double parking in the streets. Many vehicles had tickets on their windshields.

Dave flipped his cigarette into the gutter and walked over to the church. He noticed the patchwork on the damage caused by numerous earthquakes. Many buildings appeared to have similar cracks. He wondered if he was going to feel any tremors while he was staying in the city. He smiled at the thought of a major earthquake shuffling the mountains of paper reports in the research room in the penthouse of the hotel.

Dave walked around the old church. It was closed to visitors. He decided to walk down to the Nieman Marcus store and buy some candles for Ann for Valentine's Day. He then walked over to a coffee shop. He sat and drank a cup of coffee and watched people walk by on the street. There was never a lack of variety in the crowds that marched up and down the street on their way to work or running errands. Most were dressed in business attire and walked with a sense of purpose. There were the homeless who ambled aimlessly up the sidewalks with sleeping bags strapped to their shoulders looking for handouts and loose change. Dave tried to imagine where he would fit among all these people who were just trying to make their way in this unwieldy city. He longed for the safe and relatively quiet days at Norbank.

He finished his coffee and looked at his watch. He thought he had time for a nap before the evening's festivities. He grabbed his candles and walked back up the steep sidewalk to the hotel.

The following morning Dave sat at a long conference table surrounded by his coworkers. On the other side of the table were the employees from Verdura Bank. This institution was considered the most likely to purchase National Assets. Will Eagleton urged his management team to put on the presentation of their lives for this group. Bob Whiting was in charge of the loan servicing presentation. He fumbled nervously through the introductions and made an awkward attempt at humor. Then he turned the floor over to Bud Murphy who walked up to the front of the room with his overhead slides and a stack of handouts.

Predictably the Verdura employees started leafing through the presentation packet instead of listening to Bud. Bud mumbled nervously and the audience shifted in their seats as he took them through the organization chart and the recent accomplishments of his unit. He talked briefly about the history of National Assets move from Chicago and their building the first servicing center on the west coast for the company. Bud also tried to throw in some humor. It came across as insulting and arrogant. When he moved into the productivity numbers and the accounts per employee, the Verdura group started asking their questions.

In the beginning the questions were easy to answer and established comparisons with the industry standards. As time went on the questions became more pointed and Bud struggled for the answers. Bob Whiting jumped in on some of the answers. He talked around the questions and gave his philosophical point of view on some of the issues. This type of response made the Verdura employees grow impatient. They turned to the packet of information and started making notes. Dave knew that they were planning to do their own research in the records library once the presentation was over. One of the Verdura employees waved for Bud's attention.

"It's my understanding that you started a home improvement loan servicing center about a year ago," he stated. "Are we going to get a presentation on that operation?"

"What we thought we would do is combine the numbers from both of the operations so that you wouldn't have to sit through two similar presentations," Bob fielded the question. "Was there something in particular that you were looking for? We have Dave Jenkins here. He's the manager of that operation and can handle any questions you may have."

"I would like to hear from him about the start up process and his experiences with spinning off a separate operation from the existing one," The employee answered. "It's my understanding he came to you from Norbank and would have a valuable perspective on your efforts to build a new operation."

Bob reluctantly nodded for Dave to take over the presentation and talk.

"I'm sure Dave would be happy to enlighten you on his experience this past year," Bob said. "Dave, why don't you take them through the start up of your operation?"

Dave stood and walked to the front of the room. He began by introducing himself and giving some of his background. He carefully walked them through the history of his operation and some of the obstacles he faced in getting it running. Then he cautiously took them through some of his concerns about the growth in delinquency and what was being done to address the issue.

The Verdura employees nodded with interest as Dave spoke. Their appreciation showed as Dave gave them facts and didn't stray to far into the philosophical ramblings they had experienced with both Bob and Bud.

"If you'll turn to page thirty-one of your hand out," Dave continued, "you see the growth in the more serious delinquency categories." He paused a moment while everyone found the page. "In our attempts to work with the delinquent customers we've purposely allowed the delinquent accounts to remain on the books rather than write those accounts off. This was our attempt to refinance and to modify the loan payments to accommodate the customers when they faced temporary periods of unemployment or unforeseen medical expenses. It's a risk that we thought was well worth taking in light of the loss mitigation programs being promoted by the industry."

"Do you have formal charge off policy?" the Verdura employee asked. One of the key questions was out on the table. A thin smile crossed Dave's face as he prepared to answer. He wasn't quick enough. Bob Whiting stood from his chair to field the question.

"We've been working on a formal charge off policy that will be compatible to both Bud's and Dave's operations. We do not want to indiscriminately write off loans that may turn out to be performing receivables." Bob was gaining momentum. "You have to remember that this isn't a first mortgage operation. The loans we make are consumer loans. It's a different animal than what you are probably used to."

Dave saw the impatience in their eyes. Not only was Bob wandering off into philosophy again, he was talking in a condescending manner. Dave waited for a pause to interrupt him.

"If you would like to discuss this further after the presentation, I'll be available for questions," Dave said. He noticed the anger on Bob's face.

"Actually," Bob said, "I am coordinating all requests for information outside the formal presentations. If you have any requests for further information, please coordinate them through me."

"It seems to me," the Verdura employee persisted, "that a charge off policy would be one off the first things you would want to implement."

There was silence in the room until John Fremont cleared his throat and prepared to speak.

"In defense of Dave," John said, "he proposed a comprehensive charge off policy before his operation ever went live. It was one of his major concerns when he started the servicing plant." A longer, awkward silence followed John's comment.

"Well, if there are no more questions, why don't we adjourn for now," Bob said nervously. "Thank you for your attention."

The group of Verdura employees quietly stood and walked out of the room. The National Assets team sat looking down at the table until they were gone. Bob glared in John's direction.

"Just what was that all about?" Bob asked indignantly. He tried to gather his papers off the table with his shaking hands.

"I was keeping all of us from looking like complete idiots," John answered. "Telling them that we didn't have a charge off policy damaged our credibility. I guarantee you that they will be drilling deeply on that issue."

"You were instructed to observe this presentation," Bob answered. "If anything destroys our credibility, it's giving the appearance that we are divided among ourselves."

"I think that we owe them the truth, if we have the answer," John said.

"I disagree," Bob said flatly. "That's why they are here. They need to find things out for themselves. We don't offer them everything on a silver platter." Bob struggled to control his impatience. He turned to Bud Murphy. "You did a fine job on your presentation, Bud. Superb, simply superb."

Dave looked at John and rolled his eyes. He gathered up his documents and left the conference room with John.

"How about a cup of coffee in private?" John asked.

"Sounds good to me," Dave answered. "I'm going to call the office and see what's going on. I'll meet you in about fifteen minutes in the coffee shop."

"While you're doing that, I need to order some delinquency reports," John said. "I'll meet you down there."

Since there was an abundance of fresh coffee in several of the conference rooms, the coffee shop was empty of any employees from either company. John and Dave found a quiet corner and ordered the coffee that they really didn't want. They went over the presentation shaking their heads in disbelief at the bad information that had been presented.

"I believe in putting your best foot forward," John said, "but that went too far. They'll have grounds for a lawsuit if we keep pumping them with all these lies."

Dave was surprised to hear John so vehement in his criticism. Evidently Bob had broken through his patience and John didn't keep his usual reserve in his words.

"By the way Bert Gunderson said that he talked to you," John said changing subjects.

"That's true," Dave said. "He talked to me. I didn't talk to him. He wanted me to, but I didn't see any upside to that. It would just put me in more danger."

"Not if he had something to trade," John said mysteriously. "Information is a powerful commodity in this business."

"I wasn't thinking about that at the time," Dave said a little defensively. "I didn't want any more complication in my life that day."

"He thinks that we're trapped in a bad company. He thinks we're trying to do the right thing. He knows that we are outsiders." John stirred his coffee slowly. "He knows a lot about the National Assets organization and its history. He was willing to tell me about some of it in exchange for my help." John looked over at Dave waiting to see if he wanted to hear the rest of his story.

"Okay," Dave smiled. "Let's hear it. I can tell you're dying to tell it."

"Poor choice of words, Dave," John returned his smile. He took a drink of his coffee and began.

"It seems that Leo Pecunia and the CEO of Verdura bank, Jim Stratton, are life-long business associates. Back in the sixties when National Assets was just a fledgling business, Jim funded a lot of their first loans. And they've stayed close ever since. Verdura Bank even looked the other way when large sums of money were mysteriously flowing through the accounts of National Assets. The money laundering may have started back then. And Jim Stratton may have been a beneficiary to those transactions, both personally and professionally.

"When Leo retired and left the company to his son, Leo Jr., the relationship between the two companies continued. Leo Jr. wasn't as good a businessman as his father. By the time they knew that National Assets was in trouble, Verdura Bank was a major buyer of loans. Now they own the majority of loans that National Assets services. If the company were to take a fall, Verdura would face big losses and possibly a lot of embarrassment. And that's why they are looking at buying the company. If Verdura can win the bid, they can control the publicity, the losses and the quiet demise of the company. No one will ever be the wiser."

"So the other two companies who are coming in to perform due diligence have no idea that the sale may already be a foregone conclusion," Dave finished the thought. "Verdura can't afford to let anyone else acquire National Assets. Leo Pecunia and Jim Stratton may have all of this sewn up. All they have to do is to advise their respective boards of directors to go along with the transaction."

"That's right," John said. "Everything looks legitimate. The perfect white collar crime. Or the perfect white collar cover up."

"I called the Sacramento FBI office," Dave said, "and they didn't know Bert Gunderson."

"He knows," John said. "He's out of the Virginia office."

"Why didn't he straighten me out on that?" Dave asked.

"Maybe he thought you were a little too unreceptive. Maybe he decided to leave it alone when I started talking with him. He didn't need to pursue you anymore."

Dave stared out the window thinking about that for a minute. It made sense. But there was still a lot of danger attached to a relationship with him. And it was becoming more dangerous as pieces of information were put together, he thought.

"I'm thinking about the millions of dollars that are being spent on a deal that's already done," Dave mused. "A lot of people would be angry if they knew what was going on. I wonder how many lawsuits will spring up in the aftermath of this acquisition. Duping the National Assets stockholders is one thing. Trying to fool all of the Verdura stockholders is a much tougher task. There must be a lot at stake."

"The initial bid for the company is over two billion dollars," John said slowly. "Leo Jr. owns forty percent of the stock. That makes him a very rich man instead of the leader of a bankrupt company."

"I understand how Buster and Shane would have to be dealt with in order to keep this going," Dave said.

"And what lengths would they go to now that they are close to the finish line on this transaction?" John asked.

Both looked around the coffee shop at the same time. Dave realized that he knew enough to be very dangerous to the company. He knew that his risk had just increased ten fold after this conversation with John. Whether he liked it or not, he was in deep, maybe two billion dollars deep.

The following week Jim Stratton, several board members, and the financial team from Verdura sat in the executive conference room discussing the details of their bid. They had been meeting for the last two hours listening to the executive summary of the due diligence findings. They moved on to the profit projections and found themselves in a heated discussion on the financial reports that National Assets had given them.

"We've got to move ahead on the numbers that we have," Jim Stratton said impatiently. "If we go back and ask for more information we're going to lose this opportunity to acquire the biggest equity lender to one of those other banks."

"But the numbers just don't add up," Tom Brooks, the chief financial officer, stated evenly. "Our pricing and revenue models indicate that their profit and cash flow projections are way off."

"Our pricing and revenue models are built for the first mortgage business," Jim almost shouted. "National Assets is a different business. Our models are imperfect. We don't understand that business as well as we do our own."

The board members and the remaining financial analysts looked on in confusion. They were uncomfortable with the way this discussion was going. The board was split on its decision to acquire National Assets. And they only had until midnight to submit their bid. Jim Stratton sat back in his chair in an attempt to appear calmer, more reasonable to the group. He knew that there was more at stake here. He knew about the money laundering. And he knew that he had to cover up Verdura's involvement by acquiring National Assets and slowly absorbing the losses into the bank's balance sheet somehow.

"This company represents the number one market shareholder of the equity business in the country. We're buying a lot more than their estimates on future profits. We buy the biggest car in the race. They have the plant, the personnel, and the market share. All we have to do is run it intelligently." Jim folded his hands on the table and looked around the table.

"Something just doesn't look right." Tom Brooks was not going to back down. He had been over these numbers eighteen hours a day for the past four days. He was convinced that the whole story was not out on the table, and certainly not depicted accurately in these numbers.

"Gentlemen, I leave it up to you," Jim said finally. "We have before us the opportunity of a lifetime. I strongly recommend that we take it. The board can vote now and decide our future."

David Shipley, the chairman of the board, was the oldest man in the room. He wore a dark, expensive suit and sat at the head of the table quietly listening to the discussion. Half the time he looked like he was asleep. When he opened his eyes he stared straight at Jim Stratton. His blue eyes were clear and intelligent with a steel like gaze. Everyone at the table knew that he probably could run the business in his sleep.

He quietly stood and addressed the group even though he kept his gaze fixed on Jim.

"We don't have the luxury of unlimited time to discuss this issue much more. And when the numbers don't corroborate the story we've been told by their executive management team, it worries me." The chairman let his eyes shift to each attendee around the table before he continued. When he resumed his speech, he was looking straight at Jim.

"But when haven't we been lied to?" He paused to clear his throat. "We have so many lawsuits pending in the aftermath of our last acquisition that it really won't matter if we have a few more. Jim, if you think this is right thing to do, the board will back you. The vote won't be unanimous, but you have your supporters. But remember this. If this acquisition turns out to be a pile of shit, you're going to be the one sitting in the middle of it for the rest of your career. This is one of those career making, or career breaking decisions."

The room was quiet for several moments after chairman Shipley sat down. The group stared at the packages in front of them waiting for someone to make the next move. Finally Jim Stratton spoke.

"Then we'll go ahead with the deal," he answered with the same conviction he had displayed throughout the discussion. He knew the consequences of not acquiring the company. The team of financial analysts looked down in defeat. Their eighteen hour days had gone for nothing.

Many cities in the country considered Sacramento a visionary for their extensive network of bicycle routes, especially the bicycle path that ran along the American River for twenty-six miles from Folsom Lake where it gently descended into downtown Sacramento. The path was paved and stayed away from city traffic. In sections of the bike path one could imagine being out in the country miles away from civilization. Candi Combs pedaled steadily along the asphalt trail staring out at the scrub oak and manzanita bushes that lined the bike path. The scent of river water mixed with the wild fennel drifted across the bike path.

The previous week she had resigned from National Assets. Everyone understood her action since they thought she was grieving over Shane. She had quietly cancelled the lease on her furnished apartment and stored her belongings in one of the ubiquitous storage facilities that line highway fifty.

This morning she had taken the bus to the Nimbus dam off of Hazel Avenue. Usually there was enough of a crowd in the parking lot of the fish hatchery to make her inconspicuous. She spotted the green bike that had been left there for her earlier that morning. Carefully she put on her leather gloves and tried the combination on the padlock. The prearranged set of numbers worked and the lock fell open.

Candi tied her small duffel bag to the back of the bike and pedaled toward downtown. She wanted to leave town as inconspicuously as possible. But she thought that Will had gone overboard. Probably his love of physical fitness, she thought, had put her on this bike. A few strands of her recently dyed and cut hair streamed in the wind. The exercise relaxed her while her breathing became deeper and measured.

Occasionally she looked out at the cold water of the American River as it hurried toward the city. She imagined the banks lined with people panning for gold one hundred and fifty years ago. People still came to the banks of this river to find their fortunes, she thought. Only they didn't squat in the hot sun any more. They sat behind their desks and plotted, planned and contrived ways to satisfy their greed. Just like in the past only a select few found their fortunes. The rest died or walked away in disillusionment trying to find a different way to survive. She pedaled faster toward her gold. Will had promised her fifteen thousand dollars.

An hour and a half later she coasted into old Sacramento, the historical district that had undergone extensive restoration. The old hotels and mercantile district housed trendy restaurants and retail stores. Boardwalks still ran the length of district and were always crowded with tourists. Candi spotted the bike rack near the train museum and slowly placed her bike next to an identical green bike. She walked into the public restroom with her duffel bag and changed out of her exercise outfit and into a short sleeve knit shirt and khaki slacks. She stood at the sink and freshened her appearance as best she could. After brushing out her hair, she added a little lipstick for good measure. She walked leisurely back to her bike and noticed that the other green bike was gone.

After looking around carefully she straddled the bike and looked down at the two new oversized water bottles on the frame of the bike. She quickly placed one of them in her duffel bag and opened the top on the remaining bottle. She smiled when she saw the neatly rolled cash stashed inside the bottle. She knew she couldn't count it now. She shrugged philosophically at the possibility that Will shorted the payoff and there was nothing she could do about it. But it still looked like a lot of money to her.

On the top of the cash was her train ticket to Stockton. Her train left in forty-five minutes and the train station was only four blocks away. She would only have to pedal on this street under interstate five and she would be there. And the trains didn't ask for picture identification like the airlines did.

Candi looked around one last time. She wondered if she was being watched and if they would make sure that she got on board the train. She needed no convincing after finding out what happened to Shane. She would have to run fast and hard in case Will and his buddies changed their minds about her. And she knew that Will was counting on her fear.

25

The weeks that followed were a gauntlet of interviews and presentations to curious employees of other institutions. Norbank came in the following week. Since Dave was a former employee of Norbank, National Assets tried to keep him secluded during the week. Bob Whiting specifically warned Dave about not making this "old home" week. But Dave saw no way to avoid it. He renewed old acquaintances without compromising the integrity of the due diligence exercise.

After they left, Cooper Bank came in for a look at the National Assets operation. It was nearing the end of February and the company waited to hear who the buyer was. There was a lot of talk about selecting a company that would leave the National Assets operations intact. They wanted a buyer who valued the staff. That was the public relations line that they put out to their employees.

Dave's suspicions were confirmed when Will Eagleton announced that the company had agreed to sell to Verdura Bank. Will made the announcement during the first week of March. The sale would take place as of the close of business on June 30th. All employee stock plans as well as the publicly held stock would convert to Verdura Bank stock at the closing price for that day.

Memos, emails and public announcements heralded the merger. New releases publicized the fact that two financial leaders stood poised with the resources and the vision necessary to go forward into future markets with a full array of financial products for the consumer. Employees were excited about the benefits offered by merging with Verdura Bank.

Dave and John were a little more cynical about the merger. They found it interesting that the company referred to it as a merger when in reality it was an outright sale. Both knew employees in the banking industry who had been acquired by Verdura. The story was that Verdura left acquired institutions alone for about a year after the purchase. Then they came in and took control with a vengeance, cutting jobs and demanding unattainable goals on budget controls and revenues. When those weren't met, they started cutting back operations, closing offices and laying off employees. It was a subtle form of conquest and destruction of the competition. Dave had seen it too many times to be surprised by their methods. His contract offered him insulation from the changes that would probably come if Verdura held to its pattern.

In the meantime John was working with Bert Gunderson handing over critical information that helped the government in their pursuit of National Assets' illegal activities. Dave decided to stay neutral. He worried about John's safety yet admired his courage and integrity. Dave knew that there might yet be a better way to resolve the reporting issues if he worked openly with the new management that Verdura was slowly sending in to the company. These Verdura employees were portrayed as advisors who couldn't set policy until the sale was complete, yet helped to align key procedures such as reporting and personnel administration. When Verdura did step in, there would be less adjustment needed.

One of these lead managers was Zack Peters, a senior vice president who had been with Verdura for three years. He managed the mortgage servicing operations for Verdura at their headquarters in North Carolina. He was about forty years old. He was short and energetic. He had dark eyes that shifted around a lot taking in everything they could. He had dark hair tinged with gray and long in the back. Dave remembered him from the due diligence meetings in San Francisco. He had paced around the room during much of the presentation. His nervous energy seldom allowed him to sit in a chair for very long. It was apparent to Dave that he was well informed about the mortgage business. Dave usually had to educate a superior on the business before he could get an informed decision on a proposal. It had been one of his greatest frustrations at Norbank where the bank held fast track promotions for certain individuals. They would expose these high potential people to short assignments in every facet of the business before they settled them in some executive capacity for the rest of their career.

When Dave introduced himself to Zack at the due diligence meeting, both knew each other by reputation.

"What in the world are you doing working at National Assets?" Zack asked him in a quiet corner of the room before the presentation began.

Dave laughed quietly while he wondered if the company's reputation was that maligned in the industry.

"The opportunity to build a servicing operation from the ground up attracted me here," Dave said evenly.

The smile faded from Zack's face. He shook his head and rolled his eyes.

"I hope it was worth it," Zack answered. "The first thing I would do is to combine all of the servicing into one unit. Save money and staff." Zack was already outlining his strategy.

"National Assets thought that it would work better with two operations," Dave said.

"They just didn't have enough faith in Bud Murphy to do the job," Zack said. "That's probably why they brought you in."

Dave was surprised by Zack's directness. He wondered if Verdura had figured all of this out, or whether someone had briefed them already.

"The pay is good, as you probably already know," Dave answered and smiled. Zack returned his smile and walked to the other side of the room. He stood out in the room because he was the only person among the twenty people who wasn't dressed in a suit. Zack had worn a plaid shirt and khaki slacks every day of the weeklong due diligence meeting. Dave took it as a sign of self-confidence. Zack didn't need the clothes to impress anyone. He preferred to rely on his wits.

Weeks later with the sale announced and everyone waiting for July 1st to arrive, Zack stood in the doorway of Dave's office dressed in a sport shirt and slacks.

"Good to see you again, Dave," Zack said cheerfully. "I'm looking forward to working with you."

Dave stood and shook his hand. He motioned for Zack to sit down. Zack smiled but remained standing. He shoved his hands in his pockets and leaned back against the wall.

"So how are things going?" Zack asked casually. Dave figured that Zack never asked a casual question. He was always looking for insights to the business operations and to the people who managed them.

"We're going to have a good month. Delinquency is on the way down and we're coming in under budget on expenses."

"I'm glad to hear about delinquency dropping," Zack said. "It looks like that's been a problem over the past year."

Dave went into his explanation about the company not taking losses promptly that overstated the delinquency for the majority of last year. Zack listened carefully. Dave knew he was getting a chance to present a more accurate picture of the delinquency and loss problem than he had been able to give at the due diligence meetings.

"Wow, I had no idea," Zack said after listening to Dave's struggles to get the losses taken in a timely manner. "Why didn't any of this come out at the due diligence meetings?"

"One doesn't make a point of airing dirty laundry at presentations to strangers," Dave answered carefully. "Besides, I was asked not to speak at the due diligence presentations."

"I noticed that," Zack nodded. "Can you get me a report that shows the total amount of loans that should be charged off to loss and your plan for getting them charged off? Maybe you can put together a little of the history of your attempts to correct the problem while you're at it."

"Sure," Dave said. "I've been putting that report together for the last year. The only problem is that the list of non-performing loans grows each time I pull the report."

Zack shook his head in concern. He paced the small area in front of Dave's desk and looked at him.

"I appreciate your openness about this issue, Dave. I will remember it when we take control of the company this summer." Zack walked to the door as if preparing to leave. He turned in the doorway toward Dave. "You know, I never did feel a level of confidence with Bud Murphy. I never trusted what he said."

Dave smiled and shrugged. He didn't want to say anything that could come back on him later. And he still wanted to appear loyal to the company that was paying him. After all, he thought, there's a lot of money at stake.

After Zack left Dave dove into his work with renewed enthusiasm that comes from the hope of a better working environment by July. Maybe all of this was going to work out fine. He knew he needed to be careful until the sale was completed. A lot could happen in the meantime.

26

John Fremont decided to meet with Bert Gunderson outside the office. They held their first meeting since the acquisition at a restaurant near the office. They agreed to meet for lunch. John brought a briefcase full of reports and findings that validated some of the inconsistencies in the business operations of National Assets.

Bert arrived at the restaurant about ten minutes later than John. His eyes constantly moved around taking in everything in the dining room. He greeted John warmly and seated himself across the table from him. Bert's gaze moved from John to the stack of papers and then again around the room to make sure that they weren't being watched.

John spent the next half hour talking about his time with National Assets and what he had observed since he had been there. John also emphasized his experience in fraud detection. He told about Buster's confrontation with the headquarters staff, especially with Mort Smalley. This information peaked Bert's interest. Bert asked several follow up questions about the incident. For good measure John related the story about Shane, even though it may be just coincidence. Finally, John gave his opinions on what he thought was going on. He expressed a lot of concern about the friction between Bud Murphy and Dave Jenkins. He hoped it would be enough to keep Dave in a good light with the FBI even though Dave had not cooperated with Bert.

Bert quietly ate his lunch when the food was served. He thoughtfully reviewed some of the information that John had brought. After the table was cleared Bert put his hand on the stack of reports.

"You know, I can't take these without a subpoena," he said. "I appreciate your bringing them along but they would be useless as evidence."

"Would you like to borrow them?" John asked. "You could keep them long enough to look at them. Even though they are internal reports, they back up what I've told you. And when you do subpoena records, it's likely that you could get a conflicting version with what's here on the table."

"I'm almost sure that would be the case," Bert said dryly. "I think I'll have you hold on to these for now. But don't destroy them. Keep them in a safe place. When the time comes, I'll figure out a way to get a hold of them legally, as long as you haven't decided to shred them."

John laughed and took the papers back. "Okay. I'll find a nice safe place for these."

"I'll pay for my own lunch," Bert said. "I don't want anyone misunderstanding our intentions here."

"I understand," John said graciously. "I'm used to the same restrictions under the FDIC rules when I was with a bank."

Bert pocketed his notebook and left his portion of the check on the table. He stood and shook hands with John. After quick thanks, he walked out of the restaurant leaving John sitting at the table to finish his coffee.

After lunch John walked out into the bright midday sunlight of the parking lot and got into his car. As he pulled out of the lot he didn't notice the white BMW sitting in the back corner of the lot. Nor did he notice the man standing next to the BMW with a small digital camera. He drove back to the office. About a half a block behind him the BMW followed in the same lane. Once John pulled into his parking place at the office building the BMW sped away and headed for the downtown area. John never saw a thing.

A half hour later the BMW pulled into the parking lot at the downtown headquarters of National Assets. The driver walked to his office and downloaded several digital pictures from his camera on to his computer. Then he typed a brief report and sent the report along with the pictures to Leo Pecunia's and Mort Smalley's offices in Chicago. He cleared the pictures from the camera and deleted his copy of the file from his computer.

Leo Pecunia opened the file and looked at the pictures in his office. He stared at the pictures for a long time as if looking at a distasteful scene from a bad movie. He muttered a string of curses and slammed his fist on to his desk. He stared out the window and scowled at the traffic on the highway in the distance.

"If he thinks that he is going to get away with this," he whispered to himself. "I'll show him what loyalty is before he ruins this sale." He turned toward his phone and picked up the receiver. "Get me Will Eagleton, immediately," he barked to his assistant.

He printed out the pictures and the email. Then he deleted the file from his computer. He shoved the documents and pictures into his briefcase and waited for the phone to ring.

While Leo waited for Will to call, John Fremont called Dave.

"I've got some interesting news to tell you about. Do you have a minute?" John asked.

"Sure," Dave said. "Let me finish up with this letter and I'll be right over."

"Why don't we meet downstairs for a cigarette in about ten minutes," John said cautiously. "Does that give you enough time?"

"I'll meet you downstairs in ten," Dave answered.

Dave put the finishing touches on his report to Zack. He had constructed the chronology of his efforts to institute a formal charge off policy and his meetings with the credit committee to get the non-performing loans charged off. He had most of the material available. It was just a matter of updating it and rewriting some of his words to sound a little more diplomatic and understated so that Zack could draw his own conclusions. The total of non-performing loans was now at seventeen million dollars and would go to twenty million dollars by the end of the month according to Dave's forecast.

"This should get his attention," Dave smiled to himself as he sealed the envelope. "I think I'll send it through the interoffice mail since he's in town," he said staring at the envelope. He knew that this was dynamite. This was not information that they had learned during the due diligence examination. Dave felt a sense of relief knowing that he had finally had a chance to let the new owners know what was really going on. At least he was in the clear without talking to the FBI. He would leave that to John. He wondered if John had taken the initiative to talk to the FBI in order to shield Dave from the potentially dangerous consequences. He placed the heavy envelope in the interoffice mail basket outside his door and walked downstairs to meet with John.

After John had filled him in on his lunch with Bert Gunderson, Dave let out a low whistle. He enjoyed the timing. John had given the FBI information at the same time as Dave was sending most of the same information to Zack. He knew that something had to happen. And he wasn't holding on to the secret any more. All he could do was wait until he heard the commotion, or until the sale date passed.

"Someone's going to spend some time in jail," Dave said. "And fortunately it won't be us."

"Yeah," John answered, "but that doesn't take us out of harm's way. We are still easy targets. And there is no assurance that Will Eagleton or Leo Pecunia won't figure out who is leaking information."

"Is there any chance that someone followed you while you were having lunch?" Dave asked. "You know, you can't assume that it was a safe meeting."

"Good point," John said thoughtfully. "Maybe I need to cover my tracks, just in case."

"What are you planning on doing?" Dave looked around the parking lot suspiciously. He tried to see if anyone was sitting in a car watching. There were too many cars and the sun reflected so brightly off of the windshields, that he knew he was wasting his efforts.

"I'll think of something," John said casually. "I'll think of something." John looked out at the cars in the parking lot and smiled broadly hoping that someone was watching. He had a plan.

Suddenly Dave had an uneasy feeling. He envisioned Zack calling him in to talk about this in a conference room full of defensive executives. He imagined the sale going bad and lawsuits flying back and forth. Suddenly he was questioning his own decision to give the information to Zack. He rationalized that he had no choice. The sale had been announced and the management had been instructed to work with the lead team from Verdura Bank.

He figured that he probably wouldn't be put on the spot in some meeting now that they had the information. The fact is they could have pulled those reports themselves now that they had access to the pertinent databases. Dave figured that they would probably bring up the information in a series of questions right before they wrote the final check for the transaction of sale. Maybe, he thought, they would simply adjust the price.

He couldn't shake the feeling that something was wrong as he finished his workday and headed home. He kept going over what had happened and wondered what he was missing. Eventually it will come to me, he thought as he headed home.

27

The sale date finally arrived. There were meetings and rallies and announcements all over Sacramento. The executive team from Verdura Bank came to Sacramento for a week to hold a series of informational meetings. Will Eagleton scheduled various groups within the company to attend at different times so that the business would suffer minimal disruption.

The employees were showered with coffee cups and green tee shirts at the rallies. Everyone received desk clocks in the mail quickly followed by new benefits packages. Representatives from Verdura Bank spoke at gatherings painting images of a utopian future for the National Assets employees designed to make them impatient for the changes to come. The rallies were infectious and morale soared among the employees. They were glad to see the changing of the guard and looked forward to a more progressive and professional management of the company.

Dave had seen the routine too many times to know that the good feelings wouldn't last. And he knew from his industry associates that it would be just a matter of time before these same cheering employees would feel the heavy hand of budget cuts, productivity improvements and intolerance for inefficiency to take root. Some day soon they would long for the paternalistic and protective atmosphere of National Assets. Although the Verdura executives were saying that they didn't want to interfere, Dave knew that they couldn't wait to get their hands on the operations. And one missed forecast would give them all the reason they needed to step in and to take control of the company.

On several occasions Will Eagleton had called on Dave to give a little talk at these rallies to show support for the sale. Will wanted to prolong the carnival atmosphere for as long as possible. Dave usually found a way to respectfully decline these invitations to speak. His heart wasn't in it. And he knew that the lies would eventually come back to haunt him through the disillusionment of his employees. The company was changing. The effort he had put into the new operation could soon become a moot incident in the history of the National Assets climb to the top of the industry. Soon it would be hidden in the smothering embrace of a giant banking firm that didn't believe in entrepreneurial spirit or individual innovation. He realized that there was nowhere to go now that the company was taking over.

It wasn't long after the sale closed that Verdura Bank announced that the OCC, Office of the Comptroller of the Currency, planned to visit for what they refer to as an entrance examination. They would spend the last two weeks in July inspecting the operations and performing a full-scale audit of procedures. The result would be that the OCC would issue a report of deficiencies to be corrected in order to bring the company into compliance with the regulations of the OCC. This examination started the first major rift between the two companies.

The senior management team of National Assets was called together in a headquarters conference room to prepare for the examination. The mood was somber and reluctant. National Assets had always prided itself on answering to no one. They always ran the business as they saw fit. Now that they were under the umbrella of a federally regulated institution, they would have to comply with all of the regulations that went along with that association. Verdura Bank assured everyone repeatedly that they wanted to leave the National Assets operation intact mainly because they would have a way to conduct business outside the umbrella of federal regulation.

Zack chaired the meeting and went around the room assigning projects that would prepare not only the management team, but also the employees for the examination. Zack ended the meeting with some assuring comments about being open to the regulators. The OCC was visiting to help the company with their compliance efforts. Then, in a couple of months, the OCC team would return to see if National Assets had taken the necessary corrective actions to address the deficiencies found in the entrance examination.

Dave left the conference with a checklist as long as the legal page in his tablet. He felt confident and vindicated that he had always run his operation according to good banking practices. The discipline was built in to the procedures and the training that his staff attended. It would be an opportunity to showcase his business unit. He was already in compliance. The only point of criticism would be the delinquency reporting and the backlog of charge off that the company had been slow to address. But Dave had documented his efforts well enough to keep himself out of trouble.

When he returned to his office he called a meeting with his management team. He carefully distributed assignments to his managers to make sure that all facets of the operation were covered. He had hired his own compliance officer as a member of his team. The position reported directly to Dave.

Dave instructed Dean, the compliance manager, to have all the recent audits available for inspection. He also had an extra copy of the fourteen volume procedures manuals prepared for inspection by the OCC. He was sure that his operation would show well in comparison to the other business units. He was looking forward to the audit, a rare thing for any manager.

After the meeting he walked over to John Fremont's office to tell him about the actions he was taking in preparation for the audit. He was surprised to see John packing boxes in his office.

"What's going on with you?" Dave asked. He looked at John quietly packing his notebooks and the contents of his desk drawers.

"I've been transferred to the headquarters building," John said tersely. "I guess they want to keep a close eye on me. As a matter of fact there is a senior manager from the audit department at Verdura Bank who is coming out next week to talk to me about taking a job with him in North Carolina."

"You mean they want you to move to North Carolina?" Dave asked.

"Something like that," John said. "I think that would be their first choice. But I'm going to press for taking the job but staying in Sacramento. With computers and telephones I don't see why I need to move across the country."

Especially with a company you don't know that much about," Dave finished the thought for him. "Besides, I know how much you like California. I didn't think that anyone could get you to move away from here."

"They haven't yet," John assured him. "They haven't yet."

"Do they know that you talked to the FBI?" Dave asked.

"No one but you and me," John said. "But somehow I think they know." John reflexively scanned the walls of his office as if looking for listening devices.

"Maybe someone's trying to get you out of harm's way," Dave suggested.

"And maybe they're trying to keep me quiet." John continued to thumb through his file folders briefly scanning the contents before placing them in the boxes.

"Either way, it's all about control. Isn't it?" Dave stared at the half filled boxes placed around the floor of John's office. His gaze rested on the certificates and trophies that John had acquired during his career. Dave knew that things were changing again. He already missed the old routine, the infighting and the pep rallies that National Assets held regularly. Anger and frustration swept over him until it was hard to control. All of a sudden he felt as if he had been in the financial business for too long. Maybe it was time to do something else.

"We always have our employment contracts," Dave said trying to reassure John.

"Yeah. But I'd rather have a job. It would be hard for me to go out and try to find another job. It took me a year to find this one. Not too many companies are looking for a man in his late fifties to work at their company."

Dave knew that John was right. Even in this day of prohibition against age discrimination, the older employees had the deck stacked against them. Corporations preferred the young. They were easier to delude. Not only was it an age issue. But it was also a salary issue. John would be unyielding in his price to come to work for another organization. Pride was an issue. An acquired lifestyle was at issue, too. John would find it difficult to start over. Dave knew that he could be facing the same problem in the near future.

"Well, let me know when you get settled over at the headquarters building," Dave said. "I'll come over and meet you for lunch."

"Sure thing," John said. He didn't turn around. He kept packing the boxes.

When Dave got back to his own office he had a call waiting for him from Zack. He picked up the line immediately.

"Hello Zack," Dave said.

"Hi, Dave. How's it going?" Zack's high-pitched nasal voice came across the phone line as if he were more than a few thousand miles away. "Sorry for the bad connection. I'm on my cell phone on my way home from the airport. I caught a nonstop flight after the meeting this morning."

"What's on your mind?" Dave asked. He was still upset about John moving out of the building. He wondered if Zack had anything to do with it. Dave was still trying to establish a level of trust with Zack in spite of his suspicions.

"I wanted to touch base with you on this morning's meeting," Zack started. "This conversation never happened. If you say it did, I'll deny it," Zack tried to inject some humor into his remark but it didn't come across on the phone. When Dave didn't respond, Zack continued.

"I want you to side step the write off issues when the OCC interviews you. They are going to be very interested in your operation." Dave stiffened and gripped the phone hard. He stared at the wall of his office trying to keep his temper without losing his concentration.

"You are going to present an enigma to them. You have a good resume. They know that. Your operation is visibly a better-run operation than some of the others within National Assets. But the delinquency numbers are high. And they may notice the erratic numbers in the write off history over the past twelve months."

"But we've been through all of that," Dave started to say.

"I know. I know that you and I have talked about this issue at length and you were going to send me a package," Zack tried to continue.

"I did send you a package," Dave said. "Haven't you received it?"

"No," Zack said slowly. "Where did you send it?"

"I sent it interoffice mail while you were in town," Dave said.

"Well maybe that explains it," Zack said. "I haven't been picking up my mail regularly at any of the places it's being sent. I told the temp to send my mail on to North Carolina. So I should be getting it in a few days. I'll look around for it."

An uneasy feeling came over Dave. He didn't know if it was the evasive tone in Zack's voice, or the memory of Will Eagleton's refusal to pick up a report lying on the conference room table. He had the feeling that something wasn't right.

"How exactly do I side step this issue?" Dave asked evenly. He grabbed a pad of paper and his pen and started to take some notes.

"Dave, you're a smart guy," Zack said in a condescending voice. "I'm going to leave that up to you. It's good enough that you and I know about the issue. We can work together to quietly resolve it. If it comes up, I'm not saying to deny it. You know. Just don't make a big deal out of it. We know what that problem is and we're starting to address it. There's nothing to be gained by dragging the whole history out and throwing it around in front of the OCC. In the end you'll just be making more work for everyone. You see my point, Dave?"

"I think I'm beginning to," Dave said cautiously. He thought how the issue hadn't changed with the delinquency reporting and the charge off of the non-performing accounts. He thought about how the cast of management was changing but the message was the same. Hide the problem. And it dawned on him how embarrassing this could be to Zack. He had been one of the people in charge of the due diligence and this issue had slipped by him. He had a deciding vote on whether to buy or pass on the acquisition of National Assets. He could come under a lot of criticism if this news were to get out.

"Good. Good," Zack said. His voice relaxed momentarily. "And I promise you one thing, Dave. As soon as I get back there I'll get old Bud Murphy out of your way. I've heard from others as well as yourself how much of an impediment he's been to getting the right changes made out there."

"Sounds good to me," Dave said cautiously. He was enjoying the moment. He also reminded himself how easy it was for a new manager to over commit with promises that couldn't be kept.

"And I'm also sending you a fifteen thousand dollar bonus for your work on the transition process, Dave," Zack said.

"I'd welcome that," Dave said. He absently scribbled the amount in the margin of his notes.

"I know. We've just begun the transition work getting National Assets to work like Verdura Bank. But I know that you're going to be on the team. Hell, Dave, we need you on that team," Zack said with slick enthusiasm.

"I plan on being here," Dave returned the lie. "Thanks for your vote of confidence."

"Whoops, I gotta go, Dave. Good luck with those OCC people," he said. "I'll catch you later. And remember. This conversation never happened."

As Dave hung up the phone in his office he thought of how often Zack used that phrase. He wondered how many others were hearing conversations that never happened. The ones that Zack would deny ever having. Even though Zack joked about it, Dave had no doubts that Zack would deny them if he had to.

Dave closed the door to his office and sat back down in his chair. He enjoyed his black leather chair. He had ordered it outside the normal company purchasing guidelines. And he had been criticized for buying it. It had special back supports that could be adjusted. The chair cost seven hundred dollars, but Dave wanted to be comfortable. He didn't want any more chronic back problems than he had already endured. One doctor had told him that his back pain was due to an injury. Another doctor had told him that it was caused by stress.

Dave gripped the arms of the chair and spun from side to side. He thought about the phone call with Zack. And he knew that his intuition was on target. Dave smiled to himself at the irony of it all. The company was changing hands, but hiding the same issues. It fit. Verdura Bank made the purchase to hide the deficiencies of the National Assets operations. These were deficiencies that Verdura stood to suffer from whether they bought the company or not. And just like National Assets, Verdura wanted to pay Dave for what he knew and was not telling to the wrong people. He laughed out loud and spun his chair around. This was too easy, he thought, way too easy.

He stopped the chair from its slow spin and stared out the window of his office. He knew that something wasn't flowing right in his thinking process. Something was still wrong. He thought about the meeting with the FBI agent at the coffee shop. He thought about the meetings with Will Eagleton and the rest of the credit policy committee over the write off issues. He thought about the money-laundering story that John had told him. And he remembered that the CEO's of both companies were long time friends. Something just wasn't adding up. Dave knew that he should feel on top of the world. He had a contract with stock options. He had another fifteen thousand dollars on the way in his next paycheck. He would only see about seven thousand of that after taxes. But it was still a lot of money. And that's how you keep score, he reminded himself. The one who has a lot of money and the time to enjoy it is the winner, he thought. Only he wasn't going to laugh about it until he figured out what was bothering him. He just knew that he was overlooking something.

28

The OCC team arrived one week later and quickly took over the conference rooms at the headquarters. There were sixteen auditors, mostly CPA's. The management team from National Assets used their presentations from the due diligence meetings for the opening conference. Managers presented a ten-minute overview of their operations. Once again, the servicing units were combined into one presentation with Bud Murphy giving the majority of the presentation. Dave filled in the differences for clarity but only talked for about five minutes.

After the initial meeting the group of examiners dispersed into the various buildings. Dave reserved a room in his operation for the two weeks that the team had planned on staying with them. He gave them the largest conference room and had his computer technicians hook up two lines to the mainframe so that they could do their own research online. That would eliminate the necessity of copying a lot of files and sending them into the conference room.

The first thing that they asked to see was the set of procedural manuals that Dave and his management team had written. The day before Dave had received a frantic call from Bud Murphy asking for a copy of the manuals. He was going to have his staff alter them to fit his operation as best he could before the auditors arrived. Dave relented and made the manuals available to Bud in the spirit of teamwork. He knew that Bud wasn't following the procedures anyway. So the result of producing the manuals in Bud's operation would be an embarrassing disaster. Bud seemed to overlook this problem. Or else he thought that it would be a lesser violation than being able to produce no manuals at all.

Dave walked into the conference room where the three examiners stood looking around as if they had just materialized in the room and were getting their bearings.

"Good morning," Dave greeted them cheerfully. "I hope that you'll find everything you need here. If not, please let me know."

The room was fully supplied with a coffee maker, office supplies, telephones and computers. The examiners were impressed with the accommodations and seemed delighted at the forethought of the home improvement management team for anticipating their needs.

The lead examiner was Bruce Longo, a large man with a beard. He had a round face with bushy eyebrows that appeared as one solid line across the top of his eyes. His eyes were a dark chocolate color that didn't miss much. He was quiet and didn't smile. Although he was cordial at the opening meeting at the headquarters, it was clear that he wanted to get started and wanted everyone out of his way. He walked to the end of the table and slapped his brief case down into the seat of a nearby chair.

"This looks fine, Dave," he said gruffly. "We'll go ahead and get started. One thing we'll need is a roster of your key people along with their phone numbers in the event we need to talk to them."

"They're right here." Dave reached down for a blue folder on the table and handed it to Bruce. Bruce's eyes widened in surprise that Dave had thought of this. Dave looked at the other examiners and said, "My assistant, Marilee is coordinating all of the interviews that I'm sure you'll want to have with my managers and some of the supervisors. Just let her know the times and the names and she'll be happy to arrange the meetings."

"Good. Good." Bruce nodded his approval but didn't smile. "Now if you'll excuse us, we'll get started on reading your procedures. And here's a questionnaire that I need you to fill out for us." Bruce handed Dave a thick sheaf of papers watching for any reaction. Dave took the papers and smiled.

"I'll get to work on these right away," he said. "Let me know if there is anything you need."

With those words Dave nodded to the team of examiners and walked back to his office. He left directions with Marilee to let him know if she heard from the auditors. He distributed sections of the questionnaire to department managers asking that they be returned by the end of the day. He also had his financial analyst assemble the required reports for the auditors. Dave wanted the start of this audit to go smoothly. He knew that if he did the right things at the beginning, he would win the confidence of the audit team.

The examiners plodded through the audit with minimal disruption to the staff. Dave received a status report on their findings every third day of the audit. For the most part the examiners were complimentary on their observations of the business unit. As if to affirm this finding they seemed more relaxed as the days went by. Dave knew that if auditors became more distant and less talkative during an examination, then they were finding a lot of deficiencies. He was pleased that they even accepted an invitation to lunch on the last day of their audit.

During the course of the audit the subject of loan losses came up. The examiners wanted to talk at length about the backlog of non-performing loans. Dave decided to handle the meeting and address the questions. He invited the examiners to his office one afternoon and covered the subject as objectively as he could. Fortunately there had been enough activity and meetings addressing the issue that Dave could make it look like the company had started taking a proactive stance on clearing the backlog of charge off. He purposely avoided any blame fixing and let the examiners draw their own conclusions hoping that they would see the effort that Dave had invested in getting the loss issue corrected.

The meeting had gone well and the examiners were impressed with the attention that Dave had given the loans since he had started at National Assets. Bruce Longo even commented on the procedures that he had seen over at Bud Murphy's operation. He had quickly figured out that they were a copy of the ones Dave had written and that Bud was not following them. Bruce just shook his head and frowned.

"It's apparent that he has never operated according to any set of procedures. He's probably one of the reasons that the company is in so much trouble," Bruce said in an uncharacteristic display of confidence. "We'll have to address that in our findings."

Dave knew that Bud would be angry and blame him for getting Bud's operation in trouble. Dave wondered if Bud would come up with a way to rationalize the deficiency with the new owners.

The more that the examiners compared the two operations, the better Dave looked to the OCC. Dave took it as a vindication for all of his hard work and struggle against the indifference of the senior management. He felt an immense amount of pride in his staff and his operation. Once again the way looked clear for Dave to run a profitable operation if only Verdura would leave his group intact.

Unfortunately that would not be the case. Zack heard about the conclusions of the audit. He mentioned to Dave that the company might be better off combining the two operations and letting Dave run them. All that Dave could think about was the mess he would have to clean up in Bud's operation. He was also worried about the long time loyalties of some of Bud's management staff. He wondered if they would try to sabotage his attempts to straighten out the operation. If Zack decided to combine the operations, Dave knew that he was in for some long days and hard work.

A few days after the audit was completed Zack called Dave to arrange a meeting at the headquarters. July had given way to the first days of August. The weather was hot and dry. The fields had turned a golden brown and the American River had slowed its rushing current now that the most of the snow had melted in the Sierras. It was already hot in the morning rush hour traffic as Dave made his way downtown to the headquarters of National Assets.

Dave arrived early and found a good parking place in the normally crowded parking lot. He walked around the buildings and found a bench in the shade of an oak tree. He set his briefcase down and lit a cigarette. He watched the staff slowly make their way from their cars to the buildings. The aroma of fennel and dried grass scented the air. Dave enjoyed one of the few relaxing moments he had stumbled upon over the past months.

He sat and thought of all the events that had led him to this bench. He thought that the worst was over. Zack was probably going to make some announcement about reorganization. Dave could feel the change coming. The senior management team of National Assets had been unusually silent. John Fremont still hadn't left for North Carolina. Dave knew that John was actively negotiating to stay in California. For the present Verdura had decided to give him an office in the headquarters building until they saw where he best fit in the new organization.

Dave missed the camaraderie and occasional lunches that he shared with John. It seemed to Dave that Verdura had adopted John. Bruce Curley and Will Eagleton had left him alone. Dave didn't know what had become of John's conversations with the FBI. Maybe they had all the information they were going to get from John. Maybe they had taken the investigation behind the scenes until some future date. That's usually the way it turned out, Dave thought. When everyone least expected it, the FBI would show up and cause a big disruption in the business. The only other alternative that Dave could think of was that the FBI was working with the OCC. Perhaps that would give them unprecedented access to the inner workings of the company.

A soft summer breeze whooshed through the large oak tree overhead and Dave heard the birds begin to chirp. There must be dozens of them living in this tree, he thought. Dave stood and looked at the wide trunk of the tree. He wondered how long it had been there. He wondered if some executive had planted it when the grounds used to be a cannery along the American River in days past. What changes that tree has probably seen, Dave thought. Dave stood and stretched one more time in the morning sun before heading in to the headquarters building.

"Come on in, Dave," Zack said warmly and pointed to a chair at a small round table in the corner of his office. Dave noticed that someone was already seated at the table.

"I'd like you to meet Larry Dixon," Zack said. "Larry, meet Dave Jenkins. The two shook hands and Dave sat across from Larry. "Larry comes to us from the auto division of Verdura Bank. He has a little extra time on his hands. So I thought he would be a good resource for you, Dave. Think of him as kind of an advisor as you plan your merger of the two servicing units."

Larry was about forty. He was dressed in an expensive, but conservative business suit. He was partially bald which didn't match his boyish countenance. His eyes were alert and he smiled easily. His athletic build showed through the suit. Dave could feel the energy radiate from him.

"I want you two to work together on this project," Zack continued. "I think we have an opportunity to save on salaries and other expenses by consolidating the servicing operations in National Assets. We can eliminate a lot of the redundant processes. That's what you need to ferret out and eliminate. It's a chance to save a lot of money right away."

Dave noticed that Larry was already taking notes in his leather bound folder. He wrote energetically with his lacquered pen as Zack spoke. Dave sat there and took it all in.

"Do you have a target date in mind for all of this?" Dave asked. "Our biggest task will be to combine all of the loans onto one system." The irony didn't escape Dave that he had spent his first months with the company finding a way to separate the two portfolios. Now they were working to combine them. Everything moves in cycles, he thought.

"I'd like to announce the fact that we're combining the operations next Monday," Zack said. "And I would like to target the first of December for the actual merge date. Maybe we won't have everything merged by then. But we should have the major functions such as customer service and collections merged by then."

Larry nodded as he jotted more notes to himself in his notebook. His gold cufflinks glittered in the morning sunlight coming through the office window.

"How do you want to handle the announcement to HUD?" Dave asked. He saw the puzzled look on Zack's face. "The home improvement division was started as part of the corrective action plan to remedy the servicing deficiencies that HUD found during their last audit about two years ago. I'm wondering how receptive they'll be to our plan to eliminate that part of the corrective action plan."

"Well, they certainly can't tell us how to run our business," Zack snapped. "This is a whole new ball game. We'll present the fact that a regulated institution has acquired the portfolio and the controls will be much better than before. They understand efficiency and cost containment." Zack took a moment to calm down. "Larry, why don't you and Dave set up a conference call to the regional HUD office and informally cover our strategy? It will be our first contact with the regional office since the acquisition. It will look like we are following protocol to contact them and let them know that we are managing the operation now."

Dave tried to hide the smile that was forcing its way to his face. He was always amazed at the arrogance that cloaked large companies. They considered regulatory issues a nuisance unless they fit into their plans for reorganization. He knew that the perception was that 'bigger is always better' when it comes to financial institutions. He used to strut around the office himself and think the same thing until he arrived at National Assets.

"Okay," Larry said. "We'll set up the call and let you know how it goes. I'm sure it will be a win." Once again Larry busily noted something in his notebook.

Zack looked at Dave questioningly. His look implied suspicion that Dave was going to resist some of the changes. Dave's comment had made Zack's idea sound naïve. And Dave had just lost points with Zack for bringing it up.

Slowly it dawned on Dave that Zack was looking for gophers, people who would blindly agree to his every direction without the test of argument. Dave didn't like where this was going any more than Zack liked the sound of caution and experience coming from Dave. The meeting ended as abruptly as it started. Zack stood up and retreated behind his desk.

"That's all for now," Zack announced. "I'll leave you two to get to know each other and work out the details on the reorganization. I would like to see a rough plan on my desk no later than the end of business tomorrow."

Larry turned to Dave as he put his pen back in his pocket. Dave read it as a sign that nothing noteworthy would be added to what Zack had said.

"Dave, how about my meeting you for lunch later," Larry said. "I'll swing by your office and we can eat lunch somewhere near your office, since I'm without a place of my own here."

"Sounds good," Dave said. "I usually eat about eleven thirty. Does that work for you?"

"Let's make it twelve thirty," Larry said with forced nonchalance.

Dave knew that a subtle line had been drawn in the sand with that remark. He knew how to read the signs, the implicit messages, the subtle straining for the upper hand in the slightest conversation. He shook his head slowly and smiled at Larry.

"Let's make it after lunch," Dave said. "Anytime after twelve thirty I'll be in my office." Dave saw the jaw muscles tighten in Larry's face. He noticed that Zack was trying to hide his amusement. Dave thought, *I may lose the war, but this skirmish belongs to me.*

29

In the days that followed Dave saw the slow and steady transition of the servicing units from two separate entities into one teeming organization. Some of the discussions were heated. And the management staff that had been loyal to Bud for years did not take well to the changes. There were instances of hostility and outright rebellion. Verdura Bank dealt with these occurrences swiftly. They were making their presence felt. Soon it was clear to everyone that they went along with the plans or they got out of the way in a hurry.

Larry took an active part in the reorganization. He talked to Bud and let him know that his services were no longer needed as head of a servicing organization. Larry placed him in some harmless capacity as a credit policy administrator in charge of appraisal quality. He was assigned to review property appraisals on real estate after the loans were booked. He was moved out of his office into a cubicle in the headquarters building. Larry took over his old office as a statement that things had changed for good.

The shock waves moved through Bud's servicing organization. Some of his managers resigned in indignation. Others became openly non-compliant until they were forced out of their jobs and given assignments with less responsibility. The staff was stunned that someone like Bud so well entrenched could be disposed of so quickly. A layer of fear slowly settled on the business organization as everyone realized that no one was untouchable.

In time Larry started to bring in some of his own staff from the east coast. He hired several freelance consultants, mercenaries in the mortgage banking world where loyalties ran to the next paycheck. Consultants had no investment in relationships or company politics. Their interest was in short term results regardless of long term damage to the business. The use of consultants usually implied that the current management team was not capable of correcting a deficiency in the operation. The result was inevitably lowered morale and increased resistance to change. Dave wondered where all of this was leading.

His management staff was becoming confused and frustrated. He watched his area of responsibility slowly erode in front of him in the aftermath of each meeting that was held. For the most part he maintained good relations with Larry and tried to implement the changes. Most of the changes were defensible. More importantly it was clear that the Verdura Bank transition team heavily sponsored Larry. Dave knew that he had never enjoyed full support from National Assets. Now he felt the same lack of support from the Verdura staff. He wondered how long it would be before he would be moved out of his place. He didn't have to wait long.

One morning, he stood outside of Larry's new office waiting to see him. Larry kept him waiting. Dave could hear the animated voices behind the closed door of Larry's office. Dave thought that a meeting had not gone well and was taking longer than Larry had anticipated. To Dave's surprise he saw one of his managers leaving the office when the door finally opened.

"Hi Debbie," Dave said with a surprised look on his face. Debbie Evans was the customer service manager. Dave recruited her when he started his operation. He had always admired her loyalty and her hard work. The questioning look in Dave's eyes forced Debbie to look away momentarily.

"Good morning Dave," Debbie said quickly. She was flustered. There was tension in her voice. She didn't stop to explain anything to Dave. He figured he would catch up with her back at the office. Maybe Larry would shed some light on why she was visiting here.

"Come in, Dave," Larry said from behind his desk. Dave thought that he said it rather loudly to distract him. "Come in. Have a seat. Would you like some coffee?"

Dave knew he sounded too gracious and confident. Larry was up to something. The sight of one of Dave's own employees leaving Larry's office had unnerved him. Now he knew he was the prey in a cat and mouse game with Larry.

"I wanted to go over some changes I was going to propose to Zack this afternoon. I wanted to get your input on some of them," Larry said. His friendliness was an attempt to cover his nervousness. Dave knew that the changes must affect him.

"What I thought I would do is give an analysis or summary of my observations to Zack," Larry started in. He handed Dave a draft of a presentation. "Here, I want you to look at this. But it isn't your copy. This is real confidential stuff." Larry paused for emphasis. "Since the changes would affect you, I wanted to run them by you to make sure that you were on board with them."

Dave took the papers and started to read. A lot of the analysis was information that was made known during the due diligence and the weeks of meetings that followed. The only thing that Larry added was his own opinions on opportunities for improvement.

When Dave turned to the final pages, he scanned the proposed organization charts. He noticed that Larry had put himself in charge of everything. For his new management team Larry had taken all of Dave's managers including his financial analyst. The chart proposed that Dave work directly for Larry. Dave's head snapped back when he saw his name in a box reporting directly to Larry. Dave didn't try to contain his skepticism.

Across the desk from him sat a person with only half of his experience at running a servicing operation. And Dave was expected to answer to him! Dave felt the floodgates of his disappointment open within him. He shook his head and looked up at Larry.

"You'll be in charge of all the loss mitigation activities for the combined units," Larry said. Dave thought he detected some pleading in his voice. "I'll be depending upon you for the majority of decisions that control the profitability of the organization."

"It's a little less responsibility that I have now," Dave said evenly. "And it changes my job responsibilities drastically." Dave could tell by the blank look on Larry's fact that he didn't know about the clause in Dave's contract. It stated that if his job responsibilities were to change by more than twenty-five per cent, then Dave could exercise his contract rights and be paid for the next two years while seeking another job.

"I thought you would be pleased with your new position," Larry said nervously. Dave couldn't tell if Larry was joking. He could feel the rage well up within him.

"This isn't going to work for me," Dave said finally. "It's too big a cut in my responsibilities."

"What if we added to your responsibilities," Larry pleaded. "I could put the customer service unit under you control."

"I don't think so," Dave said. "I think this is something I need to talk to Zack about." Dave saw the alarm in Larry's face. It was supposed to go smoothly. Larry wasn't supposed to make any waves with Dave. Dave could read it all in Larry's face. Dave knew that the battle for control was about to start in earnest.

For the following week Dave could not get Zack to return his calls. And he knew that Larry was talking to him every day. *It happens that quickly,* Dave thought. Once again he realized how fragile the status quo is in the business world. He was on the outside of the restructuring of the company. There was no such thing as loyalty in the corporate dictionary, no matter how many times it appeared on banners and in speeches about the core values of the organization. Anyone with the National Assets brand on them was suspect in the problems they now faced. The OCC had published a dismal report on the company citing major deficiencies in every business unit. When he was allowed to see the report on the deficiencies listed for the servicing operation he was not surprised to find that the majority of them referred to Bud Murphy's operation. The only deficiencies noted in the report that affected Dave dealt with the backlog in writing off non-performing loans. Nothing was said in the report that there was a plan in place to remedy the situation.

The recommendation from the OCC was that all of the loans totaling twenty-two million dollars should be taken to loss immediately in order to bring the company into compliance with OCC regulations. In addition to the loss projections for Dave's operation, the OCC added the uncharged losses from Albuquerque and from Bud Murphy's operation. The total came to a staggering one hundred million dollars in unrecognized losses.

It was surprising to Dave that Verdura Bank resisted the recommendation to take all of the charge off at once. Even though they led everyone to believe that they had missed the deficiency in their due diligence visit, they now owned the problem and the monetary loss it would cause. Verdura was embarrassed and unhappy about the issue. Maybe the bank was looking for a scapegoat, Dave thought. And maybe he was the scapegoat. He thought it ironic that he had fought so hard to bring the problem to everyone's attention. Now he was being blamed for it. He had produced the chronology of events and reports that vindicated him to Will Eagleton, Zack, Bruce, John Fremont and others who could have remedied the situation. At least they reflected Dave's efforts in finding and addressing the issue from the beginning of his career at National Assets. Dave was stunned at the turn of events. He was caught in a time warp while the struggle for power played out in the corporate headquarters.

In the quiet of his office he reflected on the sudden change of events and his position with the company. He suspected that employees were viewing him differently. Maybe the word was out on the grapevine that the new Verdura management team had ostracized him. He reached into one of his desk drawers and pulled out his employment contract. He slowly and carefully read each paragraph. On the second reading he placed a calculator and pencil near the contract. He carefully figured the payout that was due to him now that a proposed change of responsibilities triggered the acceleration clause.

After an hour of reading and calculating, Dave estimated the contract to be worth about five hundred thousand dollars including the stock options. He sat back and whistled to himself in amazement. Maybe I do have a chance to grab the golden ring, he thought. The one good thing about all of this bureaucracy, he thought, is that no one had taken the time to evaluate what his contract was worth if they changed his job assignment.

Dave flipped through his business cards until he found the card he was looking for. He stared at the name of an attorney, Mike Bear, he had known for most of his career. He reached for the phone but stopped short. He decided that first he would draft his letter stating the fact that his job assignment had changed and that he was demanding the payout of his employment contract.

This is the first time, he thought, that he was writing a letter that was worth almost a half million dollars to him. His hand trembled with excitement as he carefully crafted the letter. He constructed an attachment that outlined his present job responsibilities before the sale of the company. Alongside the list of responsibilities he listed the proposed changes given to him by Larry. After he finished the draft, he looked at it carefully. It was a slam-dunk, he thought. No one could argue with it. Even though no one had yet asked for a buy out of their employment contract, Dave knew that the time was right for him.

After he was satisfied with the draft and the attachment, he put it with the contract and called his attorney. He waited patiently as the phone rang and finally went to his voicemail.

"Hi Mike," Dave started talking to the voice mail recorder, "this is Dave Jenkins. I need you to look at a letter for me. I will send it to you via an overnight service. After you've had a chance to look it over, please give me a call. I want to get your opinion on this. I may need to fight a legal battle over the issue, but it's too soon to tell. I'll be in my office all day tomorrow. Call me as soon as you can. Thanks."

After he had hung up the phone Dave walked out of his office and headed for the Kinko's office down the street. He didn't want to risk exposing his request by using company resources. *Besides*, he thought, *one never knows who is watching.*

"I'm going to be gone for about an hour," he told Marilee. "I have an errand to run."

Marilee looked up from her computer screen. "I'll be glad to help you with that," she said eagerly. Dave knew that it was hard to hide anything from Marilee. She was a perceptive assistant and knew that Dave was going through a tough time. She had been in the background in all of his struggles since he had started with the company.

"No, but thanks anyway, Marilee," Dave said with a thin smile. "It's probably better for you if I don't involve you in this."

"I'm not afraid," she stated simply. Dave noticed the determination and loyalty in her expression. He wondered how loyalty could exist so strongly in a relationship, but not in the corporate reporting lines. For a moment he was tempted to trust her with the package.

"I know you're not," Dave answered. He smiled in appreciation. "But I would be afraid for you."

Marilee returned his smile and watched Dave walk out of the building. His shoulders were hunched forward in determination.

Dave walked into Kinko's and found a quiet table where he could work on his letter. He loaded it onto a word processor and made his final revisions. After copying the contract and placing it in the package along with his letter and attachments, Dave felt a sense of relief and excitement. He was in new territory. He wondered what Verdura Bank would do when they received this package. He wondered if they would agree to pay or fight it. He felt as if he were handling a package of explosives ready to go off at any moment. He stared at the envelope ready for mailing to Mike. Next to it sat a copy of everything he was mailing. He could feel the changes that would come if he sent this package. His momentum carried him forward to his decision.

As soon as he had made up his mind he called Ann and explained to her what was going on with his job. He read the letter to Ann and asked what she thought of his plan.

"It sure sounds to me like this job is coming to an end," Ann said thoughtfully.

"How do you feel about all of this?"

"Frankly I'm getting worried about your safety and your sanity. I think that this job and the situation you are in is starting to wear on you." She sighed heavily. "I would be relieved if you were to get as far away as possible from this job."

"We may have a lot to do in a very short time period if we make that decision," Dave warned.

"Then so be it," Ann said firmly. "Staying around just doesn't seem worth the risk."

He mailed the package at the counter and put the originals and his copy in his briefcase and walked out the door. The whole process had taken him less time than he had anticipated. He looked at his watch and decided to stop by a park near the American River. He needed time to think. He needed to get away from everything long enough to evaluate what he was doing. He knew there would be no turning back once he sent the letter to the personnel director at Verdura Bank.

Dave stopped at the entrance gate to the park and paid the dollar admission. He drove slowly around the quiet park. Since it was a weekday, the park was empty except for a few joggers and some retirees who were enjoying the sunshine. Dave pulled up to a picnic table near the bank of the river and walked to the edge of the water. The sharp smell of fennel mixed with the aroma of the river. Dave breathed deeply. He took in the beauty of the park. The magpies and gray squirrels filled the trees with chatter and chirping. A soft breeze whooshed through the sun-toughened leaves. A red tailed hawk lazily circled high overhead. Two deer stood silently at the edge of a tree line watching Dave warily.

Dave sat at the picnic table and silently played out the movie in his mind. He recalled his first trip to Sacramento. He was full of wonder and excitement at a new beginning in a strange city. His heart was open to the change. He had resolved to put all of his knowledge and experience to work for him. How had it all come to so many struggles, he wondered. Maybe it was just meant to be. Maybe, he thought, that there were lessons he was supposed to learn out of this that he couldn't have learned in any other situation. Maybe life was preparing him for bigger battles.

In the end all he could think of was that this episode in his life had not lived up to his expectations and that maybe it was time to move on. He felt too close to all the turmoil. He found it hard to step out of the middle of the fray into the position of an objective observer. He wondered if anyone were in control of the situation. Maybe random forces had converged as Verdura purchased National Assets and no one was big enough to stop the turmoil. He was caught in the warp of a big battle where the enemy wore matching uniforms. It was no longer about him. He needed to leave. He needed a new start.

Then he remembered the money that could give him that new start. He smiled to himself as he thought about the employment contract, the severance money and the possibilities ahead of him. He realized how quickly he could put an end to his stress and suffering. He thought how things were coming together for him. Maybe life was looking out for him after all.

Dave stretched and started walking back to his car. He looked across the park. A car caught his attention. It looked familiar. The car looked liked John Fremont's car. Dave looked around at the nearby picnic tables. At one table near the car were two men sitting across from each other. They appeared to be in an animated conversation. Suddenly Dave recognized John Fremont and Will Eagleton as the two men at the table. He stared in disbelief. He quickly walked to his car and drove back to the office trying to understand what he had just seen.

At the other end of the park John sat across the table from Will and carefully chose his words. He had asked for a meeting with Will away from the office. He told Will that he thought it would be safer if they talked somewhere outside of work. Will reluctantly agreed to the meeting. He had seen the pictures that Mort had sent and was trying to decide what to do about it when John called him.

"I've been contacted by the FBI." John decided that a straightforward approach would work best with Will. "The agent's name is Bert Gunderson. I agreed to meet him for lunch to see what he wanted."

Will stared silently at John. Since he offered no response, John took it as a sign to continue.

"He wanted my cooperation in furnishing information about the company's cash operations." John took out a cigarette and lit it. He knew that Will did not like to be around people with unhealthy habits. But John wanted to give the impression that he was nervous about coming to him with this information.

"Did he ask for documents?" Will asked evenly. He watched John's eyes for any sign of deception.

"He didn't ask for anything other than my cooperation," John said. "Gunderson said that he wanted me to think about it before the discussion went any further." John hoped that his next words sounded convincing. "Since I'm not that much in the loop on the money operations, there's really not a lot I could tell him. And since he doesn't sign my paycheck, but you do, I thought that I should bring this to your attention."

Will didn't show any signs of appreciation. He stared at John for a moment and took a drink from his water bottle.

"Why did you decide to meet him for lunch?" Will asked. "Don't you think that was a little risky?"

"I really didn't want to meet him," John sighed. "But I knew that if I had to come to you and let you know about his approaching me, I thought you would appreciate it if I took the time to find out what it was all about." John stared across the park for a moment before continuing. "As it turned out, he didn't tell me anything and I don't know anything to tell him. But I thought you would like to know about it, Will."

Will sat for a long time staring at John. He reached inside his coat pocket and ran his fingers over the photographs of John's meeting with Bert. Will didn't trust John. But he took his gesture of loyalty as a promising sign. Perhaps he didn't have to watch John so closely, he thought. After a few minutes, Will broke the strained silence.

"Don't meet with him any more. Avoid any calls from him. If he tries to contact you again, which I'm sure he will, call me." Will didn't wait for an answer. He tipped the water bottle to his mouth and emptied it. Then he threw the bottle violently at a nearby trashcan. It was apparent that he had no intention of trying to put the bottle in the can. He wanted John to know he was angry and that he wasn't going to give any explanations. He stood and brushed the wrinkles out his suit. He walked to the car without another word.

That night Dave sat at the kitchen table stabbing at his food. He told Ann about Shane. After the shock began to wear off, he told her about Buster. Although Ann hadn't met all of the executive management team, she had heard Dave talk about them occasionally. She had to interrupt him periodically to understand where they fit in at National Assets. After he had allowed some time for that to sink in, he told her about seeing Will and John in the park. Finally, he told her about sending the employment contract to Mike Bear.

"So what's next?" Ann asked. She had become concerned about Dave's brooding and prolonged silences when he was at home. Just as the business world was crushing down on Dave, she was beginning to feel the effects of his changing moods.

"We may need to get out of here in a hurry," Dave said. He sighed deeply and took a drink of coffee. "I don't want to put us in danger. I don't want to put us in any more danger," he corrected himself.

"Why don't you just go to the police or the FBI?" she asked.

"It's more complicated than that," Dave said. "I think that they are already looking into all of this criminal activity. But they have to be careful and their progress is slow. And if there is a large group of people with a lot of money behind all of this, the fact that law enforcement is looking into it won't keep us safe." He finished his coffee and set the cup down on the table. "It didn't keep Shane safe, or Buster."

"Good point," she conceded. "Let me get the kitchen cleaned up. Then we'll go over what we need to accomplish here." She stood from the table and started stacking dishes. "If this contract pay out works, we'll have a lot of choices once we sell the house."

After the table was cleared and seconds on coffee were served, Dave and Ann outlined their plan to sell the house and the countless tasks that surround moving out of a city as quickly and as quietly as possible. The prospect of money and the danger they found themselves in motivated them to work a detailed plan out over the next three hours.

By eleven o'clock they had their plan. Dave and Ann allocated the tasks, made their lists and collected phone numbers for their calls in the morning. Ann stretched and yawned.

"It's funny," she said through her yawn. "We need to make everything happen while it looks as if nothing is happening. That attracts less suspicion."

"Exactly," Dave said. He thought it funny that Verdura was trying to do the same thing with National Assets.

30

The following day was a quiet one at work. The morning was filled with the routine of returning phone calls and answering emails. Dave held a meeting with his managers every week to talk about issues in the operation. His staff was unusually quiet this morning. Dave shrugged it off to his own distraction and dismissed the meeting early. When he returned to his office he saw the message from Mike Bear. Dave quickly picked up the phone and called him.

"Dave, what the hell is going on up there?" Mike said jokingly in his Texas drawl. "Looks like they're beating the shit out of you."

"I'm beginning to think the same thing, Mike. It's good to hear your voice," Dave said calmly trying to hide his anticipation. "What do you think about what I sent you?"

"Looks like you have an airtight argument," Mike said. "I looked it over carefully and I don't see much room for them to wiggle around. They've violated the agreement. So you are due the money. I'd be real careful until you get it. You know, don't do anything that would create a performance issue. Don't get drunk in your office. That kind of stuff." Mike had a way of bringing humor into tense moments. Dave knew that from his experience with Mike. He was tough in the courtroom but always carried his sense of humor.

"I can be careful," Dave said and laughed.

"There's just a couple of things I'd change in your letter, if it were me," Mike said in more serious tone.

Dave grabbed a pencil and carefully wrote down the suggestions that Mike relayed. They talked about each other's news for a while. After lavishing him with thanks, Dave ended the conversation. Marilee was holding a message slip in front of his face that Will Eagleton's assistant was on the phone holding

164

for Dave.

"Dave, this is Will Eagleton," he said in an urgent voice. "I'd like you to come over to my office as soon as possible. Do you have some time right now?"

"Sure," Dave said. "I can be there in half an hour."

"Good. I'll look for you then." Without saying goodbye Will hung up the phone.

The late morning traffic was light and Dave made good on his commitment to be there in thirty minutes.

"Come in Dave," Will said in a serious voice. As Dave walked into his office he was surprised to see John Fremont sitting in one of the chairs in front of Will's desk. Dave couldn't read the expression on John's face. Everyone looked serious, he thought.

"Have a seat," Will pointed to the remaining chair next to John in front of his desk. Will sat in his leather high back chair behind his desk and folded his hands in front of him. Dave sat and waited for Will to begin the meeting.

"The reason I called you here, Dave, is to express my disappointment in the way that you've handled your role in this transition to Verdura Bank. The acquisition will only go as smoothly as the leaders of this organization allow it to." The pacing of Will's words made Dave think that he was forcing himself to hold his temper in check.

"What exactly have I done to obstruct the transition?" Dave asked.

"It appears to me that you haven't let go of the issue on losses, non-performing loans. It's come to my attention that you've been supplying the wrong people with your version of your efforts to bring this matter to light and to get the problem fixed."

"I've only given information to the examiners and to Zack," Dave said in his own defense. "I don't see where that could be construed as being obstructive."

Will leaned forward in his chair and stared at Dave.

"Answer this question," Will said evenly. "Did you talk to the FBI?"

Dave glanced over at John. John was staring at the floor. The hesitation in his answer was enough for Will.

"It would be more appropriate to say that the FBI tried to talk to me," Dave said. "They approached me and asked for information."

"Why didn't you tell me about this?" Will said, his face red with anger. "John came forward when they approached him."

"Because nothing came of it," Dave answered.

"Then how in the hell did they get enough information to ask questions about specific numbers in our charge off backlog? How did they get specific times and dates of meetings that are proprietary information?"

"It wasn't from me," Dave said. Dave looked over at John. He suspected that John had given the information. But John's silence confused Dave. He wondered if he was being set up for this fall. "Frankly, I resent the insinuation that I was somehow involved in passing on information to an outside source. I would know that I would have to go through our legal department."

"How can I believe that if you met with them and didn't tell me?" Will asked.

"Because that's what I'm telling you," Dave answered angrily. "When have you ever needed to question my integrity? I've always been up front about anything that concerned me. I surfaced it to you. And frankly I have found it extremely frustrating when nothing gets done about it. This is bullshit."

Dave's outburst seemed to calm Will down a little. Will stood up from behind his desk and walked over to a window. He stared out at the street for a moment. Then he turned and looked at John.

"John seems to think that you had more dealings with the FBI than you're letting on."

Dave couldn't believe what he was hearing. Once again he looked over at John who still fixed his eyes on the floor. Dave searched for the right words.

"Maybe John's concerned about his job. Maybe John's mistaken," Dave said. He looked over at John again. "John, what makes you think that I passed information on to someone outside the organization?"

John looked up and shrugged. There was no response even in his eyes. After a moment he looked back down at the carpet. Dave stood from his chair. He wondered if Will was baiting both John and him. He knew that there was nothing he could say that would put himself in a better light with Will.

"Okay, you've registered your disappointment, Will. And I've registered my answer. I would not give that information to the FBI. I would have nothing to gain by doing so. And frankly, I'm disappointed that you would think that I would do such a thing. The only information I've given out is to the OCC examiners and to Zack. And anything that I have given them can be substantiated since it is well documented in my files." Dave paused to catch his breath. "Is there anything else you wanted to discuss?"

Will stood at the window and looked at Dave for a minute as if assessing what he had just said. Will clasped his hands behind his back and shook his head. Without saying anything he turned once again and stared out the window.

Dave took that as a sign of his dismissal. He looked once more at John and walked out of the office. His hands didn't stop shaking until he got to his car. Once inside his car he closed his eyes and took several deep breaths. When he thought he was in control of himself enough, he started his car and pulled out of the lot.

As Dave drove back to his office he wondered why John was so quiet. Had he blamed his own activities on Dave to save his own job, he wondered? Was Will just on a fishing trip for information? Dave knew that friendship had limitations, especially in the business world. He couldn't believe that John hadn't come to his defense. Maybe John was desperate to keep his job. Then he remembered seeing John and Will at the park. Dave wondered what they had been talking about. He resolved to keep his activities to himself from now on. He would execute his own plan quietly and confidentially.

That afternoon Dave attended two meetings dealing with the recombining of the two servicing centers. Managers from Verdura Bank led both meetings. The managers talked about the systems issues and the organization structure. They filled whiteboards with diagrams and timelines while energetically waving the marking pens in their hands while talking. Soon the chemical fumes of the marking pens filled the room. To Dave it was if he was listening to all of his own plans in reverse from the time he worked so hard to separate the servicing centers.

Dave noticed that his own management team had grown more distant with him and with each other. He suspected it was due to the divide-and-conquer strategy of the bank. The new managers loaded his staff with assignments. They didn't feel that it was necessary to check with Dave. His direct reports were methodically pulled out from under him. And Dave understood the finality of his isolation. The bank had dealt him out. He had never been given the opportunity to talk about his new assignment with Zack. But he was certain that Larry had discussed it at length with Zack after Dave had refused to consider the new assignment.

After the meetings Dave walked to his office and mailed the letter demanding his contract payout to the director of human resources at Verdura Bank. As far as he was concerned his fate was sealed. He couldn't make Will Eagleton any more disappointed. Will would probably be glad to see Dave go. He knew that Larry and Zack probably considered him an obstacle in the reorganization plan. Dave hated to leave his staff in a new and uncertain flux. But he knew that they were seasoned managers, used to the changes of business. Now that the company was under the watchful eye of the OCC, the only interest the FBI would have in the organization would be to go after individuals like Mort Smalley or the senior management team of the old National Assets.

After Dave mailed the letter he started packing his remaining personal belongings. He decided to take a few things home every night. Maybe it would be less conspicuous, he thought. And it would be a lot easier when the day came when he did leave. He also began deleting files from his computer. He copied some of the more important ones. With every action he took to separate himself from his office, he felt more relaxed. It reminded him of his last days at Norbank.

Before he left the office for the day he called a couple of recruiters to let them know that he was interested in looking at other opportunities in the industry. He knew they would call him back at home this evening. He would have to find a realtor to list their house for sale. The market was good so they shouldn't have any trouble selling their house. And he knew that some companies interested in hiring him would buy the house and sell it for them if that's what it took to get Dave to come to work a little earlier. The only question was whether Dave wanted to continue in this line of work.

Dave picked up his briefcase and his small box of personal belongings. He sighed deeply and looked around the office. The end was about to begin, he thought. He wondered how big of a fight he was in for with Verdura Bank over his contract. A lot of money was involved. It was certainly enough money to fight over, he thought.

Dave thought about the money often. He figured that he could get by on his savings if he was able to cash out his contract. He wondered if he would miss the power and the stress of working in a large organization. He thought about how much of his life he had been working like this. He thought about all the missed opportunities to enjoy what he already possessed. He thought of the time he could spend with his family, the time he could spend getting to know himself. He had performed the role of company man for so long he wondered if he would recognize his real self.

He had wrapped himself in power and position and money for so long, he dreaded the withdrawal pains that would surely accompany an exodus from the corporate world. He had spent thirty years learning how to be correct, to dress appropriately, what seat to take in a conference room, how to speak in public, how to get staff to rally around him. He had worked hard to become good at these skills. He also admitted that they were part of the illusion. And that he would have to face the reality of his life someday. Maybe this was the opportunity life was giving him. Maybe it was all a mistake. Maybe this was his chance to correct it.

Dave thought back to the time when he entered the work force. He was just out of college. He was getting married. Life held the promise of a soulful journey into relationship with the world. He tried to remember what was important to him at that moment in time. He wondered what were his motivations for working so hard, what were his dreams. What happened to all those dreams, all that energy, he asked himself? And what had so completely cloaked those dreams and ambitions over the years? What had stifled his inner visions and voices? Were they still there? Were they still alive? Had the quest for power and control and acceptance led him to this crossroad where he had to search for the very reasons he started on this journey? Had he subordinated his own soul to the quest for security? Why was it that he always remembered being happiest when he didn't have much money? And now he stood at a place where he was questioning all of this with a pile of money at his side for the taking, his integrity hanging by a thread, and his dreams only an outline in a dense fog of corporate conditioning.

He chased the philosophical thoughts away from him. He knew he had a lot to do and didn't need the distraction of all this thinking that boiled down to his feeling sorry for himself. He knew he was responsible for getting himself into this situation. And he knew it was up to him to change things if he didn't like it.

He climbed into his car and drove away from the office building. As he pulled into the evening traffic he felt new energy flow over him. His thoughts were thick with the rush of adventure and new beginnings.

An almost full moon floated above the eastern horizon in the early evening sky as Dave drove eastward on El Camino Avenue. The rush hour was ending and traffic moved well. While he waited at a stoplight he turned on the radio and listened to the evening news. He felt at peace knowing that life for him might return to normal. After he had made the turn onto Fair Oaks Avenue, he decided to stop at a coffee shop and pick up a bag of his favorite French roast coffee.

He loved the smell of the roasted coffee beans as he entered the store. The aroma assaulted his nose and he smiled in satisfaction. With his pound of coffee under his arm he walked back out into the parking lot toward his car. The parking lot wasn't crowded, but Dave had parked on the edge of the lot out of habit. He tried to avoid the inevitable parking lot dents that were caused by car doors swinging wide into the side of his car. Tonight his habit would work against him.

As he approached his car he noticed a dark blur out of the corner of his eye. He bent slightly to grab the door handle when he heard the footsteps. Before he could turn around someone shoved him onto the grass border of the lot. The next thing he felt was a flurry of fists pounded into his body and head. He tasted his blood. A wave of nausea and dizziness mixed with the pain of the blows and he felt himself slipping from consciousness.

He lay in the grass bleeding and his ribs hurt when he tried to breathe. He barely made out the silhouettes of two men standing over him. One reached for his wallet and began looking through it. Dave wondered if he was about to die, the victim of a mugging. He licked the blood from his lip and waited. Finally one of the men said, "This is your only warning." Then he tossed the wallet at Dave's battered face. Both men trotted off toward the street. Dave lay there for a moment thankful that he was still alive. He tried to move but sharp pains shot through his side. He groaned and rested his head on the ground. A few moments later Dave heard a car pull into the lot. He heard voices and footsteps.

"Oh my God! Look at this," one of the strangers whispered. She approached Dave with caution. Her hands reflexively went up to her throat.

"I'll call for help," another stranger said. The voices belonged to women, probably going into the coffee shop, Dave thought. He finally regained control of his breathing. As long as he took shallow breaths it didn't hurt. He stared numbly into the headlights of the idling car.

"Can you help me up?" Dave asked in a raspy voice. He flexed his muscles to see what hurt and what didn't. He moved his legs. He felt most of the pain in his head and ribs.

"Just lay there until help comes," the woman's voice answered softly. Dave looked up and saw the concern on the woman's face. She was an older woman and Dave doubted she had the strength to help him up anyway. With a concentrated effort Dave rolled to his good side and pushed himself up to a sitting position with his arm. The dizziness returned momentarily. He wiped his mouth with the back of his hand smearing the blood in a pattern that streaked the left side of his face. He blinked his watery eyes and looked around.

"You should lay back down until the police get here," the woman warned. The concern in her voice was genuine.

"I'll be okay," Dave said with a hollow voice. His legs were wobbly as he stood up next to the car. As he reached his full height his head started pounding. His shirt was sticky with sweat. The dizziness gave way to nausea once again. He didn't want to throw up in front of people so he gulped down his nausea and tasted the blood. He could hear the footsteps of the other woman running toward the car.

"The police are on their way," she told her friend as she looked at Dave. "Here, let me help," she said as she reached toward Dave's face with a wet towel and began to dab the blood from his face.

"It looks worse than it is," Dave tried to make light of the whole incident. He thought it strange that he should feel embarrassed. After all, he thought, he was the victim. The cool wet towel revived Dave. Soon he could see clearly and the strength flowed back into his legs. He leaned back against his car and looked at the women.

"I'm okay now," he said weakly. "Thanks for helping me."

The manager of the coffee shop came running out to see Dave.

"He was just in my store," she said to the others. "He was just in my store not five minutes ago."

Dave wondered if she was amazed or fearful that she had been so close to the crime in both time and location.

"And you spilled the beans," the manager said forlornly as she looked around the ground. "And here's your wallet. They must have been after your money," she said decisively as if she had solved the crime. "Can you make it to my store? You can sit there and wait for the police to come. I'll replace those coffee beans for you, too. Come on."

The women carefully guided Dave into the store. After Dave thanked the two women who had found him, he went back into the restroom and washed off his face. As he toweled his face he saw that a bloody nose, a cut lip and a little bruising on his cheekbone were the only signs of the incident. Other than sore ribs and a pounding headache he thought he was okay. He was surprised that he didn't feel angry. Maybe that would come later. Right now he felt incredibly lucky to be standing here washing his cuts and feeling the bulge of his wallet back in his pocket. When he inspected the wallet his forty dollars was gone and his driver's license was on the ground near the wallet. Nothing else had been taken. He thought that maybe they were just after the money. Then he remembered one of the men saying, "This is your only warning." Dave stopped wiping his face and tried to remember if he really had heard that, or if he had imagined it.

A half hour later, after filling out a report and declining any medical attention, Dave left the store once again with a pound of French roast tucked under his arm. The deputy escorted him to his car and watched him drive off as if he expected Dave to pass out any minute. The closer Dave came to his home his mouth felt as if it had swollen to the size of a football. And his head ached. Once in his driveway he started to laugh the laugh of a survivor. And it hurt to smile.

"My God," Ann exclaimed as she put her hands up to her neck. "What on earth happened to you?" She stared in horror at Dave's bruised and cut face.

"Oh just another day at the office," Dave joked. Then he saw the tears start to form in his wife's eyes. "Let's go in the kitchen and I'll tell you the whole story."

An hour later Dave had related the recent events about Will calling him in to his office and confronting him about talking with the FBI. He held small plastic bags of crushed ice to his face while he talked. He told Ann about his conversation with Mike Bear. And he told her briefly about the mugging in the parking lot of the coffee shop. He shared his suspicions that Will was on a fishing expedition to see if he or John were talking to the FBI. He speculated that since Will couldn't tell for sure, he decided to send Dave a warning, one that would make him think twice about talking to anyone. Finally he voiced his concerns that Will was probably angry with him for deciding to leave the company. With all of his sources Will could have already found out about it.

The attack on Dave took place on Tuesday night. For the remainder of the week Dave stayed at home and worked out of his home office. He found that he was able to attend the conference calls and answer his emails just as easily from home. In fact, he doubted that most people knew that he was working out of his home. His wounds were healing quickly. Ice packs took care of the soreness and the swelling. By Monday he would have only a few bruises to explain. And if he didn't make any quick moves, his ribs didn't give him much trouble.

One early morning Dave went in to the office to pick up his mail and leave before anyone would see him. He stopped by his medical clinic on the way in order to get a tetanus shot. Dave recalled getting his last tetanus shot over ten years ago when a dog had chased him over a barbed wire fence. He had avoided the dog bite, but cut himself on the barbed wire. For some reason Dave found the image of mad dogs chasing him amusing enough to distract him while the needle went into his arm. He was out of the clinic in ten minutes.

He arrived at his office a few minutes later. After packing his briefcase full of mail and looking at some reports, he quietly left using the back stairway. Unfortunately he ran in to Marilee, his assistant, as he was walking down the stairs to his car.

"Dave, what happened to you?" she gasped with her hands over her mouth when she saw the bruising and swelling on Dave's face.

"Oh I just had a little accident," Dave said. He smiled a lopsided smile that made him feel awkward standing in the stairway looking at Marilee. "Nothing serious. Like I said in my voice mail, I'll be back on Monday. Just call me at home if you need me for anything." He could see the sympathy in her eyes. He wanted to get away before anyone else saw him.

"Marilee," he said, "can we keep this between ourselves, please? No one else needs to know about this."

"Sure, Dave," she said softly. "Just give me a call if you need anything here," she said. Her concern showed in her voice and on her face. Dave wanted to say something reassuring to her. He wanted to let her know that someone was trying to keep him quiet, to warn him. And that she didn't have to fear for her personal safety. But he knew that one word about it would demand a lengthy explanation. And he didn't feel like talking about it right now.

Dave nodded and walked down the stairs and out to his car. He was determined to keep this incident quiet. The words "this is your only warning" kept replaying in his mind. If he was the target of intimidation, he didn't want anyone to know that they got to him. He didn't want to give anyone the satisfaction. And he didn't want anyone else knowing about the incident.

After Verdura's announcement of the reorganization came the directive that the budgets would have to be revised in order to fit the structure for the coming year. Since Dave was planning on leaving the company, he couldn't get excited about the budget process like he usually did. He always liked to be inspired about the upcoming year with all of the plans and opportunities in order to give his best to the budget. Now it was like going through a meaningless exercise in forecasting. He knew that the budget would change time and again until the organization settled in. And he hoped he wouldn't be there to see it.

He laid out sheets of paper with new reporting lines and salary information. He calculated the postage and phone expenses based on the historical numbers. He estimated salaries based on the new organization structure. Then he reviewed the new business forecasts for the coming year that would dictate how much staff would have to be added in order to handle the incoming loans. He thought that by the time Verdura Bank saw these figures they would conclude that it would be cheaper to move the loans to North Carolina and close the operation in Sacramento. He smiled as he remembered the assurances from Verdura that National Assets would remain open and unencumbered by the regulatory bureaucracy that shadowed their lives. He remembered them saying that the merger would be virtually seamless from the perspective of the front line employee. He kept repeating the word seamless as his sore mouth stretched into a twisted smile.

By the end of the week he was finished with the first draft of the budget and sent the files to the chief financial officer of National Assets. He attached explanations on his calculations. It was important to let the chief financial officer know whether he was using historical or current expenses as his basis for calculation. He diligently wrote in the footnotes to explain the larger variances from previous years. Dave had a reputation for his accurate forecasting and solid reasoning on budget calculations. It was still important to him that his work reflected his professional approach to his job, even if it went unappreciated. He knew that he would be among the first ones finished. He always was. And he knew that they needed him to attend the budget meetings, because he knew the history of the servicing center and could easily explain the expenses to senior management.

On Friday evening Dave sat back in his chair and let out a satisfied sigh. All of his email was answered. He had attended all of the conference calls scheduled for him. And he had submitted the budgets. What a difference it makes when one can work undistracted, he thought. He knew how time consuming it was to handle unexpected visitors to his office, the commute time and the lunchtime. Yes, he thought, he would be ready to get back into the trenches on Monday. He would be ready for anything, he mused as he gently massaged his sore jaw.

The first item of news on Monday was that Verdura Bank had approved Dave's request for his contract buyout. The human resources department in North Carolina called to inform him. They said that a representative from National Assets human resource department would be getting in touch with him to set a final date of employment and to review the payout amounts on stock options and severance pay. Dave was elated. He felt as if he had won the lottery. He tried to grasp the idea of all that money landing in his lap in one lump sum. His mind raced. He felt as if he had just discovered a treasure but didn't know how to hide it until he could move it to safety. He tried to calm his mind and caution himself that he didn't have the money in his hands yet. Many things could happen between now and the day he could get his hands on the money. The reality hit home when he received an email confirming the earlier conversation on his buyout.

As soon as he talked to the National Assets representative, he would give his notice. He could tell everyone good-bye. He knew he would miss his staff. He appreciated the loyal employees who worked so hard for him. He would miss the power. But he wouldn't miss the headaches, the intrigues and the political infighting he had to deal with every day. The week was starting out well.

The second event that would change Dave's week happened when the mail arrived at mid morning. In the stack of mail was a thick packet marked personal and confidential. There was no return address on it. Dave inspected the postmark to find that it had been sent from Sacramento. His first thought was that it might be some kind of explosive device. The company had published warnings about opening any packages that did not contain return addresses. But Dave could tell that this package was soft and flexible. It felt as if it contained papers and something else, smaller and compact. He carefully opened the packet to find that his suspicions were correct. The bulk of the package contained a thick stack of paper. He pulled out the top sheet. It was a cover letter signed by Shane Davis, the systems technologist. Dave knew he was reading a letter from a ghost. He held his breath as he scanned the contents.

The letter started out that if Dave were reading this, then something bad had happened to Shane. As a precaution Shane had accumulated incriminating documents and correspondence about the illegal activities of several top executives with National Assets. There was also a diskette that was a key in getting into the system one time that would give Dave access to more sensitive reports and documents. Dave let out a low whistle as he read some of the pages. The papers he was holding were far more incriminating than anything Dave had in his possession. The last item in the packet was videotape. A message scribbled on the videotape described the contents. It was a short message from Shane along with some instructions for using the diskette. And the last segment of the tape contained a meeting in Will Eagleton's office with some of his Chicago associates that validated some of the findings in the documents. Shane wrote that he had successfully installed a bullet camera in the room that went undetected by any of the participants. It was explosive information.

Dave sat back in his chair and stared at the contents of the package spread out on his desk. He had everything he needed to bring the senior management team down. But he didn't know who to go to. He didn't know whom to trust. The FBI didn't seem interested now that the company was under the watchful eye of the OCC. He knew that John Fremont seemed more interested in keeping his job. He thought about going to the press, or maybe the Securities and Exchange Commission. He considered how valuable this information would be to several senior managers. But he didn't think that he would survive the transaction if he tried to sell it to them. Besides, he decided he didn't want to be a party to extortion. He realized that now he was in a very dangerous situation. If the beating were a warning, then his life would be in more danger if anyone knew that he had the contents of this package.

Dave walked over to the area of his servicing operation where his staff boarded new loans into the system. He scanned the documents onto a disk with one of the high-speed scanners used to scan loan documents into the system. He figured that the disk would be easier to hide. Most people would look for documents if they were trying to find incriminating paperwork. In a few minutes he had a complete file of the documents on disk. When he returned to his office Dave cut the lining of his briefcase and carefully slid the disk behind the lining.

Dave gathered everything up and put the contents back into the envelope. He walked across the parking lot to the Bank of America and rented a safe deposit box. After storing the package in the box, he called Ann from a pay phone outside the bank. He told her what was in the package. They agreed that she would pack what she could and drive to the San Francisco area to visit her sister. Hopefully, they thought, that would put her out of harm's way. Dave advised her not to use any charge cards in the event someone tried to trace her whereabouts. Dave promised to call every evening from a safe phone. He said his goodbye and walked back to his office.

He needed some time to think about what to do with all of this information. He needed to decide whether he would use the program to go into the system for more information, before someone deleted it, if they hadn't already. He found it hard to concentrate on anything for the rest of the morning. He had to talk to someone, but he didn't know whom to trust.

Later that afternoon he told Marilee about his plan to leave the company. Out of consideration for her, Dave wanted Marilee to have ample time to look for another position before he left. He knew that Marilee probably suspected that Dave was planning to leave. But he wanted to give her the opportunity to look after her own career. If the company considered Dave as damaged goods, then Marilee would need more time finding a job. After a few tears Marilee left his office and began working on her resume and looking at the various job postings. She agreed to keep the matter in confidence until Dave announced his departure date.

Dave stood in front of his office window and collected his thoughts for the last meeting of the day. He had to attend a meeting on the new systems architecture. Although his role at these meetings was not much more than a casual observer, he knew that they needed a subject matter expert from each business so that nothing was left out of the design. Dave found it tedious to sit through these meetings and see his world change. It discouraged him to see all the of the good work he had done over the previous two years go down the drain.

Nothing had really changed, he thought. There was just a new gang in town giving directions, trying to motivate, and attempting to be the visionaries for the coming year. They promised better benefits, better work processes, and more accountability. The company would become the premier financial organization of the new millennium. Dave had heard all of the propaganda so many times before. He had been the one preaching it some of the time. Now it sounded so hollow, almost comedic. He had to look down at his legal pad and scribble something to hide his amusement. Nothing really changes, he thought. The acquiring company destroys so that it can rebuild what was already there and working. So many lives were affected. So many families dependent on the income would be changed by what happened in these meetings. Employees became a commodity much like the computer terminals. They were just numbers in the productivity equations that hopefully would reflect a greater return on investment to the stockholders some day in the future.

31

The following morning Dave left for work at 6:30 hoping to get ahead of the rush hour traffic. The traffic was light, free of accidents, and Dave made good time. He stopped about a block from the office at a restaurant for breakfast. It was a place where he never stopped and thought it would be a good idea to break his routine in case someone was waiting for him along the way. The mugging had made him more aware of his habits. He found himself looking in his rear view mirror more often and taking different streets to and from work.

Once he was inside the restaurant he found a corner booth and ordered a big breakfast of ham and eggs and rye toast. It was the kind of place that left the pot of coffee on the table so that you wouldn't have to keep waving down the waitress for refills. Soon he was looking down at a plate of fried eggs and a savory slice of smoked ham. He inhaled the aroma for a moment before picking up his fork. He ate slowly and thought about the coming day. He was more relaxed, more detached from the daily business now that the Verdura staff was taking a more active management role. Most importantly he had more time to think, to plan.

Once the breakfast dishes were cleared away Dave poured himself another cup of coffee and took a pad of paper out of his briefcase. He studied the notes he had made the night before remembering what he could about the information that Shane had sent him. He made a rough outline of the money laundering activities. Now he was able to fill in the names based on the correspondence he had seen in the package. It was all falling into place. And it involved a couple of senior people at Verdura. It was an almost perfect scam covered up with the purchase of National Assets by Verdura Bank. Shane had even managed to get a hold of the bank routing numbers that allowed the money to flow to subsidiary corporations.

The one item that still bothered Dave was how John Fremont had suddenly become talkative with Will Eagleton. At the same time John began avoiding Dave. Dave guessed that John might be fighting his own battles for survival. Perhaps he was working his own angle to free himself from the mess they had discovered and didn't want to put Dave in harm's way. He wished that there were a way he could find out. He guessed that John was probably being watched. It was better to leave him alone and to choose his own course of action. Finally Dave paid his check and drove over to the office.

He was still early when he walked up the stairs. The early morning customer service and collections shifts were hard at work on the phones. Some of the employees smiled and nodded with their headsets on even though they were occupied talking to customers. Dave glanced at the call management electronic bulletin boards and could see that the call volume was already heavy. He stood for a moment in the middle of the customer service area taking in the activity and the hum of voices and the pieces of scripted conversations. Many of the one-sided conversations dealt with explaining the merger to worried customers. The explanations were measured and confident. Dave knew that he had built this from nothing. He stood there proud of his accomplishment and sad that he wasn't a part of it anymore.

As he walked in his office he noticed that Marilee wasn't in yet. The message light was flashing on his phone. He sat at his desk and began to retrieve the messages. One of the voicemail messages was from the human resource department. The personnel representative wanted Dave to call so that they could set a final date of employment and go over the disbursement amounts. Dave listened to the message with an air of detachment as if she were talking about someone other than Dave. The reality of his situation was sinking in. He would soon leave all of this behind. Now he wondered what, if anything, he should do with the explosive information that Shane had left him.

His pride told him to stay and fight. His common sense told him to take his money and walk away from the whole mess. And he knew that he probably would just walk out quietly. He wasn't the kind of person to make trouble. He reminded himself that he had to look for another job. And that meant that he would need a reference from National Assets or Verdura Bank.

After he had returned some calls, he heard Marilee dropping her purse on her desk and turning office equipment on. Dave thought that so many days had started like this and now it was all ending. He felt like a ghost in his own office. Marilee stood in his doorway waiting for him to notice.

"Good morning," she said cheerfully. "I'm going down to the vending cart for coffee. Would you like some?"

"Sure," Dave answered. He was over his limit on coffee from the restaurant. But he knew that Marilee was going out of her way to be helpful. Dave never expected her to get coffee for him as part of her routine. "Thanks for asking." Dave handed her a couple of dollars and smiled.

In a few minutes she was back at his desk with a steaming cup of French roast. She even took the lid off of the coffee and placed a pastry next to his cup.

"Thank you," Dave said warmly. His eyes reflected his surprise.

"No problem. My treat," Marilee said. "By the way, I need a little extra time for lunch. I've got an interview outside the company, another bank over on Madison. I may not need it. But I wanted to clear it with you." She sounded excited and pleased that she had found something so quickly.

"That's fine." Dave smiled at her conspiratorially. "Good luck."

"Thanks."

"Before you go over there today, there is something I need you to put together for me on a diskette," Dave said casually. "I need an email address list of all National Asset management, all servicing employees, the OCC team, and the executive team from Verdura. When I make the announcement that I'm leaving, I want to get the message to everyone at the same time."

"I understand," Marilee said. "It's a good idea. Maybe it will cut down on the phone calls."

"Naaa…" they both said at the same time and laughed.

"I'll write the announcement this morning," Dave said. "But don't send it out until I ask you."

"Will do," Marilee answered and walked out of his office.

A few minutes later Debbie Evans, the customer service manager, stood at Dave's door. She did not look happy. Dave had recruited her from Norbank and she had done a good job of building the customer service organization. Debbie was in her mid-forties, dyed her hair auburn and wore expensive clothes. Her employees viewed her as a tough leader. But she had a tough job keeping the phone lines going and handling most of the complaints from the customers. She knew her job well and always turned in good results. She demanded time and coaching from Dave. She viewed it as her right to use him as a resource. Dave didn't mind. He hadn't been very available lately and the look in her face reminded him of that.

"Got a minute?" she asked. She stood in the doorway with a pile of papers in one hand and a cup of coffee in the other. Dave wondered how long this was going to take.

"Sure," he said casually. "Come on in." He could tell from the pensive look on her face that she was not happy about something. Dave took a deep breath and sat back.

"What's on your mind?"

"You've been hard to get a hold of lately," Debbie chided him. "I've got a lot of things I need to bring you up to date on." She looked confused, as if she were searching for the right words.

"I had a meeting with Larry yesterday," she began with an ominous tone in her voice. "I was wondering whether you knew anything about it." Dave admired her loyalty. It was one of the traits that made him decide to recruit her.

"No, I didn't." Dave was getting used to the fact that Larry was taking a more active role in the daily management of the operation.

"He gave me a raise. He wants me to run all of customer service. Evidently his first choice didn't work out."

"Congratulations," Dave said evenly.

"Is that all? Congratulations? What's going on around here, Dave?" she said in an exasperated tone. "I'm here because you recruited me. I want to know if you plan on being around very long." Debbie liked to get to the point in a hurry.

"There are no guarantees," Dave said evasively. "I can't control things since the sale. It's all up to Verdura. We have to abide by their plans."

"I know that, Dave. I want to know what's going on with you. You're not in half the meetings that affect the servicing organization. Larry is out talking to all of your management team. And all of a sudden you're walking around here a lot more relaxed than I would have thought you would be. It isn't right."

"It's not my call anymore, Debbie."

"Are you staying?"

"I don't know yet," Dave lied.

"I heard that you were leaving." Dave knew better than to ask where she heard that. It was probably just speculation. In any event he didn't want to deal with it right now.

"Look, Debbie, there are no guarantees in this business. You've been around long enough to know that. We're all going to have to find our places in this new organization. If we don't like where they put us, then we've always got the choice to get out."

"You're side stepping me," Debbie said. "That's not like you."

"Debbie, if you're asking me if I like what's going on, then the answer is no. This isn't what I planned to have happen to our careers. Whether I stay around or not is my decision. I'll let you know when it's time to announce it."

"So you're leaving," she said finally.

"I didn't say that."

"I get the feeling that you're leaving. You don't seem interested anymore. It's like you've abandoned us."

Dave looked at her and sighed. He felt guilty about his evasiveness with Debbie. She had always counted on his integrity. He knew that if he told Debbie that he planned on leaving, he would be talking to her for another half hour minimum. And he didn't want the information floating around on the grapevine before he talked to Zack, or someone above him who would at least return his calls.

"I think that I'm the one who has been abandoned. Not by you, but the company has abandoned me. It's okay. It's their call. Now I have to decide whether I can live with that or not." Dave sat forward in his chair hoping Debbie would take it as a sign that the conversation was over. She did.

"This isn't fair," she said. Her eyes were starting to water. Dave didn't understand what she was saying. Maybe she meant the way he was treating her. Maybe she meant the way the company was treating him. Maybe she just had to be mad at someone and Dave was the easiest target. He sat in silence until Debbie realized that he wasn't going to respond. Finally she stood and walked out of his office.

Dave sat at his desk composing himself. He didn't like confrontations with his employees, especially the ones who had worked so hard for him. He felt his anger creeping up in him. He decided to channel the anger into something useful. His legal pad was on the corner of his desk. He put it in front of him and started writing his resignation letter.

Dave met with the human resources department that afternoon. He had an appointment with a young woman who had started with the company two weeks ago. He didn't know her and now he was discussing large sums of money and the end of his employment with an eighteen year old new hire fumbling through papers.

Her name was Bobbi or Terri, something that ended in an "i." Dave couldn't remember but he thought that it was Terri. She was short and wore her dark hair just below the ears. She looked too young to Dave to be handling such a large transaction. The receptionist had seated Dave in a small consultation room. There was a table and four chairs. The walls were bare. Dave thought that it would have been a good place to go insane if he were left there very long. Terri walked in after about five minutes of waiting. She held a pen in one hand and a stack of papers in the other. Her pen was fat, covered with a design of colored balloons and bears. On top of the stack of papers was Dave's letter for request of payout on his contract.

Terri nervously arranged the papers on the table and started explaining the various computations to Dave. Dave had calculated all of the disbursements several times so that he would be prepared for any discrepancies that came up during the meeting. He was glad he did. The amount that the company had come up with was a few thousand dollars more than Dave had anticipated. As Terri went through the calculations he realized that there was some unused vacation and personal time off that the company had credited to the amount. After agreeing to a departure date of January 4th, Dave signed the papers. Terri told him he could stop by on the fourth and pick up his money and final paperwork. He thanked Terri and left the building.

As he drove back to his office Dave felt a sense of excitement. A personal sense of accomplishment flooded over him. He even started singing along to the song on the radio. He hadn't felt this good since he had been released by the Marine Corps when he was twenty-one years old. He calmed down thinking that he better save his celebration for when he had the money in his hands. That was still a few days away. And anything could happen in a few days.

When he arrived at his office he walked by Marilee's cubicle and gave a thumbs up and smiled.

"Go ahead and send out the notice," he said. Marilee nodded and smiled.

Dave felt so expansive he decided to call John Fremont and tell him personally.

"You did what?" John sounded surprised.

"That's right," Dave answered. "I sent a letter requesting the payout on my contract and Verdura agreed to it. My last day is next week."

"What are you going to do for a job?" John asked.

"I don't know. Now that I have some money, I may just take some time off and relax. I'm sure that something will come along."

"I think that you would have been better off finding another job before you resigned," John said. Dave could hear the anxiety in John's voice as if he were the one going through this.

"I'm not worried about anything except getting out of here in one piece."

"I'm really sorry that things didn't work out. I feel partially responsible for recruiting you for this job. I had no idea that things would turn out this way."

"I never expected any guarantees," Dave said reassuringly. "It was my choice. I take responsibility for it."

"Have you told Eagleton yet?"

"No. I think he'll be glad to see me go."

"You better start getting the things you want to keep out of there. They may usher you out of the building once they find out."

"I've already taken care of it," Dave said smugly.

"Keep in touch."

Dave hung up the phone. That was it, he thought. John didn't offer to take him to lunch. He didn't even seem interested in getting together before Dave left. Dave shrugged it off philosophically. Maybe John's fighting his own battles. Maybe he's envious, he thought. Maybe he has an exit plan of his own.

Everyone met the news of Dave's resignation with the same casual interest. There were no offers of parties or lunches. Verdura had made their intimidating presence felt too soon. Everyone had their attention riveted to the changes that were going on. Most of his change-numbed employees took it as an ominous sign. They knew that things were going to get worse if the senior management of National Assets started leaving. And Dave had started a trend among the management. Those under contract who had seen their jobs change started writing letters to request payouts on their contracts. Within the next few days there were over twenty requests from managers filed with the human resources department.

Dave enjoyed hearing about it. He had blazed the trail for an onslaught of resignations. Verdura was starting to take notice. One person resigning didn't bother them. A whole group resigning grabbed their attention. Soon Dave received a call from Larry requesting a meeting that afternoon. Larry gave the pretext of wanting to talk about some budget issues.

When Larry arrived he asked Dave to meet him on the patio of the employee lounge so that they could have a cigarette. After a casual start to the conversation Larry quickly got to the point of his visit.

"Is there anything I can say or do that would get you to stay?" Larry asked. "This whole operation could be yours by the end of the year. I'm just an interim manager for the merger."

"No thanks," Dave said dryly. "I was promised that before you arrived on the scene. Why would I believe that promise again?"

"This really looks bad that I lose the most senior person in servicing management," Larry said.

"You should have thought about that before you changed my duties."

"I didn't know that you were under contract."

"So your real concern is that your decision cost the bank a lot of money, not my services," Dave said with too much satisfaction in his voice.

Larry looked at him for a moment. He stabbed his cigarette in the ashtray repeatedly. Then he immediately took a fresh one out of the pack and lit it. Dave realized that he was either forming a response or calming down. Dave waited quietly. The look on Larry's face changed subtly. He seemed to release the tautness in his face and he looked defeated.

"I don't know that much about servicing management," he admitted. "Verdura just wanted someone in here that they knew wasn't going to be loyal to National Assets and fight all the changes."

Dave looked at him and laughed out loud. He flipped his cigarette into the ashtray and shoved his hands into his pockets.

"After all of the documentation you've seen, you thought that I was going to attach my loyalties to a group that got this company in such a jam?" Dave stared at him and shook his head. "You don't think that I welcomed the change?"

"No one knew where you stood," Larry said. "And everyone wondered why, with your experience, things like the charge off backlog could happen on your watch."

Dave looked away in frustration. He couldn't believe what he was hearing. There was no way that they could have come to that conclusion without help. Someone had to be twisting the story. Exasperation and revulsion swept over Dave. He knew that this wasn't the time or the person to straighten things out with. His explanation would just get buried in an attempt to look better in some superior's eyes. And Dave couldn't afford to look any worse than he already did.

Dave thought that they all deserved each other. They could spend their workdays rewriting the history of the company and who did what to whom. But Dave was out. And he was getting angry as he stood there and thought of all the backstabbing and infighting that must have taken place in order to bring his career to this discussion with Larry. Now he was determined to make a statement. He wanted to put his story on a billboard and let everyone hear his version, the one backed up by facts, for everyone to hear at the same time, unbiased, unfiltered, just once.

It took Dave a while to calm down after his meeting with Larry. What frustrated him even more was the fact that it wasn't worth the effort to try to set the record straight. Something in his conversation with Larry opened a dark, dangerous cavern in Dave's mind. It was a darkness he never knew existed. The cold, dark cave full of hatred and rage beckoned Dave inward. He struggled. He resisted the temptation to give in to its easy pull.

He walked back to his office and started throwing things in the trash. He thumbed through the old reports and correspondence that no one would be interested in. He pulled personal phone lists off of the wall and threw them away. Soon he calmed down and sat at his desk. He looked around at the almost bare office. He felt despondent. He had to do something before he started getting too depressed. The he noticed that his message light was flashing.

He was surprised to hear a message summoning him to Will Eagleton's office. Everyone had steered clear of Dave lately. They considered him damaged goods. Verdura would question anyone's loyalty who spent too much time consorting with a pariah. Dave returned the call. Will's assistant said that Dave was scheduled for an exit interview with Will at nine o'clock tomorrow morning.

Dave was late due to traffic. Will seemed impatient that Dave had kept him waiting and took it as a sign of indifference from Dave now that he was leaving. Dave saw Will's jaw muscles flexing when he entered Will's office.

"Come in. Have a seat," Will said more as an order than an invitation. Dave noticed that Will seemed to have aged over the past few weeks. He didn't exude the confidence and energy he was known for. The lines on his face appeared deeper and his frown darker. His eyes had a wary look to them, as if he were waiting for someone to ambush him at any minute. He knows, Dave thought, he knows that he is useful to Verdura only as a transition tool. Once the acquisition is complete they will throw him out like an old ladder that's no longer needed because the new stairway has been built. Dave wondered if Will was dealing with that realization. Maybe he was in that place where he can no longer define himself by the power he wields, Dave thought. Fallen angels are the most tragic figures, he mused. But he guessed that Will was no angel.

"I wanted to touch base with you before you leave," Will said. "Do you have any plans?"

"Not really." Dave thought that he would try to be polite as long as the conversation drifted in that direction. "I thought I would take some time off to catch my breath, process a few of life's lessons and then decide what to do next." Dave knew that sounded weak. He didn't feel the need to collapse in front of Will in an emotional farewell. Nor did he feel the need to tell him off, to tell him how difficult he had made Dave's life by not supporting him. But Dave understood the issues were more complex than that.

"I'm sorry that things didn't work out for you in the new administration," Will said feigning sympathy.

"It's just life telling me to move on," Dave said evenly as if he wanted to keep this discussion on a philosophical level. Will rocked back in his leather chair and steepled his hands in a prayer-like pose.

"I hope you respect the confidentiality of our trade secrets," Will said. "There are a lot of things that you know that should not be discussed outside the company."

Dave felt the rage flash through his body. Once again he felt the dark cavern yawn in his mind. He knew that Will was cautioning him about talking about the company's dirty secrets once he had left. He imagined that some computer technician was deleting his access to the system as he sat here. He wondered if the meeting with Will was a ruse to get him out of his own office. He fought to control his temper.

"You didn't seem to be that interested in what I know. Why should anyone else be interested in it?" Dave said slowly. He was trying to control his anger.

"Let's just cut the cat and mouse bullshit," Will said abruptly. "You keep what you know to yourself. It doesn't leave the company. Is that clear enough?" Will's face tensed and flushed a dark shade of red. Dave knew that the limits of civility had been reached. There was nothing more to say.

"It doesn't leave the company," Dave parroted Will's last remark back to him. "Or else what? You'll have me beat up again?"

He stood and walked out of the office. No wishes of good luck, no good byes, just move away. He could feel Will's hostile stare as he walked out into the hallway. Will's words kept echoing in his mind, "it doesn't leave the company." Dave kept rolling that phrase over in his mind all the way down on the elevator and as he walked to the parking lot. Then the idea struck him. He would gladly comply with Will's wishes because Will had planted the perfect idea in Dave's head. Dave burst out laughing at the simplicity of the idea.

Dave's scheme unfolded in every detail. He called directory assistance on his cell phone for two numbers. Then he made his calls. One of the calls successfully got him the appointment he needed today. All he had to do now was to stop by the bank.

Dave heard the roar of a big car engine behind him. He stepped quickly next to his car and turned to look. John Fremont pulled up next to him in his white Lincoln town car. He motioned for Dave to get in. Dave pushed the remote button and locked his car before getting in with John.

They drove quickly out of the lot and onto the city streets. John drove through the residential neighborhoods. The streets were lined with old oak trees shading the street a dark, cavernous look. Joggers and walkers patrolled the sidewalks. Dave looked out and wondered what they all did for a living that allowed them time to exercise in the middle of the day. Maybe they took early lunch hours to avoid the midday heat. Maybe they were unemployed. His thoughts were interrupted when John cleared his throat.

"I wanted to talk to you before you left," he started in a formal tone. "Before I say anything else I want you to know that I'm wearing a wire. I've been cooperating with the FBI in their investigation. They're hoping to get something incriminating at one of the meetings that are scheduled this week. Nothing may come of it. But at least they will know that I was on their side trying to do the right thing."

Dave stared at his chest wondering if there was a network of wires crisscrossing his upper body like a chain link fence. He wondered if the wire was on and who was listening to their conversation. The thought bordered on the bizarre for Dave and he found it hard to take seriously.

"They don't care anymore," Dave said finally. "The FBI knows that National Assets is going to behave now that they are under the regulatory eyes of the OCC. There's no need."

"There are certain individuals, not the company, that they are investigating," John said. Dave thought that he would elaborate but no more explanation was coming out of John.

"Why are you telling me about all of this?"

"I know that you were wondering why I've been distant, why I haven't come to your defense at some of the meetings. I need to befriend some of the executives. I needed to get certain people to say more," John said. Dave thought that in his own way John was apologizing. He was trying to explain his actions. Dave was flattered that John thought it was important enough to go out of his way for this conversation.

"Why didn't you just tell me after work?" Dave asked.

"I didn't know what your plans were. I thought that maybe you would be gone before I had a chance to talk to you," John said. Dave was moved by the sincerity in his voice. He had always valued his friendship with John. Corporate life had muddled so many things. Dave knew that they had lost the way in their friendship. He wondered whether this incident would make the friendship stronger or weaker over time.

"There's one other thing you need to know about," John said hesitantly. "The FBI wants to subpoena you. They're willing to bring this out in the open to get a hold of what you know."

Dave felt his stomach begin to churn as the panic welled up inside of him. He was too close to the finish line for this big of an obstacle, he thought. It would blow everything he had worked for. And he wouldn't be able to go ahead with his plan. He saw the five hundred thousand dollars evaporating before his eyes.

"This isn't the time for that," Dave said.

"What if something were to happen to you?"

"No," Dave said emphatically. "You've got to convince them not to do this."

"But it's for your own safety, your personal safety as well as protection from prosecution," John pleaded.

"Look," Dave said finally. "Tell them if they'll wait a week they'll have more information than I could give them right now. You've got to convince them to hold off."

"I can't promise anything, Dave. I'm in no position to make promises. I think they've made up their minds. This is the way they want to go."

"You've got to try," Dave whispered. "It will make all the difference. You've got to convince them to wait. Have Gunderson leave me his email address at my home number. If he doesn't get an answer, tell him to leave it on the answering machine."

Both were quiet as John drove back to the parking lot. The sat in the silence of friendship one more time before things changed for good. As John pulled up to Dave's car he extended his hand and looked him in the eye. Dave returned the look that told two friends they were still friends.

"Watch out for yourself," John said with a husky voice.

"You, too," Dave replied. He stepped out of John's car and didn't look back. He heard the town car roar away. Dave stood in the silence of the parking lot and finally opened his car door. The pent up heat escaped from the car's interior and blasted Dave in the face. Dave grimaced at the heat and sat down in his car. He couldn't wait until the air conditioner made it bearable. As he waited Dave rested his forehead against the steering wheel and closed his eyes. For the first time he felt like crying. He never cried over anything. The childhood tapes started playing in his mind, "big boys don't cry." He gulped hard and drove to the bank. Once out of the bank he headed east toward a small business district. He took the piece of paper out of his pocket and read the address one more time.

The place he was looking for was in the back area of a strip shopping center. The only sign to the store was on the door. Dave had to park his car and look around for the address. Within a few minutes he saw the business name painted on the door, *Digital Bytes*. He walked in the lobby. The air conditioning was cranked to a low setting and the cold air was a shock. The lobby was decorated with posters of hard rock bands. The counters were gray and the carpet was a mint green, plush and smelled new. Beyond the counter was a large work area that looked like a computer tech lab. Long tables filled with hardware lined the bare walls of the room. Electrical cords snaked across the floor in a web of confusion. One man in his mid-forties bent over a circuit board jabbing at it with a small tool.

"I'll be right with you," he said without looking up. After a few minutes the man smiled at the circuit board as if it were alive and put the small tool back in the pocket protector of his shirt pocket. He walked toward the counter in an easy manner and smiled.

"You are Mr. Jenkins?" he asked. Dave noticed his long gray beard and the balding spot on the top of his head. They contrasted with the youthful look in his face.

"Yes, I'm Dave Jenkins," Dave said holding out his hand. The computer technician's name was Starkey and he shook Dave's hand warmly.

"I figure what I have to teach you will take about an hour. That will be forty dollars in advance."

Dave pulled two twenty-dollar bills out of his pocket and placed them on the counter.

"It could be more," Starkey said grabbing up the money. "But let's see how it goes. Did you bring the diskette?"

Dave pulled the diskette that Shane had sent him out of his coat pocket and handed it to Starkey.

"First thing we do is copy this sucker just in case we have an accident,"

Starkey said. He looked like he was talking more to the diskette than to Dave. Starkey worked with almost a slight of hand and in seconds he had made a back up copy of the diskette and gave the original back to Dave.

"Here's the paperwork I want to scan in," Dave put the package on the counter that Shane had sent him. As an afterthought he put the diskette containing all of the email addresses of the management team, the OCC personnel and the servicing employees that Marilee had prepared on the counter alongside the papers.

"Okay, let's go to work," Starkey said. Over the next hour Dave and Starkey built a complete electronic file of all the incriminating paperwork along with links to other important documents on the system. He wrote a lengthy letter explaining his efforts to address the deficiencies in the bookkeeping at National Assets and the subsequent efforts to hide these discrepancies. He was going public with his story. But he was only circulating the story within the company. He smiled as he thought how he was complying with Will Eagleton's directive to keep what he knew within the company. *It would go no farther*, Dave thought.

"Can I include some transcripts from this video tape?" Dave held the cassette in front of Starkey.

"I can do better than that," Starkey said confidently. "I can make some file attachments that will have actual video clips. Your mail recipients can click on the icon and watch a thirty second movie. We can do as many as you like."

A little more than an hour later Dave had what he wanted. He held the diskettes tightly as he listened to Starkey's final instructions.

"Now once this is loaded the program will write the information permanently to the system. No one can destroy it. They can only delete it from their mailbox. Your only problem will be if too many people try to access the library of documents and video files I've created. It will jam up the company's system temporarily and handle the requests in chronological order. It will be like a long line at the movie theater," Starkey said laughing. "They'll just have to wait their turn for the information."

"Thanks," Dave said. He put another forty dollars on the counter. Starkey grabbed it as quickly as he had the first money.

"Thanks for the tip," Starkey smiled. "Just remember. We never met if this thing blows up."

"I'm leaving the company anyway," Dave said. "I won't be around to tell anyone." Dave made a move toward the door. He noticed that Starkey wanted to tell him something more. He paused for a moment.

"I knew Shane," Starkey said. "He used to come in here for personal stuff. It's the least I could do for him."

"He would have appreciated it," Dave said and walked out the door into the sunlight.

By the time Dave returned to the office the afternoon shift was going home and the evening shifts were logging on to their computers. There was a lot of activity at that time of day. Dave walked to his office and noticed that two strangers were sitting at his desk. One was reading a book. Another was working on his computer.

"What's going on?" Dave asked trying to control the surprise in his voice.

"We have a disconnect order," the young man working at his computer said. He turned in his chair to face Dave. "We thought we'd get a jump on it."

"I don't leave until tomorrow," Dave said angrily. "Why the hell didn't you call?"

"We left a voicemail," the one with the book said as if that would absolve them of barging into Dave's office and cutting off his access to the system.

"I still have a lot of work to do," Dave said as evenly as he could manage. "Now get that computer back on line."

"Part of it is already down in my car," the one behind the keyboard said.

"I'm waiting," Dave said. He struggled to control his temper. He had to get access to the system, to his email. Otherwise he couldn't get his message out.

"I'm going to go get a cup of coffee," he said in measured voice. "And when I come back, I want this thing working."

Without waiting for an answer Dave walked out of his office and down the stairway to the coffee stand. Before he ordered, he thought of an idea. He walked hurriedly toward the conference room where the OCC auditors had worked. He walked in and flipped on the lights. The harsh florescent rays flooded the room and allowed Dave to see through squinting eyes that the computers he had set up for them were still in place. He walked over and turned one on. To his surprise and relief it was still working. He quickly signed on with a user name and password that someone had taped to the side of the monitor for easy reference. He smiled at the irony of the situation. He had preached password security to his staff since the first day of operation and here he was taking advantage of a clear violation of his own policy. Then he loaded the information and program on the diskette.

The seconds ticked by like hours. Dave sat at the computer hoping no one walked in. He wondered if the computer technicians in his office could detect that he was somewhere within the company using another terminal. Since it was late in the day he figured that the email would not get to people's mailboxes until morning. And he was scheduled to pick up his money and sign the final papers in the human resources office in the morning. It would be close. On one hand there was almost a half million dollars at stake. On the other hand was his compulsion to get the truth out on the system in so detailed a story that no one could deny the truth. Finally the computer indicated that the file had been transferred.

Dave jumped up from the computer, popped the diskette out of the slot and hurried back to the coffee counter. He had just picked his coffee up and was sitting down at a table when one of the computer technicians approached him.

"Mr. Jenkins?" he said timidly. "We're having trouble getting your computer back on line. We can do it, but it's going to take a while. We have to be somewhere else right now. So we thought that we could come back later, or in the morning if that's more convenient." He waited wondering if Dave was going to lose his temper. As an after thought he said, "We're really sorry about the inconvenience we caused you."

Dave took a sip of the hot coffee. He looked out the windows of the coffee lounge for a moment.

"I've been sitting here this whole time wondering how something like this could happen," he said slowly just loud enough for the technician to hear him. "Just come back tonight when you can. That way I can use it first thing in the morning," Dave said calmly. He thought he better not let them off the hook tonight. Otherwise it may look suspicious later on if anyone were to ask them.

Before Dave left the office that night he cleared out the rest of the items in his office. He knew he wouldn't be back. He planned to go to his meeting with the human resources representative, pick up his money and leave. There would be no time for good byes in the morning. He wanted to get clear of the chaos that his email would cause. And he wanted to cash his checks before the company decided to take punitive action. He was walking a tightrope. He only hoped that the email wouldn't circulate until after he left in the morning.

Later that evening Dave stood in the back of his house on the patio. He lit a cigarette and stared out at the sky. He missed seeing the stars. There was so much ambient light around the city that only the brightest stars shone in the night sky. A soft wind blew in from the foothills and he could smell the heady spices of the pines and the fennel.

The house sold quickly and the movers would arrive tomorrow to put his furniture in storage. Dave and Ann planned to tour the country and look for a place to work and to live. In the meantime they would stay with his brother in Florida. His brother had plenty of room and Florida was about as far away from California as Dave could get. He needed to put some distance between himself and all of this business.

In the distance he heard the wail of sirens. He heard the loud mufflers growling up Hazel Avenue. Over his backyard fence he could hear the soft nasal tones of his neighbor talking to someone on his cell phone. He scanned the backyard landscaping. He looked out at all the rose bushes he had nurtured for so long. He would miss all of this. But he knew that it would take more than a nice yard and big house for him to be happy. Or maybe it would take less. It all changes anyway, he thought. Nothing's permanent.

He sat down on one of the patio chairs and watched the night breeze move the tree branches. They looked like they were waving good-bye to him. As he stared up at the trees he noticed that the stars seemed brighter tonight. He wondered how bright they would be as he drove across the Mojave Desert in southern California. Dave wanted to stand by the side of the road of Interstate 40 near the Tehachapi Pass and look back down on California. It would be his farewell gesture to a state he liked except for the job. He wanted a ritual that would give him closure. He thought of pulling into a motel somewhere around Needles after his first full day on the road. He would be tired and ready for a good night's sleep. He would walk in the parking lot of the motel and look up at the sky knowing that the stars would be brighter, knowing that he wouldn't have to face all the stress of this job anymore. In his mind he was already there. He only needed to finish the last piece of business at the office tomorrow. Then he would be on his way.

In the distance he heard the hoot of an owl. He remembered his first night in this house when he heard owls all night long. As new houses were constructed the wildlife had migrated more toward the foothills. Now one was back. Maybe, he thought, it was one of the owls that greeted him on his first night in this house over two years ago. He was beginning to believe in omens.

Dave didn't remember sleeping that night. He lay in bed imagining his visit to the human resources office to sign his papers and pick up his checks. He rehearsed his plan as he lay in bed staring up at the ceiling. He would stop by the bank and deposit the checks. Then he would call and have the money transferred into his investment portfolio and an array of trusts. He would divide the large amount of the check into several investments and let the money earn more money for him. He wanted the money to hide in multiple investments so that Verdura would think hard about stopping payment on it for any reason. Dave knew that it was an irrational fear, but he didn't want to take any chances. He wanted as much peace of mind as he could summon.

He last looked at his clock at four-thirty. He decided to get up and start the day. He moved like a robot through his shower and shave. He dressed in a dark blue suit and deep red tie. He decided to look important even if he wasn't any more in the eyes of the company. He knew that suits demanded respect. And he wanted every advantage. His appointment was for nine o'clock and it shouldn't take more than thirty minutes, he thought.

He went out to the kitchen and fixed a cup of coffee and a bowl of instant oatmeal. He had packed his car last night and just had a few things he needed to bring out to the trunk this morning. He put the house key in an envelope for the neighbor who was going to let the movers into the house. For one last time Dave looked around the house and the yards. He felt as if he should thank the house for sheltering them so well over the past two years and for selling so quickly. In the end he just nodded at the air, whispered a thank you, and walked out to his car. He glanced around the neighborhood to see if there were any strange cars in the street and to silently bid his indifferent neighbors farewell. He slipped the house key under a planter near the garage and drove into the city.

He was early enough that he missed most of the rush hour traffic. He parked in a public lot and walked down the block to a coffee shop. It was a little before eight o'clock and he sat three blocks away from his appointment. To pass the time he bought a copy of the *Sacramento Bee* along with warm Danish pastry dripping with icing and let the hour pass by leisurely.

After what seemed like half a day to Dave it was time to head down the street. He forced himself to breathe deeply as he walked. He knew that this was the moment he had been waiting for. He hoped that there would be no interruptions, no complications, and no last minute requests for meetings with Will Eagleton or anyone else.

In the end his fears were unfounded. The representative was waiting for him in the lobby. She led him into one of the interview rooms and in ten minutes he was back out on the street walking toward his car. He clutched the envelope full of checks and had to fight the urge to run. By ten o'clock he had finished his banking and investment transactions and was driving south on interstate five toward Bakersfield. He kept checking his rearview mirror as a precaution.

When National Assets opened for business the morning that Dave left town, the computer system barely functioned. His email went out to an audience of four hundred employees, managers and regulators. It was like a computer virus with the clock set for the opening of business. The normal office work slowed to a standstill as employees read the history of fraudulent transactions and subsequent attempts to cover up the trail of fraud left in the wake of their activities. Some employees gave up on their attempts to sign on to the system and looked over the shoulders of their coworkers in adjoining cubicles. Copies were printed and read in the employee lounges. Staff was stunned and angry at the report. Productivity gave way to the discussions and reactions of groups of employees.

Impromptu meetings sprang up in the aftermath of the news. Disgruntled employees vented their anger in the smoking areas and lunchrooms. Middle managers and supervisors held meetings among themselves in an attempt to plan some type of damage control over the freewheeling situation. Some employees simply went home without checking out with their supervisors. The electronic bulletin boards were overloaded with unanswered calls. Senior managers stopped taking phone calls until they had all the facts. A tidal wave of chaos washed over the long rows of cubicles.

It was noon before senior management could react to the shockwaves. Will Eagleton stood at the end of a conference table interrogating the two computer technicians who had worked on Dave's computer.

"Are you sure that he didn't come back and use the computer?" he asked for the third time. His hands wrung an imaginary towel anxiously as he paced a short distance back and forth.

"We're sure," one of the technicians said in a timid voice. "There's no way he could have had access until this morning. And we've checked."

"Can you tell where the message originated?" Will asked.

"We think it was a computer terminal in a conference room on the first floor of the servicing center." The other technician offered.

"What do you mean 'you think'?" Will pounded the table in frustration. He grabbed his water bottle and squeezed it. The computer technicians cringed in their chairs wondering if Will was planning on throwing the bottle at them.

"The system is so overloaded that we have to wait in line for the verification on our research," one of them said in small voice.

"Why can't we bring the system down and do the research?" Will asked.

"That would be pretty risky in the middle of the day. We may lose financial transactions that have been entered in the system. And there's no guarantee that we could bring the system back up with all of the traffic that's slowing down normal business operations."

Will looked up at the doorway to see his assistant waiting for him to acknowledge her. She leaned against the door frame with the hint of a smile on her face.

"What?" Will asked. He resented the intrusion but he knew it must be important for her to interrupt him.

"Mr. Eagleton, there's a reporter from the *Sacramento Bee* on your line. He wants a word with you," she said staying in the doorway.

"Refer it to public relations," he said impatiently. He squeezed his water bottle so tightly that the computer technicians thought it was going to burst in his hand.

"I've tried," she said. "He said if you won't talk to him, he'd be out here with a photographer and team of reporters."

"Shit," Will whispered in frustration. He turned his anger on the two technicians. The dark look in his eyes made them both lean back in their chairs. "Get me some answers and get back here as soon as you get them," he snapped. Without dismissing them he stormed out of the conference room. His assistant followed at a safe distance.

Both technicians sat at the conference table for a moment and smiled at each other. It took them a minute to calm down.

"Serves the sonofabitch right," one said to the other. They stood and sauntered out of the room in no particular hurry.

32

Two days later Dave and his wife woke up in their motel bed in Prescott, Arizona. He had picked Ann up on his way south. With each mile he put behind him he felt the weight of the last two years lift from his shoulders. By the time they pulled into Prescott it was late. That night he slept soundly without waking during the predawn hours. For the first time since Dave could remember he awoke because he was rested. He dressed quickly in a pair of jeans and a sweatshirt. He laced on a pair of hiking boots, brushed his teeth and packed his small duffel bag. After they checked out they drove out to the highway to find a cup of coffee. The streets were quiet and full of morning shadow and the sky was such a deep blue it hurt his eyes.

After a quick breakfast Dave drove out to the base of Thumb Butte. He parked his car in a small dusty parking lot bordered by old logs lying on their sides. A weathered picnic table stood in the shade of a bent pine tree. Beyond the table the trail to the top of the butte opened inconspicuously. Dave grabbed his water bottle and started up the trail. It took him about thirty minutes to make it to the top. The view was breath taking as was the climb. He sat back against a rock and looked out at horizon. The change of scenery was a welcome shock to his system. His eyes rested on the small junipers and pinions that dotted the surrounding hills that had been worn smooth and gray be the centuries of wind and snow. He could feel the silence. Overhead a jet cut across the sky leaving its quiet contrail as the only evidence that it was even there. Even though Dave could still see his breath, the warmth of the sun and the exertion from the climb had warmed him.

After a few minutes of silence he reached inside his jacket and pulled out a national newspaper. He found a section that carried other news stories from across the nation. He smiled when he saw the article. All of his efforts condensed into ten paragraphs. National Assets had shut down for the week.

Arrests had been made. Others were being questioned at Verdura Bank. Verdura had entered into a supervisory agreement with the OCC. That meant the regulators were running the company now.

Dave smiled at his sense of vindication. But he felt the sadness that something had ended. Something that had carried the possibilities of success and self-fulfillment. Then he thought about the money. He knew that there still loomed the possibility of retaliation by any one of the executive team at National Assets, not to mention Verdura. Hopefully they would be too busy fighting their own battles to spend much time coming after him. He wondered if it had been worth the money. He knew it would take some time before he decided whether that was true.

Dave walked back down the butte at a leisurely pace. When he reached his car he saw his wife standing by the picnic table enjoying her coffee and a cigarette. She was reading the news story in a different newspaper. Dave saw her shaking her head and laughing. He took out a map and studied the road to Granite Dells. Now there's something that's lasted a long time, he thought. After a brief look at the map Dave and Ann packed their things off of the picnic table back into the car. They both commented that the picnic table had a fresh coat of green paint. They looked at each other and laughed. He started the car and drove down the highway taking in the colors of the desert with fresh eyes.

* * * * *

Printed in the United States
19247LVS00007B/1-51